Reiziger

KIRK GRAHAM

ISBN: 0991793404

ISBN 13: 9780991793402

Library of Congress Control Number: 2012922947
Chapter 24 Publishing

www.kirkgraham.com

www.chapter-24-publishing.com

For Jackie –
thanks for your patience.

About the Reiziger

Stretching three hundred and twenty feet from bow to stern, the Reiziger was an impressively large ship. Built in 1958 by Dutch shipbuilders, her original design was that of a modern day stern trawler, though she was never used for such a purpose.

Considering her size and shape, the Reiziger was not a swift vessel. Even though she was a dual propped ship, her maximum speed topped out at eighteen knots. For most excursions, she was more suited to cruising at around fifteen knots. Power came from two eight-cylinder, four-cycle turbo diesel engines, boasting an operating push of nearly fifteen hundred horsepower. The engines were strong, reliable, and easy to maintain, a tribute to her first-rate builders from the Netherlands.

Originally painted off-white with blue, orange, green and red accents, she wasn't an overly striking ship; rather, she looked somewhat awkward on the water. Noticeable from her obscure markings, she was easy to spot on the open seas from miles away. Yet, she still managed to become a true envy of other sea going vessels; thanks to her capabilities, operating range, style, and design. Particularly on the Atlantic, the Reiziger was one of the most noticeable ships throughout the sixties and seventies. To this day, the Reiziger is *still* considered one of the finest naval exploration vessels ever built.

Upon completion, she was sold to the German government, who had great intentions for the mighty ship. Assigned to the German Navy, the Reiziger was predominantly used for marine biology and naval technological trials and research. Technically not armed, the ship was equipped with single torpedo launch capability, although a trial of this feature was never put to the test.

In the year she was set to sea, the Reiziger was outfitted with the latest technological advances available at the time: deep penetration sonar, short and long wave radio systems, a complete marine research laboratory, as well as retractable stabilization arms for the rougher seas.

She was dubbed "The Queen of the Atlantic" by her first commander, Fregattenkapitan Helmet A. Klaustzman. When Klaustzman was discharged from his duties aboard the Reiziger over a decade later, he further commented that the Reiziger was the 'finest seagoing vessel' he'd ever had the pleasure to command - a statement that was reiterated by all who ever had the privilege to work aboard the ship.

Ten years after her initial launch, in late 1968, the ship was once again updated and retrofitted. This time, a dual-pronged crane arm built by a Canadian manufacturer was installed. The new crane allowed for the simultaneous release and retraction of ROK and MIG IV - the Reiziger's single-manned submersible vessels. The German Navy built the submersibles designed to resemble Otis Barton's Bathysphere, only larger and much more capable. Each unit came equipped with two dexterous control arms and a battery-powered system for self-propulsion, allowing ROK and MIG IV to reach diving depths of nearly five miles below the ocean's surface.

Other refit additions to be installed within the coming years included: bioacoustics sonar, single room cabins on the main deck for passengers, and a fully equipped medical centre situated behind the cabins.

Disaster struck the Reiziger in the fall of 1971 when she was run aground off the coast of Morocco. The damage to the ship was extensive: including a six foot split in the port-side section of the hull, one of the massive props was torn off, and the main rudder was bent. As well, the engine room and adjacent meter room were substantially destroyed by fire.

The crew at the time questioned if bad weather was the culprit that led to the ruin of the Reiziger, or if it was because of human error.

A long internal investigation into the cause of the accident concluded that in fact, human error led to the Reiziger's downfall. Consequently, a naval tribunal revealed that Fregattenkapitan Klaustzman was incompetent, irresponsible, and an alcoholic. He was discharged from the navy with extreme prejudice. Six months later, he committed suicide by hanging.

Sadly, the German government didn't see it fiscally responsible to repair the Reiziger after her grounding. And so, the majestic 'Queen of the Atlantic' sat laying waste in a dry dock off the coast of northern Africa for nearly two years. Ultimately, in July 1974, the Reiziger was decommissioned and retired from the German Navy before being put to auction.

The ship was an embarrassment for the German government at this point and they wanted to be rid of her completely. Nevertheless, they were still hoping to obtain at minimum the scrap metal value for the ship - a small redemption for such a great loss.

A pleasant surprise came from South Africa in the form of a rich oil tycoon named Leon Kirkus. He bought the Reiziger for a whopping four hundred thousand Deutsche Marks.

The ship's new owner spared no expense bringing the Reiziger back to her former glory. Kirkus had the boat re-welded, repainted, redecorated, retrofitted, and refinished from bow to stern. The Reiziger now stood a glorious bright white with majestic navy blue accents to her exterior. Across both sides of the superstructure and on the rear of the ship emblazed the Reiziger's name in massive teal lettering. As well, a new symbol was designed specifically for the ship's rebirth – the Sun surrounded by the twelve signs of the zodiac – to signify the ship's 'traveler' namesake. This new symbol was painted broadly across the sides, back, walking decks and exhaust stack of the ship. Every lifeboat, life raft, fire extinguisher, or any other item attached to the vessel was also stamped with the new symbol. Guard rails extending the perimeter of the ship were painted gloss black to compliment the Reiziger's black underbelly which was barely visible at the waterline. Carpets of red, white and blue were installed to the interior cabins, the mess hall and the research lab; all sporting the ship's new insignia five meters in every direction. All windows and portholes throughout the ship were replaced with fresh triple-paned glass. The glass itself displayed the pride of the Reiziger, as they were acid-etched with the ship's logo and namesake to each interior panel. Retractable blinds were also inset to the windows within the command center and sleeping cabins for privacy and protection from the raging equatorial sun. The finished look was truly amazing. The Reiziger had been given a new lease on life. After her updates; which took nearly a year to complete, she resembled more of a cruise ship than a former navy vessel – but once again, the Reiziger became the envy of the Atlantic sea going vessels.

No longer part of the German naval fleet, the Reiziger was transferred to the port of Cape Town, South Africa; which became her home berthing location. From there, the vessel was hired out for private charters, research missions, or on occasion; commercial fishing excursions. Whatever the purpose, it didn't matter - not to Kirkus. As long as those hiring the Reiziger paid the going rate, he was happy...and fortunately for Kirkus, they all paid well.

Not being a seaman himself, Kirkus, hired a former merchant sea captain named Devon Grey to command the ship. Grey's initial duties were to captain the ship for required voyages, and hire the necessary crew. Within a few short months, Grey's list of responsibilities multiplied. He managed the cargo operations, making sure the ship complied with local and international laws, overseeing that the ship's company and state flag policies were followed, as well as immigration and custom regulations. In addition, he supervised the ship's inventory, accounting, and payroll divisions. The only aspect Captain Grey didn't worry about was the Reiziger's fiscal productivity; that remained a matter for Kirkus.

At full complement, the Reiziger research vessel could comfortably accommodate twenty crew and thirty-two passengers. When she departed Cape Town on October 14th, 1985, for a private charter mission to the British overseas colony of St. Helena, the ship's manifest listed eight crewmembers, seven scientists and one dog.

Four days after departure, all communication with the Reiziger ceased. What follows is the story of the Reiziger.

....

"Is she going to die?"

"I don't know. She's been shot.

She's lost a lot of blood.

It doesn't look good."

"She didn't deserve this."

"I know, but none of us did."

....

1

The night air was cool and almost completely still. A saltwater fog danced through the darkness of night, passing gently over the Reiziger's exterior. The fine mist surrounded the ship like an aura. The salt water tried to eat at the ship's steel exterior, but thanks to the Reiziger's multiple layers of paint, the effort was futile.

Aside from the odd splash of water breaking on the bow of the ship, the only audible sound was the purr of the Reiziger's engines working in cadence to an imaginary metronome.

Looming darkness stretched the Atlantic Ocean like a massive black tarp pulled across a backyard swimming pool. The overcast October sky concealed the moon and stars. For miles, the only visible light emanated from the Reiziger.

The ship's powerful forward lights illuminated almost thirty feet ahead. Despite the darkness, the lights were relatively unnecessary. The Reiziger almost seemed to plot its own course through the abyss like an arrow in midflight, straight and true. Even if she strayed a bit, it didn't matter. There were no other ships for miles.

Captain Grey entered the command center bridge with his dog at his side. Grey was tall and well-built. Standing six-foot two, he stood proud, with a solid jaw and piercing blue-green eyes. His skin-tone, though Caucasian, was darkened and weathered, a sign of a man who spent most of his life at sea. As always, he wore a short-sleeved white button-down shirt decorated with the ship's logo on the left breast pocket. His white and blue captain's cap complimented the Reiziger's colors while also sporting the Reiziger's sun and zodiac logo. His neatly trimmed blondish-gray hair transitioned in front of his ears into symmetrical sideburns that ran down along his jaw line into a completely gray trimmed beard. The gray hair made him look older than his current fifty-two years, yet he didn't dye the color out. Instead, he rather enjoyed his distinguished look. That and he didn't care what others thought of him; he was Captain.

Cody, his noble white malamute cocked her head up towards her master for quick reassurance that all was well as they proceeded into the command center. She always waited for her master's signal before she carried on to her corner. Captain Grey nodded in affirmation to Cody. Off she padded to her bed of blankets tossed in the corner of the room. She circled around a couple of times and then settled down to rest, tucking her nose under her paw.

It was during a SCUBA expedition off the uninhabited island of St. Paul, Nova Scotia back in nineteen seventy nine when Captain Grey found the abandoned pup, near death. She was malnourished, her hind legs were broken and she was suffering from severe retinal deterioration in her one blue eye. Being a man who loved nature and most of Mother Earth's non-human creatures, the Captain just couldn't bear to leave the poor dog to die. He rushed the young malamute pup to nearby Cape Breton for critical veterinary care.

The Mi'kmaq doctor who ran the Cape Breton Animal Hospital took in the near lifeless pup right away. Over the next several weeks, the doctor, along with Captain Grey, worked relentlessly to nurse the pup back to health. Grey assisted the doctor everywhere he could with the young pup: helping with her feeding, bathing, grooming and exercising. He was at her side during the entire recovery process, and played a significant role in the dog's recuperation. The Mi'kmaq doctor gave her the name 'Ogoti', which in the Mi'kmaq language meant 'partner'. Captain Grey liked the name and chose to use it as well. Though, in the days that followed, he started calling the dog by a shortened version, simply referring to her as 'Cody'.

As the weeks passed, the Mi'kMaq doctor could see that a strong bond was forming between the Captain and the dog. When the young Ogoti was well enough to leave veterinary care, the doctor suggested that the Captain adopt her. At first, Grey was reluctant, but secretly he knew in his heart that he had fallen in love with the malamute. There was no question - he simply had to take her home with him aboard the Reiziger.

Cody hadn't left the Captain's side ever since. For the last six years, she was his faithful companion and friend, always there - wherever he went.

Captain Grey looked at his dog curled up in her bed and nodded to her with a smile. 'Life of a dog', he thought.

He then focused his attention to the task at hand. He scanned over the displays of the computer monitors; everything looked in order. Silently, he glanced over First Officer Tom Bailey's shoulder to check the navigational report. Captain Grey smiled to himself. As always, the Reiziger was right on course.

Modern technology aboard the vessel had simplified the job of travelling the seas. Sextants were replaced by computerized navigational systems. Charts, graphs, callipers, and engine order telegraphs were barely used in today's era of commanding a ship. Frankly, most ships could almost guide themselves in this modern age. Captain Grey was well aware of this, but he also knew that there was far more to being a captain than just sailing from port to port.

Confident of his ship's abilities, Captain Grey sat back in his captain's chair, kicked his heels up onto the console, and lit his pipe. He casually flipped through a magazine while soft jazz quietly hummed in the background. After a few minutes, Grey snuffed out his pipe and closed his eyes.

* * *

The waves of the Atlantic gently broke on the Reiziger's steel hull. The bow of the ship sliced through the water, tossing up a fine mist and leaving behind a rippling of white waves. As the boat heaved in the water, hollow groans sounded out from the ship's steel framework, echoing through the still night air.

Then the alarms sounded.

"Report!" called Captain Grey as he bolted upright.

Frantically checking a status report from one of the computer monitors, First Officer Bailey responded, "Captain, it looks as if Savior One through Four were released!"

Tom Bailey had worked with the Captain for nearly five years now. He was hired onto the Reiziger straight out of nautical college along with his identical twin brother, Drew. The brothers quickly became the Captain's most trusted and respected crewmen. Initially, the Captain had a hard time telling the two brothers apart, but then he found a way to distinguish one from the other. He simply asked that Tom grow a moustache. That remedied the problem.

Captain Grey grabbed the CB microphone while he simultaneously reached over to turn off the cassette player.

Clicking on the mic, he called out, "Second Officer Medupé."

Grey was in the zone now. He was focused. He furrowed his eyebrows and waited for a response. Barely five seconds passed before a voice came back through the CB speaker.

"Medupé here, sir," replied a voice with a heavy South African accent.

"Check on the storage bays for Savior One through Four immediately."

"Yes, sir."

Clicking on the mic again, Captain Grey called to his crew, "Attention all crew - this is the Captain. This is not a drill. I repeat. Not a drill. We have alarms. Report on Saviors One through Four? Over."

No response came across the CB. Captain Grey got the answer he expected - none of his crew would purposely tamper with the life rafts. Nobody in his command would do a thing like that, and he knew it.

Captain Grey watched as Tom carefully documented everything happening into a logbook.

Then, waiting a beat, he clicked on his CB again, "Officer Medupé, come in."

"Yes, sir. Medupé here. Captain, I'm by the storage bays for Savior One through Four. It's affirmative sir. They are missing. I repeat – they are missing."

The Captain slammed his fist against the Plexiglas cover of the control console. "Damn it!" he said. Cody jumped up from her bed, but Grey quickly waved her back down. He hadn't meant to startle her. She didn't like excitement. Tom was still busy documenting and checking status reports on the computer consoles, but he *too* was slightly started by the Captain's actions.

Grey clicked on the CB once again. "Officer Medupé, gather the passengers in the mess deck immediately. We have a situation."

"Yes sir. Right away. Medupé, out."

* * *

Amy awoke to the wail of the ship's alarms. The clock on her nightstand showed that it was precisely three-eleven a.m. - too early for her. Trying to muffle the blaring alarms, she covered her head with a pillow. After what seemed like hours, the alarms finally subsided. Amy rolled over and tried to fall back asleep, but even without the alarms sounding, the ringing continued to resonate in her ears.

Shortly after the alarms had stopped, a South African voice called out through the overhead speaker system, "Your attention, please. All passengers and crew must report to the mess deck immediately – this is not a drill"

"Son of a bitch!" Amy muttered to herself as the announcement was repeated four more times.

Rolling out of bed, she stood up and stumbled through the darkness to the bathroom. Just before she reached the bathroom, her forehead collided with an open cabinet door.

"Son of a bitch!" Amy yelled out, this time much louder than the first.

She stepped into the locker-sized bathroom and flicked on the light. Amy grabbed her black, wire-rimmed glasses off the counter and put them on. "Just great!" she said, looking at the bright red bump forming in the middle of her forehead. This made Amy even angrier and more put off by being awakened at such an ungodly hour.

Grabbing her cosmetics bag, she pulled out a few things, applied a scant amount of makeup and quickly tied back her shoulder length auburn hair. Appearance was not something she paid attention to at the best of times. Her natural beauty didn't need much highlighting, even at three in the morning.

She was slim and fit and endowed with envious proportions for a woman of twenty-seven. Her eyes were a deep jade green, and her skin was pale and smooth. Freckles dotted across the bridge of her nose, cute and flirty at the same time. If Amy had chosen a different profession from scientist, she could have pulled off being a model. However, genetics gave her one strike: she never grew taller than five foot one.

Hoping the meeting wouldn't take too take long, and not caring what anybody thought, Amy simply wrapped herself in a robe, pulled on her slippers, and left her cabin.

* * *

Captain Grey stood at the front of the room studying the passengers as they shuffled into the mess deck. He looked sternly at the tired and worried faces as everyone walked unassuming across the carpeted dining area and took a seat. While the Captain remained silent, the passengers watched him, trying to get a feel from him as to what this was all about.

Seven scientists and five crewmembers sat before him. Missing were Fenyang, the cook, and the two Bailey brothers, Tom and Drew, the First Officer and Navigator, respectively.

Captain Grey continued to survey the crowd in silence. He examined people systematically, paying close attention to their movements and their mannerisms. He studied every individual's weary eyes, looking for an answer to the question he had yet to ask. With every face that he intently looked to, eyes quickly avoided his stare. Who was responsible for the alarms? Who was responsible for releasing the life rafts? The Captain was determined to find out.

For the past nine years of commanding the Reiziger, Captain Grey had worked with many passengers and crew. Over time, he had become a master of the silent cross-examination that he was presently conducting. Grey had the ability to stare deeply into someone's eyes, taking a glimpse into their soul and ultimately uncovering their true character, their desires, and their intentions. Of all the skills essential to the captain of a ship, Captain Grey felt that this was the most valuable talent for a man in his position.

The Captain's face remained expressionless despite the fact that the passengers were growing impatient. Cody sat respectfully beside her master, wagging her tail as he studied the small crowd sitting before him. It wasn't long before tension could be felt throughout the room. The passengers could sense that Captain Grey was angry. Yet, no one dared to speak - too fearful that any comment would draw his anger in their direction. Unfortunately, this made the situation even more uncomfortable.

Geophysicist Stephan Woodley and biologist Amy Masterson finally broke the silence as they began to chatter quietly to each other. Amy was pointing to the mark on her forehead, while Stephan leaned forward to examine it. All eyes in the mess deck had shifted to the pair, but neither Amy nor Stephan took notice.

Not seeing that there was any harm in their casual chitchat, the two continued with their conversation, getting livelier by the minute. They gestured, smiled, and at one point, they even laughed out loud.

Distracted by the nonsense talk between the two scientists, Captain Grey shot an angry look at the pair and loudly cleared his throat. His piercing blue-green eyes dilated to an intense black.

When the two scientists finally caught on that the rest of the room was watching them, they quickly stopped talking. Amy was first to realize that all eyes were on them and promptly tapped Stephan on the leg, urging him to stop talking. He glanced around, feeling slightly embarrassed.

Again, the room was silent. Not a sound was heard except for the swish of Cody's tail on the floor and the tick, tick, tick of the clock that hung above the door to the galley. The minutes marched on in the mess deck, yet time seemed to stand still.

Captain Grey kept his eyes fixed on the two scientists. Woodley couldn't compete with the scorn of Captain Grey's stare, and like a dog being broken by its master; he lowered his eyes to the floor. Amy, on the other hand was brazen. She stared back at him through her wire-rimmed glasses, while thinking to herself, 'I didn't do anything wrong. You were the one who woke me up, Captain. It's even your fault that I bumped my head.'

Amy kept her eyes locked with the Captain's and kept her expression blank, stone-faced. Captain Grey finally looked away and shifted his focus to a porthole window to his left. He made a mental note that Amy was a person of interest in his investigation.

Amy muttered almost inaudibly, "Ha! This is such bullshit, Captain. Don't think for a second that you can intimidate me!"

Stephan leaned over and whispered to her, "I'd be careful if I were you. This Captain Grey guy seems like a real asshole. I wouldn't want to get on his bad side."

Still looking out the porthole window, Captain Grey spoke at last, "I'm sure you all heard the alarms from your cabins?" he said as he adjusted his belt.

The small crowd confirmed this, as the group of crew and passengers said yes and nodded.

"Ladies and gentlemen," the Captain continued, "We have a problem. We're currently positioned four days from Cape Town. We're almost nineteen hundred miles from our home port - about a third of the way between Africa and South America. Fortunately, for all of you, we're not far from the destination for your mission. However, I must inform you that, in my role as Captain, I have decided that we are stopping here until the situation at hand is resolved."

A murmur rose from the assembly.

Captain Grey looked back at the crowd before him. Anger rose in his chest, deep lines furrowed across his brow while he clenched his fists tightly.

"Within the last half hour, four of our canister life rafts were put to sea. There's no way we can go back to retrieve them. I wish we could, but unfortunately, the canisters were not properly released. They did not have their locating beacons secured before release, and without the beacons to signal their exact whereabouts, we don't stand a chance to find them. Any search effort would be futile. The consequence of this negligent act presents two threats to all of us on board this ship. First, we have a potential saboteur aboard, and second, there is only a single life boat remaining."

"Not much need for life rafts aboard the Reiziger?" laughed Doctor Baruti, standing up from his seat near the back of the room, "This ship is unsinkable! Surely, we can continue our voyage?"

"I'm sorry, Doctor Baruti, but we cannot. Not until I have some answers. This is my ship. I decide when and where this vessel will travel."

"But Captain..." urged Baruti.

Cody jumped up and barked at the doctor, as if to tell him that was enough, her master had spoken.

The dog had startled Baruti who fell back in surprise and almost knocked over his chair. Slightly embarrassed, the rosy-cheeked physician sat down warily, not taking an eye off Cody.

"Don't worry, Doctor, she won't attack unless ordered to," Captain Grey assured.

Nervously, Doctor Baruti nodded and then looked down, still a little embarrassed from the commotion he had caused.

Before Captain Grey could continue, Amy stood up from her seat and spoke. "So, what are you going to do? Captain, with all due respect, *we* are on a scientific mission and you and the owner of this ship, Mr. Kirkus, have been paid generously to take us to our destination. I'm most certain that our benefactor would not appreciate this delay."

"Miss Masterson, Amy, correct?" asked the Captain.

Amy nodded.

"The issue is not whether or not we can continue without the life rafts. I have complete confidence in my ship. As Doctor Baruti alluded to, the Reiziger will not fail us. I feel completely safe, as should you. Besides, the remaining lifeboat is in reality a *boat* – not a raft. Its capacity is fifteen passengers, but in an emergency, would accommodate all on board. No, Miss Masterson, that is not the problem. The real problem is why someone aboard this vessel, someone in this very room, would be working against us. Why would somebody in this room be jeopardizing your mission?"

Suddenly, Stephan Woodley stood up, removed his glasses and blurted out, "Where are the Bailey brothers? And, the cook... what's his name? Fenyang?"

Captain Grey cast a sharp glance back at Woodley, but didn't speak.

Woodley was as tall as Captain Grey, but lost out to him by about twenty-five pounds. He was actually *too* thin for his height. His hair was greasy and unkempt, grown long at the bangs and pulled back across the top of his head. As he spoke, he constantly had to slide his hand across his forehead to keep his hair from falling in front of his eyes. He wore corduroy pants too short at the ankles revealing white sneakers that looked out of place against his black socks. Fashion was not his strong suit - in fact, everything about Woodley was actually quite awkward.

Captain Grey's face turned red as he finally exploded at the gauche scientist. "Mr. Woodley, sir. Do not interrupt or question my crew like that ever again. These men have worked for me for years and would have no part in sabotaging this vessel. I take extreme offence to your insinuation."

Woodley quickly realized that he had said the wrong thing. His bravado was deflated and his legs began to quiver. Slowly he sat back down.

Still insulted, Grey grabbed the portable radio off his belt clip and clicked on the mic.

"First Officer Bailey?" he called out.

Seconds later a voice responded, "Bailey here, sir. Go ahead."

"Officer Bailey, please put Navigation Officer Bailey on the radio."

Again, only seconds passed before a distinctly different voice responded, "Navigational Officer Bailey here, sir. Go ahead."

"Thank you. As you were, men."

Captain Grey double-clicked the transmitter control and then called for Fenyang.

"Fenyang here, sir. How can I help you?" a sharp Asian voice replied.

"Thank you, Fenyang, that's all. Grey out."

Captain Grey then looked back to Stephan Woodley. "You see, Mr. Woodley," Captain Grey said in a dark whisper, "I trust my men. I know where they are and exactly what they're doing at all times. Now, as for you and your research team..."

"Captain!" Amy interrupted as she clapped her hands together to break the tension that had begun to rise between the two men. "Don't turn this into an 'us against them' battle. Stephan was wrong to implicate your crew, but let's keep our heads about us and try to keep this civil."

"Yes, please, Captain, let's work together. I'm sure we can figure this out," said Doctor Baruti, his eyes still focused on Cody.

Captain Grey patted Cody on her head as she stood faithfully beside her master. Before Grey could respond to Amy or the doctor, the room suddenly fell completely silent. The ship stopped humming. The engines had just shut down.

2

"Toss him overboard," Lefu said, kicking the bloody, lifeless body of Ramon Diez. "There's no need for this piece of shit anymore."

Lefu put his pistol back into his hip holster.

Jako grabbed the dead body by the ankles while Percy lifted it up under its arms. On the count of three, the two muscular men heaved Diez's corpse over the edge of the boat to the dark waters of the Atlantic below.

"Let the crabs eat that lying son of a bitch," laughed Jako.

"I'm sure a shark will get him first," said Percy smacking his partner on the back.

Lefu watched as his minions had their laugh, but refused to join in on the banter.

"Carlito," called Lefu, "I thought you said this was a fast ship?"

"Fastest patrol boat in South Africa. Don't worry, my friend. With this old gal, we'll be on top of them within the next six to eight hours." Carlito said confidently, a cigar dangling from the corner of his lips.

"Can you get us there any faster? I'll double your pay if you can." said Lefu.

"Double? How about triple?" Carlito said smiling back at Lefu, revealing his yellow stained teeth.

Lefu looked at Carlito in disgust. Lefu didn't like Enzo Carlito, and Carlito didn't like Lefu.

The mismatched pair met years earlier while in Koton-Karifi prison in Nigeria. Lefu was serving a twelve year sentence for attempted murder while Carlito was serving fifteen years for drug trafficking.

It was truly by chance that the pair had met. One afternoon, returning from an exercise break in the prison yard, Lefu came across Carlito just outside the shower room. The middle-aged, stocky Italian man had been severely beaten and left in a crumpled heap on the ground. As it turned out, the prison guards didn't think much of their white prisoners and frequently demonstrated their hate towards them. On that particular day, Carlito was their chosen victim.

Lefu never liked *any* of the prisoners inside Koton-Karafi and normally kept to himself. But on this particular day, he chose to help a man - a white man.

As he glanced around the yard and saw that no one was around, Lefu knelt down beside the wounded man and tried to offer him a sip from his water bottle. Struggling to breathe, Carlito gripped Lefu's arm and pulled him near. Carlito had a secret that he did not intend on taking to the grave that day. Between gasps for air, Carlito sputtered details into Lefu's ear of a prison escape route. Lefu tried to catch every detail that the dying man was trying to tell him, but some of the information Lefu just couldn't make sense of.

From that moment, Lefu knew he had to keep Carlito alive – lured by any possibility of a breakout from the horrible prison.

In a panic, Lefu tucked his towel under Carlito's head and left him briefly as he went to alert the medical staff of the man dying by the showers. If it had not been for Lefu, Carlito never would have received the necessary medical attention and emergency surgery that saved his life.

After three weeks of recuperation in infirmary, Carlito was reintegrated back into the prison population where Lefu became his new bodyguard. Lefu stood six foot four with almost zero body fat. His body bulged with muscles and was covered with tattoos and scars. He could fight, he could intimidate, and he would gladly kill. In short, he was a very dangerous and mean-looking thug. With Lefu as protection, nobody came near Carlito again.

Carlito on the other hand, had never planned on sharing his plan of escape with anyone, nor did he want a companion. But ever since his near-death experience in the yard that afternoon, he felt he had to include Lefu.

When the time was right, Carlito offered Lefu the opportunity to join him on the flight to freedom. Carlito felt it was the least he could do since Lefu saved his life. This was exactly what Lefu had been waiting and hoping for.

Ten days and many secret conversations later, the two men escaped. In the wake of their escape, four guards, including the two responsible for Carlito's beating, were left dead.

Heading to South Africa, the pair left their time in Koton-Karafi prison and Nigeria far behind. Grateful for his freedom, Lefu promised to repay Carlito for his inclusion in such an ingenious plan. The repayment came easy.

Before entering prison, Enzo Carlito had spent many years commanding merchant vessels at sea. When Lefu learned of this, he found a way to utilize Carlito's nautical expertise by landing him the position of Captain of the "Pemba Koningin".

The Pemba Koningin was a decommissioned patrol boat of the South African coast guard owned and operated by an associate of Lefu. The ship was two hundred and twenty-three feet long, capable of a top speed of nearly twenty-eight knots, twice the top travelling speed of the Reiziger.

As captain of the Pemba Koningin, Carlito would run drugs, diamonds, or sometimes even human cargo. Carlito did whatever he was asked to do by Lefu or the ship's owner. He did almost anything - and he did it very well. The portly Italian man's biggest shortcoming however, was his greed.

"Triple? Carlito, you're a greedy bastard. Fine. Get us there in four hours and I'll triple your payment," Lefu grumbled as he lit his cigar.

Carlito slapped his thigh and laughed heartily.

"That's what I like to hear, Lefu. Always willing to get the job done...no matter the cost. Remember my friend, it's just business."

Lefu grimaced at the comment. Those were the same words Carlito used as the pair killed the guards in the prison. Lefu shook his head and walked to the bow of the ship.

Carlito grabbed his CB, glanced at Lefu and laughed again.

"Mr. Asunda, engine set, full speed!"

"Yes, sir. Full speed," replied a voice.

"Mr. Hogg, bring me a coffee!" Carlito yelled into the CB.

"Yes, sir, right away," Hogg replied meekly over the CB.

Carlito put down the CB and called to Lefu as he was heading away.

"Smooth sailing, Lefu. Don't you worry, my friend, we're going to be there in no time."

Lefu didn't look back at Carlito, instead he gazed beyond the bow of the patrol boat to the open water before him; not a single ship was in sight.

"We'd better be."

3

Shortly before five o'clock in the morning, the clouds began to scatter. As the sun crept up on the eastern horizon, the morning light was breaking across the ocean. Flecks of gold glimmered off the water as if the sun was licking the tops of the waves. The once dark and turbulent water now appeared glassy, almost peaceful. The mist in the air was cool and fresh with a tinge of saltiness.

The Reiziger rocked silently on the ocean as gentle waves rolled beneath the vessel, only to fade away beyond the other side of the ship. The morning was still and quiet except for the occasional splash of water breaking on the Reiziger's steel frame.

Amy stood on the main deck at the front of the ship. She scanned the immense nothingness of the ocean before her, hoping to catch a glimpse of St. Helena, but it was still too early, St. Helena was too far off. Amy was both mentally and physically exhausted, thanks to the early morning commotion, but she knew that she wouldn't have been able to fall back asleep. Instead, she watched the dawning sky in solitude, wondering if her mission was doomed.

"Can't sleep?" asked Officer Medupé, as he came up behind her.

Startled, Amy jumped a little and turned around to find Medupé standing there. The Second Officer was a well-groomed, attractive man with handsome dark eyes, dark skin, and a warm, friendly smile.

"Oh, hi, Medupé, I didn't hear you come up," said Amy, forgetting to address the ship's second-in-command properly.

"I'm sorry - I didn't mean to frighten you,"

"No, I'm fine. I'm a little on edge, I admit," she said pausing, "I'm just concerned about - do you have any idea when we might get moving again? We have get to St. Helena within the next couple of days. We absolutely must. If we don't, this whole trip and years of research will be a complete waste."

"I wish I could answer that for you, my dear, but unfortunately I can't. We'll be sailing again as soon as the Captain gives the word. That's about all I can offer."

Worry and frustration overwhelmed Amy. Her eyes welled up with tears and her cheeks grew hot and flushed. Amy pulled off her glasses and dabbed at the corners of her eyes with her fingertips.

Without her glasses, Medupé could appreciate how truly beautiful Amy was. Her skin was soft and almost flawless. Her features were quite fine and feminine. Her deep green eyes were flecked with yellow, tiny sparks reflective of her vivacity and intensity.

"I'm sorry, I feel like a fool crying in front of you," Amy blubbered.

"No, please don't. Here, take this." Medupé pulled a handkerchief from his breast pocket and offered it to her. Amy accepted and unfolded the soft linen hankie. The ship's logo was embroidered on the bottom left corner. As Amy delicately wiped away her tears, Medupé tried to comfort her.

"My dear, you have to take in the situation," he said as he gently placed a hand on her shoulder.

"Thank you, Officer Medupé. I hate to lose it like this, but you've got to understand - I've been waiting seven years to get to St. Helena. If we don't make it there within the next few days, then all of my work will be lost. Seven years wasted."

"That is a long time invested in your work, my dear. But the Captain has his way of doing things. I must say that I don't always approve of them, but unfortunately, he is the Captain. Tell me, what is the purpose of your work?"

"You mean Captain Grey hasn't told you?"

"No. I'm not in a position to make it my business as to why the Reiziger has been hired out. Only the owner of this ship, Mr. Kirkus and Captain Grey are privy to where and why we travel. That information is considered confidential." Medupé said it as if he was a bit sour about the captain and ship's owner excluding him from that information.

"Wow, your captain really is quite the enigma, isn't he?" said Amy, cracking a smile.

Medupé grinned back. "You have no idea, my dear."

"Well, to be honest, it's part of my doctorate thesis. I've been studying micro-organisms that survive and thrive in extreme environments. For the past four years, I've concentrated on one in particular called the *Ferroplasma acidiphilum*."

"I'm sorry," replied Medupé, "But I have no idea what you just said."

Amy laughed, wiping another tear from her cheek with Medupé's handkerchief. "I should have expected that reaction."

"A common response?" asked Medupé.

"More often than you could imagine," she laughed. "Well, you see, the *Ferroplasma acidiphilum* is a certain type of microbe that can survive in a highly sulphuric environment, near a volcano for example. But what makes this organism so unique is its relationship to iron. It basically eats iron for energy and passes rust for its waste."

"It sounds fascinating," smiled Medupé as he raised an eyebrow.

"Really, it is. And the truly amazing part is that this particular microbe uses the iron as a structure organizing element, making it unique from all known organisms. I know it's hard to grasp or appreciate if you haven't studied it like I have, but it's possible that this microbe retained these primordial characteristics from early evolution on our planet. It expands beyond biology. This could lead to so many other discoveries."

"You know, Miss Masterson, if we were talking mathematics or finance, I'd probably be as excited as you. As much as I can appreciate your enthusiasm towards your research, I don't understand why it's so important that we reach St. Helena within the next few days."

Amy put her glasses back on and looked at Medupé. He seemed genuinely interested in her work. She was a little taken aback – she usually didn't get much attention from anyone outside of the scientific community.

"Oh, well, because Saint Helena has not erupted since 1962. If the lithosphere studies of Doctor Conte and Doctor Athens are correct, which I believe they are, then St. Helena is expected to have another eruption within the next few days – perfect timing for myself and the others to do our important work, to see how these organisms adapt to an altering harsh environment."

"I see. Time *is* of the essence then. I wish that I could do more for you, but unfortunately, I can't. The Captain commands the ship and I must follow his orders," Medupé said.

Amy's head dropped and her heart sank. Her anticipation was dampened by the lack of reassurance the Second Officer could give her.

Neither spoke after that. An uncomfortable silence fell upon them. On a personal level, they genuinely liked and respected each other. However, considering their respective positions, one was an officer lacking the power to sort out their current situation, and the other was a scientist badly needing assurance that her mission will carry on.

All of a sudden, Captain Grey's voice broke the awkward silence as it came through Medupé's portable radio.

"Officer Medupé, please escort Miss Masterson to the command center."

Captain Grey was determined to find out who was behind the discharged life rafts. He was in the process of questioning every passenger one by one, and Amy was next in line for interviewing.

Suddenly, Amy felt sick with worry. She had nothing to hide, yet she still felt uneasy. What if her cockiness earlier in the morning in the mess deck came back to haunt her, she wondered. She tried not to think about it any longer. She knew that she was not involved in any wrongdoing. All she wanted was to complete her research mission.

"Yes, sir. Right away," replied Medupé, holding out his right arm to Amy. "Miss Masterson, would you please accompany me to the command center?"

Before taking his arm, she handed him back his handkerchief. Medupé shook his head and advised her to keep it.

"So, the captain sent you to find me and you knew I was here?"

Medupé nodded.

"Wow. This is such a big ship. And you found me here? You guys are good."

Medupé smiled.

"Just one thing, please tell me Captain Grey doesn't use interrogation techniques from the Spanish Inquisition. Although, I have to admit, right about now I'd be willing to suffer through just about anything to get to St. Helena."

Medupé politely chuckled at her comments.

* * *

The command center bridge was one of only two locations where Captain Grey controlled the ship. The original teak floors gave the space a warm and inviting glow. Captain Devon Grey sat in his chestnut leather captain's chair in the middle of the room. He quietly puffed on his pipe as he glanced though some notes he had jotted down on a clipboard. Control panels sat before him and extended along the width of the bridge beneath the forward windows. Levers and control buttons flashed red and green while computer monitors displayed various numbers and symbols. A small cassette player was set on the window ledge together with a stack of tapes. The captain tapped his pen to the rhythm of the smooth jazz of Dollar Brand playing out from the speaker. Devon Grey was completely in his element.

As Medupé and Amy entered the bridge, Cody jumped to her feet and gave a low growl. The Captain was abruptly pulled from his thoughts and looked up.

"It's okay, Cody. Lie down, girl." said the Captain. He reached over and turned down the music before waving to an empty chair positioned near his. "Hello, Miss Masterson. Please, have a seat. Thank you, Officer Medupé, as you were."

Medupé turned and left the command center bridge.

Amy slowly approached the empty seat near the Captain.

"Please, call me Amy," she said timidly as she sat down on the edge of the seat. "Wow," she said as she pointed out the front-facing windows.

"I know," said the Captain, putting down his clipboard and re-lighting his pipe that had almost gone out.

The view from the superstructure was breathtaking. The Atlantic Ocean's enormous waves appeared minuscule in size from this vantage point, at least compared to their true size as seen from the main deck level. From the command centre, the waves didn't seem frightening at all.

Amy leaned across the console in front of her, accidentally pressing a button. "Omigod!" she exclaimed.

Captain Grey reached across Amy and pushed a different button. "It's okay," he assured her.

Amy eased back into her chair and sat on her hands as she drew in a deep breath and then slowly exhaled, letting her shoulders drop.

The seascape before her was mesmerizing and beautiful. The sun was shining across the sky turning the clouds that lingered from the night before to a radiant pink. Amy felt as though she could almost see the curvature of the earth on the horizon. It was astonishing.

"I never knew how magnificent it could be," said Amy.

The Captain smiled. "Anytime I doubt why I do this for a living...all I need to do is to look out there."

Amy began to relax as she straightened her glasses and tucked her hair behind her ears, "So, how can I help you, Captain?"

"Yes, of course. I only have a few questions for you, Miss Masterson. Please don't take it personally - these are the same questions I'm asking everyone. I'm just looking for some answers." He picked up his clipboard and pen.

"No, that's fine. Please, go ahead."

"Do you know where we're going, Miss Masterson?"

"Yes, we're headed for St. Helena. My colleagues and I are on a research assignment."

"How familiar are you with your colleagues on board this vessel?"

"I know most of them quite well. Let's see...I've worked along-side Dr. Athans and Dr. Conte for the past four years. They're probably the best seismologist and geologist I've ever had the privilege of working with. They are the duo responsible for pre-dicting that St. Helena is due to erupt."

Gently, Amy bit at her lip as she paused. Captain Grey paused with her; his pen stopped recording, but he never looked up.

"Stuart Radcliff, I've known a long time. We were friends back in high school. Stephan Woodley - I've known forever. I know he can sometimes be a bit of a pain, Captain, but he is one of the best geophysicists in the world, and he really is quite harmless." Amy paused again.

Captain Grey still didn't look up from his clipboard. He held his pen on the page, patiently waiting for Amy to continue.

"Um, Dr. Baruti is a long-time friend – a great physician and biologist. I'd say the only person I don't know very well is Dr. Uuka Duiker. I met him when we left Cape Town. But Dr. Conte knows him well and he says he's a world class oceanographer."

"Is there anyone on board that you can think of who would have had a reason to release the life rafts?" Captain Grey continued with the questioning.

"No. Not that I can think of. Why would anyone want to do that? It doesn't make any sense, Captain," Amy pleaded.

"Well, thank you, Miss Masterson. That is all."

"Okay? But, Captain?"

"Yes?"

"When are we going to be moving again?"

Captain Grey finally looked up from his clipboard and turned to look directly at Amy. She felt a cold shiver run down her spine. Earlier in the mess deck, in the company of the others, Amy had no trouble standing up to him. However, here, at his command post, she felt small and pathetic beneath his authoritarian stare.

"I am well aware of the urgency you have in reaching your destination, Miss Masterson. Dr. Athans already stressed that during his interview. However, I don't have an answer for you yet. This is my ship and I will only give the orders to proceed once I find out who released the life rafts and why. Hopefully, I'll know soon enough, and then we can be on our way again. That's all I can say for now."

"I understand, Captain. If I can be of any assistance in speeding up the matter, please let me know."

"Duly noted. Thank you, Miss Masterson."

"Please, call me Amy."

Amy got up from her chair and started walking to the door of the command center. She was crushed. Years of her work and dedication were at risk of being destroyed by a saboteur.

Just as she reached the door, it flung open and deck hand Winston Deedat rushed in past her. The young African crewman's clothes were rumpled, his hair was dishevelled, and his breathing was rapid and shallow.

"Captain, come quick! Main deck, port side...we have a problem!" he yelled.

4

B lood coursed across the portside main deck, pooling in thick ooze against one of the vacant life raft bays. The puddle of blood was over three feet wide and nearly a quarter inch deep. By the stairway leading to and from the superstructure, a spray of blood covered the wall. The splatter looked as if a high-pressured paint sprayer had exploded.

It was obvious that this didn't just happen, and although a time frame was hard to determine as to how long the blood had been present, Captain Grey was certain it must have happened sometime after the alarms rang out in the early morning as coagulation had set in on both sets of blood.

Captain Grey recalled how everyone aboard was accounted for during the meeting in the mess deck. Briefly, he wondered if everyone *had* been accounted for, but quickly chased the idea from his mind. He also recalled how Medupé was by the life raft bay after the alarms and reported their deployment. He was sure of himself, which meant that this must have happened sometime afterward. Grey knew that whomever the blood came from, human or otherwise, they or it would not have survived this volume of blood loss.

"Mr. Deedat, please summon Dr. Baruti from the passenger cabins immediately. Tell him it's urgent."

"Yes, sir," said Deedat as he gave a salute and ran off.

Captain Grey slowly inched around the spill, cautioning Cody with his hand to keep her distance. She stayed close by her master. Her tail curled between her legs and her ears lay flat against her head – she was obviously frightened.

The Captain removed his hat as he crouched down beside the pool of blood and began to look for clues. As he stared at the bloody puddle on the deck, his eyes caught a glimpse of something. Stuck in the middle of the puddle of blood was a dark mass.

Captain Grey grabbed a pen from his pocket and very carefully fished the mysterious item from the blood. As he pulled it close, a thick drop of blood fell from the end of his pen narrowly missing his perfectly polished black boot. Cody whimpered and cowered away from the blood. She was not comfortable with the sight of blood and the Captain understood.

"It's okay, girl. You go sit over there."

Cody willingly took the order from her master and padded over to an open area beside the single remaining lifeboat, Savior 5.

Careful not to touch the blood, Captain Grey examined the twisted piece of material hanging from the end of his pen. He turned the pen around and around trying to get a good look at the item while careful not to drip anymore blood from the end. It didn't take long before the Captain was certain of what he was looking at. The material was a badly torn swatch of clothing. It was navy blue polyester – identical to the material his crew outfitted themselves with.

"Oh my God," he whispered quietly.

Just then, Dr. Baruti arrived on scene with the deckhand Deedat. Cody growled at the doctor as he walked past her.

"Easy, girl." the Captain said.

"Oh my word," exclaimed Dr. Baruti as he approached the mass of blood, while making sure to distance himself from the Captain's dog. "What's happened?"

"I'm not sure," Captain Grey replied, still studying the material dangling from the end of his pen. "What can you tell me, doctor?"

"I can say that is a lot of blood. Where did it come from?"

"That, I don't know," said Captain Grey.

"Well, to be definitive, sir, I hate to say that nobody could survive that amount of blood loss."

"That's what I was afraid of, Doctor. We need to do a passenger assessment immediately."

Captain Grey grabbed his black portable transmitter and gave it a double click. "First Officer Bailey from the Captain,"

Ten seconds passed.

"First Officer Bailey from Captain Grey. Over."

No answer.

"Navigational Officer Bailey from the Captain. Over."

Ten seconds passed again.

Under his command, no subordinate had ever delayed in responding. Captain Grey grew frustrated - his mind began to race, playing out potential horrible scenarios. He shook the thoughts out of his head and stared back at the bloody pen in his hand.

"I repeat, Navigational Officer Bailey, this is the Captain. Over."

No answer.

Puzzled and growing with concern, Deedat and Dr. Baruti looked at one another.

"First Officer Bailey or Navigational Officer Bailey, answer - this is the Captain speaking!"

No answer.

"Tom, Drew...come in...over!"

"Fenyang, this is the Captain. Over."

No answer.

"Officer Medupé! Come in!"

No answer.

Captain Grey looked at Deedat and Dr. Baruti in shock and disbelief. His frantic eyes scanned the blood spatter, then the sky, and finally toward the ocean. His hand trembled and he accidentally dropped the blood soaked pen and the material back into the pool of blood. He felt a sickening feeling in the pit of his stomach. Keep it together, he thought. A man in his position must maintain composure.

Trying to assure himself that there was a reasonable explanation for the events of the day; Captain Grey put his hat back on and wiped his hands on his pants, even though they weren't dirty.

"Deedat, head to the command center and check the communications. There seems to be a problem with the radio."

Deedat gave a salute and was about to run off, but then the Captain stopped him.

"And while you're there, if you see the Baileys, Medupé, or anyone else from the crew, send them to the mess deck immediately. Doctor, I would also ask that you assemble your entire team in the mess at once. If anybody is found injured along the way, tend to them. Otherwise, wait there until I arrive...and do not mention *this* to anyone! Thank you, now go!"

The two men left Captain Grey standing by the morbid mess with Cody nearby.

Sweat began to bead on the Captain's forehead. His steel blue eyes watched the two men leave. He then shifted his focus to the ocean. No land, ship, or enemy was visible - yet something was wrong in his world. The Captain felt uneasy. After nearly twenty-six years of working at sea, the worst things he'd ever dealt with were bad weather, sea-sick passengers or stale provisions. Today, he'd lost four life rafts and someone on board was injured, or worse...dead.

The Reiziger continued to rock gently with the sea. A small trickle of blood broke free from the pool of coagulation and streamed towards the Captain's boots. Noticing it, he backed away slowly, bracing himself against the guardrail of the ship. The blood narrowly missed his boots and dribbled over the edge. Grey's eyes followed the blood's trail as it dropped to the waters below. Looking down, as it hit the water, he noticed something he wasn't exactly sure he'd ever seen before. Pressed up against the Reiziger was a colorful array of jellyfish.

"What the hell?" the Captain said out loud, but then was distracted.

"Captain, come quickly" Deedat called from the top of the stairway leading to the command center.

Looking away from the jellyfish, "What is it, Mr. Deedat?" Grey replied.

"Please, sir, just come. It's so horrible, I can't explain. I need you to see for yourself."

5

It was the second time that the passengers were assembled in the mess deck that morning. Doctor Baruti didn't give an explanation as to why the Captain had called for them. But most of the passengers half expected an update on the life raft fiasco, so any further explanation wasn't required. Baruti was grateful for that.

As the tired bodies entered the grand room of the mess deck, faces quickly perked up and a few smiles appeared. The smell of fresh bread and the aroma of sausages and eggs wafting into the room instantly eased their minds.

Fenyang, the cook, stood behind a long table draped in a red tablecloth boldly displaying the Reiziger's sun and zodiac logo. Working his craft with two small frying pans, he served up the morning fare for the ravenous crowd. A small white cap partially covered his ponytailed mane of grey hair and a hairnet kept the rest from falling through. Peering through steamed up glasses, the Chinese cook waited for the passengers to select their breakfast meal. He didn't speak to anyone. Instead, he held up two ladles: one was filled with scrambled eggs and the other with a slop of oatmeal. Impatiently, he waited for his patrons to point to which item they wanted. Cooking was his specialty, hospitality was not.

Coffee, juice and disposable cups were set out on a separate table. Next to that, on another table, two platters were set out. One was filled with fresh fruit: strawberries, orange and apple slices, grapes, and bananas. The other platter was toppling with a variety of scones and muffins.

The seven scientists grabbed their morning fare and gathered around three small round tables at the back of the room. Stefan Woodley, Dr. Nombeko Conte, and Dr. Uuka Duiker sat at one table. While Amy Masterson, Dr. Elon Athans, and Stuart Radcliff sat at another. Dr. Baruti chose to sit alone at a third table. Dr. Athans beckoned Dr. Baruti to join them, but he politely declined, claiming he preferred solitude this morning to silently contemplate his work.

Of course, the explanation given by Dr. Baruti wasn't truthful. After seeing the horrific scene of blood, Dr. Baruti was extremely shaken, and for the moment, preferred to sit by himself. He was trying to figure how so much bloodshed could have taken place.

The Reiziger crew seemed sparse within the room. Fenyang was doing the cooking. The chief engineer Alan Ruiz and deck-hand Nelson Blomkamp sat opposite each other at a square table near the main entrance, while Second Officer Medupé sat alone at the officers' table near the center of the room.

Shortly after seven o'clock in the morning, the Captain entered the mess hall with deckhand Winston Deedat on his left and his dog Cody on his right. No one spoke as the trio entered the room. Deedat left the Captain and quickly took a seat with Ruiz and Blomkamp. Captain Grey stopped and looked over the crowd in the room. All eyes in the room were looking back at him.

The Captain looked worried, ragged and tired. His face was drawn and pale. His normally perfect white uniform seemed tattered and loose against his body. He looked sick. Though the Captain hadn't slept since the alarms of the early morning, he looked more like he had just been in a fight – and lost.

As the Captain headed towards the food station, his gait was noticeably slow and assuming. He passed by the officers' table, and tossed his hat on it without saying a word to Medupé. He bypassed Fenyang, not even giving the cook the courtesy of a nod. Instead, the Captain grabbed a food tray and carried on to fill up a plate with fruit and a couple of scones.

Even though his hat was at the officers' table with Medupé, the Captain took a seat at an empty table off to the side of the room. Cody was confused by her master going to sit at a different location, but she followed his lead regardless.

Grey bit into a piece of apple and chewed with his eyes closed. His right boot tapped on the floor with a rapid cadence. Once he realized the noise he was making, he stopped. It was then that he felt the stillness in the room. He opened his eyes and glanced about the room. Everybody was still watching the Captain. Slowly he put down the apple and looked back at the group.

The engineer, Alan Ruiz was a middle-aged man with long, dark hair and a patch over one eye. He'd worked with the Captain longer than any other crewmember aboard the Reiziger and couldn't recall ever seeing the Captain like this. Concerned by the Captain's atypical behavior, Ruiz leaned over and quietly asked Deedat if he knew what was going on. Deedat shook his head and didn't offer any suggestions to his friend.

Suddenly and without warning, Captain Grey broke the silence of the room as he slammed his fist on the table. His plate and contents went flying up into the air only to crash back to the ground where the plate broke into several pieces.

The group was shocked, but the Captain wasn't finished. He quickly stood up and threw his table over. "Goddamnit!" he yelled as the table crashed to the floor.

Cody jumped up and scampered to the opposite side of the room from her master.

Second Officer Medupé got up from his seat and cautiously watched the Captain. Like Ruiz, Medupé had worked with Captain Grey for many years. During that time, he had never seen the Captain lose his composure or his temper. Something was dreadfully wrong. Medupé knew this wasn't just about the life rafts.

The entire room froze at the Captain's outburst. Woodley almost choked on a piece of apple he was chewing. Dr. Conte sprayed out her drink by accident and Fenyang dropped his ladles. The only person that didn't react to the Captain's outburst was Dr. Baruti. Instead, he just closed his eyes and bowed his head to the table.

Realizing that his eruption must have brought a fright to everyone, the Captain was suddenly embarrassed. He straightened his shirt and tucked it back neatly into his pants. He ran his hand across his silver hair and softly began to speak.

"Ladies and Gentlemen, I guess I have your attention?"

Captain Grey paused. The room was still. Images of the blood, the pen, the material, and the rafts danced in the Captain's head.

He took a deep breath, "I apologize for my outburst - that was completely unprofessional and rather out of character," he paused once again. Giving a wave to Medupé, the Captain motioned for his third in command to sit down. Medupé obliged. The Captain patted his leg and beckoned Cody to come back to his side. Unfortunately, for the Captain, she kept her distance. She had seen angry men before and she didn't like men when they were angry.

"I'm sorry, Cody. Please come here, girl," he said, patting his leg.

Cody saw that the Captain's composure was regained, but still wary of him, she approached with extreme caution. When she was close enough, he held out his hand. Her nose sniffed out his palm, wondering if this man really was her master and not the stranger she was watching moments before. He seemed okay. Once Cody felt safe again, she rubbed up close to the Captain, but was prepared to dash again if necessary.

"Good girl, Cody. I'm sorry," he said.

Turning back to the group, the Captain spoke as he patted Cody's head. "Once again, I'm sorry for the outburst. As you can see, even my pup doesn't like me when I'm angry. It doesn't happen often, and I promise, it won't happen again. You have my word."

A few tentative smiles flashed back at him.

"I really don't know where to start..."

"Tell us what the hell is going on...that's a start!" blurted out Stuart Radcliff from the back of the room.

Stuart Radcliff was the youngest of the scientists aboard the ship. He was in his mid-twenties but usually acted below his age and education level. He wore a grey hooded sweatshirt with khaki shorts and leather sandals. His casually tousled blonde hair was medium-length. He was tall, handsome and looked more like a surfer than a scientist.

The whole room was waiting for Captain Grey to explode on Stuart, just as he had done earlier in the morning toward Stephan Woodley. But this time he didn't.

"Fair enough, you do deserve an explanation. Mister? um...I'm sorry," said the Captain.

"It's Radcliff." Stuart sneered.

"My apology, Mr. Radcliff. I should have remembered you from our meeting this morning. I guess you didn't make much of an impression."

Stuart didn't catch the insult. He just nodded back to the Captain.

Captain Grey smiled to himself, despite still being distraught. "Well, Mr. Radcliff, as you well know, earlier this morning someone aboard this ship released our life rafts. I know for a fact that this was not a mechanical malfunction. Our rafts can only be manually released. With that in mind, I decided that it was in the best interest of the Reiziger and my crew, that we suspend our voyage to St. Helena until I found who was responsible for this heinous action. I regret to inform you all - that it is something I have yet to figure out. While searching for a guilty party in that matter, one of my men made a grisly discovery. It's something so very upsetting and something I can't explain. And if this distressing matter wasn't enough..." The Captain's hands began to shake. His eyes narrowed into tiny slits. Cody sensed trouble and slowly moved away from her master.

"...during that time, while I was away from the command center bridge, this unknown saboteur struck the Reiziger a second time."

The audience in the mess hall gasped in shock.

"Yes," continued Captain Grey, anger rising in his voice. "Someone entered the command center and intentionally destroyed our communications system. Our long and short-range radio transmitters are damaged, as well as our navigational system, sonar, and computers. Everything is ruined!"

No one moved. The silence was so heavy it was suffocating.

"Captain, what are we going to do?" Dr. Athans finally asked, "Are we stranded?"

Deedat discretely got up and helped the Captain pick up the table and set it back in place. Captain Grey spoke again, thanking Deedat for his help as he gave him a pat on the back.

"Fortunately no, doctor. The Reiziger can still be guided without modern technology - but to do so, I must heavily rely on my crew. This brings me to a very grave and serious matter: without our communications I do not have immediate contact with my crew. I need to be in contact with them; it's imperative. I'm afraid we're also dealing with something much more serious than the lack of communications." Captain Grey's eyes began to tear up as he scratched his head and looked up at the ceiling.

"What is it, Captain?" asked Ruiz.

"Chief Officer Tom Bailey and Navigational Officer Bailey have not reported in. I don't know where they are. I'm sure this is just a communications issue. I did have trouble getting in touch with Fenyang and Officer Medupé earlier, but as you can see, these two men are present and accounted for. I still haven't heard from the remainder of my crew."

"What are you saying? Are they hurt? Missing? What are you saying?" asked Conte.

"We could help you look for them, Captain," Athans said. "It's not *that* big of a ship!"

The Captain looked across the room at Amy. Her eyes were beginning to well up with tears. The Captain wasn't sure if Amy's reaction was out of empathy for the missing men, or due to the fact that her mission was further in jeopardy of being ruined. Grey felt it was the latter.

"Please, everyone – I'm requesting that you return to your cabins and remain there until further notice. My crew will take care of all matters. I assure you that there's an explanation for everything. Tom and Drew are aboard, I'm sure, but they have yet to report in. They probably don't know anything about the communications being down. They could be working on a multitude of things, and we just haven't crossed paths yet. They're okay, you'll see," he whispered the last part as he knelt down and began to pick up the pieces of the broken plate. Cody flinched at the movement. Grey reached out a hand to calm her, but she backed away even further.

The Captain felt bad. He didn't mean to alarm Cody or the passengers with his hostile behaviour. He shook his head and tossed his hand into the air with an apologetic gesture to Cody.

He had to remain in control. Everyone depended on him to keep cool. Realizing this, he snapped back into his captain mode and began by giving some orders as he placed the broken plate on the table.

"Mr. Deedat, return to the command center and see if we can fix our communications. Whatever it takes, get something working. Mr. Ruiz, tend to the engines, we'll be putting them back online shortly. Mr. Blomkamp and Officer Medupé, I have an urgent matter that needs attention. If you would please come with me, I will fill you in along the way."

"Captain, is there anything our team can help with?" offered Dr. Athans.

"I thank you Doctor, but no. Right now, please just finish your breakfast. When you are done your meal, I kindly request that you return to your quarters. My men will take care of the Reiziger. When all is in order, I will send for your team. That's all. Thank you."

"Captain!" Dr. Baruti spoke from the back of the room.

"I request that I assist Mr. Blomkamp and Officer Medupé."

As Dr. Baruti got up from his table at the back of the room, Cody turned toward the jolly-faced doctor and gave him a growl. Dr. Baruti froze. His eyes met Cody's and then quickly shifted to the Captain for his protection.

"Cody! Leave the doctor alone," ordered Captain Grey.

Both the Captain and Baruti knew that the doctor's assistance with the 'urgent matter' would definitely be beneficial. The doctor had already seen the blood and any further examination into who, what, why, and how's, would definitely require his professional expertise. Captain Grey needed to know if the blood was human or otherwise. He needed many answers.

"Yes, Doctor," the Captain nodded, "you know the location. Please take my men and use them as required. The rest of you, thank you for your patience and understanding. I will keep you informed."

Captain Grey turned and left the mess deck room. As he walked by the head table, he scooped up his hat and slapped it on his head. He patted his thigh and Cody obediently followed the Captain from the room. She seemed to have forgiven his outburst.

Winston Deedat and Alan Ruiz quickly followed behind the Captain, while the remainder of the room sat in silence.

"Bruno! What is going on?" asked Dr. Athans, grabbing Dr. Baruti's wrist as he walked past the other scientists at their table.

Dr. Athans was a fifty-two year old Caucasian man. He was slim, tall and always quick with a disarming smile. He always wore a wool sweater over a white collared shirt topped off with a bow-tie.

Dr. Baruti looked at his friend, realizing he'd never seen Athans not wearing a bow-tie. He tapped Dr. Athans gently on the hand as he pulled his wrist free. "It is a very serious matter, my friend," replied Dr. Baruti, "but with respect to the Captain, I cannot say what it is about. I will assemble the team later and explain everything to the best of my ability."

"Are we in any danger?" asked Stuart Radcliff.

"No, my young man, I don't believe so. Please, just go to your cabins. I'll come by shortly and see you all."

"Where are the Baileys'? What's going on? What you are helping the crew in trying to figure out?" asked Dr. Conte.

"I don't know...no, Doctor, please...I will explain everything once I know more. I must leave with Officer Medupé and

Mr. Blomkamp now. Please respect the Captain and return to your rooms. I'll be along shortly."

Doctor Baruti left the room with Officer Medupé and Nelson Blomkamp in tow.

The six remaining scientists sat at the back of the mess hall feeling isolated.

"What the hell is going on?" Stuart Radcliff asked as he banged a fork against the table. "Why are we being kept in the dark about something? We're all stuck on this damn ship together. I think that son of a bitch Captain is crazy. He's putting our mission in jeopardy and I don't think he's giving us the whole story. He wouldn't even give me a straight answer. In fact, he just danced around the whole thing. And now, the communications are down. That's just great. We're sitting in the middle of the Atlantic Ocean, and he wants to play investigator? Bullshit! I say we tell the Captain he'd better get us moving or we'll inform our benefactor to withhold all payment."

Peter Woodley, Amy Masterson, Dr. Athans, and Dr. Conte, said nothing. They knew that Stuart might be right, but nobody had anything else to add.

They looked to each other for reassurance, but found none.

Dr. Uuka Duiker kept his head bowed towards the table. He hadn't moved during the entire episode with the Captain. Then very slowly and methodically, the elderly scientist pushed his tray of food away as he spoke up to nobody in particular.

"Everything happens for a reason. That is the pattern of life."

The group of scientists all turned toward the old man. They were all very surprised to hear him speak.

The scientists sat waiting...waiting for him to speak again, hoping he was the voice of reason. Perhaps his wisdom would shed some light on their situation. Perhaps he could offer some words of optimism and insight. The room was still as they all listened intently. Finally Dr. Duiker spoke again.

"Have any of you considered that maybe, just maybe, we were not meant to get to St. Helena? Perhaps God does not *want* us to do our work. Perhaps our work would lead to discoveries we are not meant to find," he paused, lifting his head to examine the group of scientists – his so-called peers.

Uuka Duiker was definitely the eldest member of the group. He looked older than Methuselah, though he was only seventy-one. Dr. Duiker and Dr. Conte were close friends and had spent many years working together. It was Dr. Conte who offered him the opportunity to assist the other, younger scientists on this mission. It was a chance for Dr. Duiker to share his expertise and knowledge...to pass on his legacy.

He rarely spoke, but when he did, it was quite unsettling, especially for the younger scientists. His voice was deep, raspy and powerful.

"Man was not meant to develop nuclear power. Man was not meant to rape mother Earth of her natural resources, but man did! People like us, people of science did! Day after day, we are paying dearly for those discoveries. Perhaps these events are happening for a reason. Part of a master design...a plan. I don't know. I can't convince you on what to believe. But I believe they are what they are, and happening for a reason. Therefore, I won't fight it. No, instead, I'll go to my room, and I will wait. If God does not want me to reach St. Helena, then I won't. I'll just wait for another tomorrow. I will see another day and I'll find my answers then..."

Doctor Duiker grabbed his brass cane and struggled against his arthritic body to get up from his seat. Once standing, he had to pause to catch his breath.

Without another word, he slowly walked from the room, while the remaining scientists watched him leave. Nobody knew what to say. They were in shock by the doctor's comments.

"Perhaps he's right," said Dr. Athans, "maybe we should do exactly as the doctor says and..."

"Perhaps he's right?" Stuart exclaimed. "That was psychobabble from a geriatric has-been. That was complete bullshit! That's what that was. Are you kidding me? Half of what he said didn't even make sense."

"That's quite enough, Mr. Radcliff," Dr. Conte cut in, visibly upset at Stuart belittling her friend. Dr. Conte was a heavy-set black woman in her mid-fifties. Normally not one to raise her voice, she couldn't contain herself at the moment.

"If you took the time to listen, you'd understand what the good doctor was saying. Doctor Duiker is a wise man and you should respect him."

"Ah, bullshit," Stuart said waving his hand in the air at Dr. Conte. He didn't want to talk to her, and she didn't want to say anything more to Stuart, but simply returned his gesture.

"What do you think, Amy?" asked Dr. Athans, trying to divert a battle that was brewing between two of his team members.

Amy wasn't expecting to have her opinion asked, but for some reason, Dr. Athans, the leader of her expedition wanted her opinion. She wondered if her feigned confidence with the Captain earlier had made an impression with her colleagues. Obviously, it had with Dr. Athans.

"I don't know, Doctor. I appreciate what Dr. Duiker is saying, but I can't say I fully agree," Amy said as she dabbed tears from her eyes, again using Medupé's handkerchief from earlier in the day. "I believe we were sent here for a reason, and I believe we have to fulfill our mission - for ourselves and for science in general. If we wait for divine intervention, we may miss our opportunity. No, I think we have to find a way to convince the Captain to get us to St. Helena – all of us need to work on him. We must find a way to persuade him. Either that or we need to find another way to get there. If we don't...this mission is lost."

6

Lefu stood at the bow of the Pemba Koningin like a statue: godlike, bronzed and powerful. The early morning sun beat upon his bald head. Mirrored sunglasses hid his eyes and partially covered a large scar that ran just below his right eye. His sleeveless shirt exposed an array of tattoos stretching the length of both of his muscular arms. With an unlit cigar hanging from the corner of his mouth, he watched the horizon, searching for the Reiziger.

Enzo Carlito steadied the Pemba Koningin across the water from the bridge of the command center. He constantly checked charts, gauges, and monitors. Everything was as it should be.

Meanwhile, Percy and Jako sat at opposite each other at a large overturned spool of rope near the bow of the ship. The pair played cards, a game of "Crazy Eights" – a game almost too difficult for their IQ's. Jako won every time and Percy was growing increasingly frustrated with the outcome, but continued to play regardless.

Lefu walked past his minions. The two brutes offered their leader to join in, but Lefu didn't have the patience or mindset for games right now. It was only a month ago that Lefu visited the Dorrondon mines, where he decided to play a couple of hands of poker with some of the miners. The men there always made sure Lefu won, as they were fearful of what might happen if he ever lost. Lefu didn't like losing, but he hated being patronized even more. At the end of the game, four of the miners ended up dead and Lefu walked away three hundred dollars richer. Lefu didn't wish the same outcome to his men and simply walked away from Jako and Percy.

"Carlito, you dumb son of a bitch! You said we'd be on top of them within a few hours," Lefu yelled up to the command center from the deck below.

Carlito walked out on the catwalk beside the command center to yell back. He was holding a sandwich and chewing. He held up a finger and paused for a moment before he spoke, "I can't hear you up here, you dumb son of a bitch."

Lefu shot him a look and yelled back, "I said, what is taking so long? Why aren't we on top of them?"

"I don't know! Something has happened!"

"What do you mean?"

"How the hell would I know? I can't make sense of it."

Lefu was annoyed with the yelling back and forth. He climbed his way up the side stairs to the catwalk and into the command center to speak with Carlito.

"Now tell me again, what's going on?" demanded Lefu.

"I don't know. You probably wouldn't understand either," Carlito laughed.

"Give me a try." Lefu didn't return a laugh or a smile.

Percy and Jako had heard the commotion and saw Lefu yelling at Carlito. The pair stopped playing their game and climbed up to the command center to listen in. Percy was the bigger of the two black henchmen. He stood over six feet six and weighed in at easily three hundred pounds of pure muscle. He was a monster. Jako was shorter and at least a hundred pounds lighter than Percy, but his stocky frame made him a solid, immovable black brick wall.

The two men positioned themselves on either side of Lefu to show their allegiance. Carlito looked at the three big men. He'd always been able to get away with being crass with Lefu - they had a history, but the other two men, he didn't trust. Ever since his beating in prison, he secretly feared most black men.

"Okay...I don't know why, but for some reason, this Reiziger ship is not moving. And, I can't pick up their radio signals anymore."

"Do they know we're coming?" asked Percy.

"I don't know...No radio frequencies are being emitted from their location so we can't intercept what they're up to, where they're going, or who they're talking to, if anyone. All we know for sure is that their ship is not moving."

Lefu lit his cigar and gently traced his finger along the pistol harnessed into his belt. "Is it possible they found out we were following them?" Lefu asked.

"Joost could have warned them," said Percy.

"Exactly," said Jako.

The three men watched Carlito. The sloppily dressed, rotund Italian man began to feel uneasy. He placed his sandwich on the console beside the radar monitor. Flipping switches and pressing random buttons, he tried to make himself seem busy. He knew he needed to make himself indispensable. Hours before, he'd seen the handiwork of these men and what they did to Ramon Diez. It was obvious that they were capable of horrible things.

"Of course, it's possible. We send out pulses and signals as a vessel on the water. As a solid moving mass, their radar would be able to read that we've been travelling almost their exact route since Cape Town, but I have no control over that. The only way to avoid partial or complete detection would be to travel a different route," said Carlito as beads of sweat formed across his brow.

The three black men did not look happy.

"I wouldn't worry though. We're travelling along a secondary shipping route. A few ships would travel this pathway. If they did see us – they shouldn't feel threatened. They'd have no reason to feel threatened; unless, as you said, they were warned of someone looking for them."

Lefu snubbed out his cigar ash onto Carlito's greasy sandwich. "For your sake, they'd better not know we're coming."

* * *

The remaining scientists finished their breakfast and placed their trays into a bin at the end of the serving table, next to a can. One by one, they filed out of the mess hall and walked back to their cabins as requested by the captain. Everyone left except Amy Masterson and Stephan Woodley. Earlier, while they were eating, Stephan had quietly asked Amy to stay behind after the others had left.

Stuart Radcliff was the last to leave besides Amy and Stephan. As he walked from the mess hall, he turned and yelled back at Fenyang, "This is complete bullshit, you know? Your Captain is a lunatic!"

The small cook struck a warrior pose, wielding his ladles as though they were swords. Stephan thought Fenyang was ready to attack. Instead, Fenyang straightened himself back up and just smiled at Radcliff before returning to his duties of cleaning up.

"What was that about?" Stephan asked.

"I don't know. Stu has some real anger issues. To be honest, that's kind of why I'm not with him anymore," Amy replied.

Fenyang was the only person left in the mess hall besides the two scientists. The little cook went about cleaning up from the breakfast session and paid no attention to Stephan and Amy. As he cleared and wiped the tables, he mumbled to himself in Chinese.

Stephan watched him intently. When he felt certain that Fenyang wasn't paying attention to them, he reached into his leather messenger bag tucked beneath his seat and pulled out a pair of binoculars. He placed them on the table in front of Amy.

"Here, take these and have a look directly out that window beside you," he said.

"Where did you get these?" Amy asked.

"Never mind that right now. Just look out that window."

Amy reached across the table and grabbed the black binoculars. As she picked them up, she noticed the inscription on their side – 'Reiziger'.

"Please tell me you didn't steal these Stephan," whispered Amy.

"Don't worry about that. Let's just say I found them. Come on, just look out the window!"

Amy removed her glasses and lifted the heavy binoculars to her eyes. Her eyes struggled for a moment to focus through the large binoculars, panning her view back and forth across the seascape. "What am I looking for?" she said as she peered out the window to the right of her, scanning the western horizon.

"You'll see it...just keep looking," he said.

Suddenly, Amy pulled the binoculars away. Her mouth opened wide in disbelief. She looked again through the binoculars. "Please tell me that's what I think it is!?!"

"It is indeed!"

"Holy crap!" Amy screamed, "St. Helena! How far away do you think it is?"

"I'm guessing maybe thirty or forty miles at best, maybe a bit more," said Stephan matching her excitement.

"What are we going to do? I mean, there it is, right there beside us, and we're sitting here. We have to get there, Stephan. We have to tell the Captain to get us there."

"That's the problem. I don't think the Captain is going to let us go anywhere."

"Oh Stephan, you know as well as I do, we must get to St. Helena. I have to finish my research! You do too. There's not much time!" Amy exclaimed.

Fenyang dropped a plate. It shattered on the floor and the sound rattled through the mess hall. Kneeling down to pick up the mess, he stopped and glanced over at the scientists, mumbling something under his breath. He then gave a simple headshake of disapproval towards the scientists, and went back to his work.

"Do you think he noticed the binoculars?" asked Amy.

"I didn't steal them. Besides, who gives a shit? He's part of this damn crew. They haven't been anything but a headache this whole trip." Stephan took the binoculars and placed them back inside his leather bag just in case Fenyang *was* watching them.

"Where did you get them?" Amy prodded, pointing to the case.

Stephan Woodley checked over his shoulder and slowly leaned close to Amy. "I found them on the main deck of the ship. They were lying on the ground by where the life rafts once were. You know the rafts that are missing? Anyway, they were just sitting by a big pool of blood...and I didn't want to hang around there, so I just grabbed them."

Amy's eyes rushed with fear.

"Blood?" she said, "From whom?"

"I don't know."

"Do you think the Captain knows about it?"

"Considering the way he acted at breakfast, I'd say so. Remember he mentioned the Bailey's? They're missing, and then there's this blood. Now somebody has sabotaged the ship by destroying the communications," Stephan considered what he was saying. "Holy shit, Amy, if the Captain is dealing with all these problems: the life boats, the communications, the Baileys, and now this blood, I can tell you we're definitely *not* going to reach St. Helena. He'll probably scrap the entire mission and take us back to Cape Town."

"What about the Coast Guard? Couldn't he just signal for them to come and help?" Amy suggested.

"There's no radio to signal anybody with, Amy. And there's no coast nearby. We're in the middle of the Atlantic. There's no Coast Guard out this far."

"This can't be happening," said Amy.

Stephan gently grabbed onto Amy's wrist and held it. He leaned across the table very close to her and spoke in a whisper, "I know a way we can get to Saint Helena."

7

Winston Deedat sat at the main console beside the high frequency radio transmitter; his eyes weary from the task before him. An HF radio dangled precariously from the side of the console, smashed into several pieces. From its mounting bracket, hung blue, green and yellow wires needed for the unit to work. The wires were ripped unceremoniously from their harness and lay slack on the floor. The unit seemed beyond repair, yet Deedat fumbled with the mess of wires in a desperate attempt to fix the communications.

Captain Grey crouched down near Deedat. He tried to piece together the pieces of the ship's CB radio and VHF radio receivers. Both were shattered beyond recognition. He grabbed the portable CB receiver from his belt clip and clicked it to see if he could conjure a response from the main units. He hoped for a signal, a noise, anything...but nothing happened.

Cody paced the room in a panic. Her blanket bed had been tossed about and she was afraid to go near it. Captain Grey noticed her uneasiness and tried to reassure her that everything was okay, but the dog continued to pace, still frightened by all of the morning's strange events.

Coming back from cleaning up the bloody mess on the main deck, Nelson Blomkamp and Second Officer Medupé entered the command center. It was the first time they had seen the ransacked room. Both men were shocked at the sight before them.

Blomkamp didn't speak, but quickly went to work sweeping up pieces of glass and debris. Medupé surveyed the damaged computer systems.

The computer display monitors were smashed in and the thick tinted glass from the units covered the command center floor. Letters and numbers from the keyboards decorated the room in a nonsensical jumble of scrabble words.

Upon further inspection, Captain Grey noticed that even *if* the monitors and keyboards were not ruined, the main power supply cords were severed. The saboteur made sure that any repair would be next to impossible.

"I don't understand," said Captain Grey, tossing a broken handheld receiver across the room.

"Captain," whispered Blomkamp as he pointed to a fire extinguisher discarded at the corner of the room.

Captain Grey slowly walked over to the extinguisher. The red powder coating finish on the extinguisher was worn away in sections. Large dents occupied most of its once smooth exterior. The squeeze trigger and its pressure valve were missing. Fine particulates of a yellowish calcium carbonate poured from top of the canister as the Captain picked it up. He let the yellow dust flow through his fingers as he dropped the extinguisher to the ground.

As the extinguisher clinked against the ground, engineer Alan Ruiz entered the command center. He was out of breath, his face red, looking as if he just ran a marathon. "Holy shit!" he exclaimed as he rested his hands on his thighs and continued panting.

Captain Grey didn't mean to lose his temper with Ruiz, but he did. "I thought I gave you a direct order to attend to the engine room, Mr. Ruiz!"

Ruiz tried to defend himself as he spoke while catching his breath. "You did, sir...but Captain, we have a problem. You have to come quickly."

8

Shortly after eleven a.m., Amy and Stefan left the mess hall, inconspicuously exiting so not to be noticed by Fenyang. Fortunately, the cook was in the galley, too busy going about his business preparing for the lunch service to pay any attention to the two scientists.

A strong westerly wind blew across the main deck. The wind was so powerful that the two scientists walked the perimeter of the ship leaning into the wind, as if marching into a gale at a forty-five degree angle. Amy tucked in close behind Stephan, using his body to keep herself somewhat sheltered from the gusts. With her small frame, she thought it possible she might get blown overboard.

En route, Stephan wanted to tell Amy where he was taking her, but the wind was too loud. Instead he used hand signals and gestures in an attempt to plead with Amy that what he wanted to show her was very important. But Amy separated from Stephan and made her way to the cabins. When the pair reached Amy's cabin, they both stepped inside.

"I was trying to tell you that I need to show you something. Come on. We don't have time to stop here right now!" Stephan pleaded.

"I know. Okay. I know. I'm well aware that you were trying to tell me something back there, but I'm sick of running around this ship in my pajamas. Just give me a second."

Stephan smacked his forehead and gave out a yell of frustration.

Amy disregarded Stephan and began to change in front of him. She threw on some jeans, runners and a hooded sweatshirt. She ran to the bathroom and did a quick glance in the bathroom mirror. She decided that she looked okay. For her own vanity, she stuffed a tube of lipstick into her pocket before she left.

"Ready now?" Stephan said sarcastically.

"Don't be an ass. You would've done the same."

Once outside Amy's room, Stephan took the lead as the pair left the cabin area. He walked in a suspicious manner. His eyes scanned the main deck and command center towering above from the superstructure for any signs of someone watching. Amy mimicked his every move.

Since the alert earlier in the morning, everyone aboard the Reiziger had become suspicious of one another – at least it seemed that way. No one spoke. Amy realized why Stephan was being cautious. Only four days ago, the research team walked this ship carefree. Now they felt that their every move was under scrutiny. A new set of circumstances presented danger to them. A new strangeness and fear was felt amongst the stranded passengers.

Stephan waved Amy to a stop when they came upon the lifeboat. She stood behind him and kept a lookout.

A carefully painted stencil on the side of the boat read: "Savior 5 Rescue". The free fall, fully enclosed lifeboat rested on top of two tubular steel rails reaching out towards the ocean. The lifeboat was a bright orange, a sharp contrast to the blue and white of the Reiziger. The bow of the lifeboat rested at a forty-five degree downward angle positioned away from its mother ship. This allowed for a fast and direct drop to the ocean below. Such was the beauty of a free fall lifeboat.

None of the other four life rafts that were lost earlier in the morning were anything quite like 'Savior 5'. The life rafts were compressed air inflatable units. They were small drifting boats that had no motors or capability of propulsion. The Savior 5 on the other hand, was a fully enclosed lifeboat that resembled a tiny submarine. Its rescue capacity was listed at fifteen passengers, though as the Captain had mentioned earlier, it could carry more if need be. It was fully stocked with water and food rations to last for five days at sea. Boasting two heavy-duty batteries to power up the single inboard diesel engine, the boat was capable of six knots undisturbed for twenty-four hours. Made entirely of specially designed fibreglass, the lifeboat was lightweight, waterproof, rustproof, and fireproof.

Woodley traced his hand across the boat, "This is our answer."

Amy looked at him with shock. This was the first time she'd ever seen a dark side to Stephan.

"We can't," whispered Amy.

"Yes, we can! And we should. Think about it - we're trapped on a boat that isn't going anywhere anytime soon. Our destination is thirty miles away. You and I both know that the Captain isn't going to take us there. He's stranded us in the middle of the South Atlantic, and he's not going to make a move to benefit us until he has an explanation for what's going on. But nobody knows what's going on – including the Captain!"

Stephan placed a hand on Amy's shoulder as she turned to face where St. Helena would be, hidden somewhere off in the distance.

"I know that St. Helena is the only thing that matters to you, Amy. We need to get into this lifeboat, reach St. Helena, do our work, and arrange for new transport home from there. Screw the Captain and screw the Reiziger. Our mission is more important. I don't care what Dr. Duiker said either. Stuart's right, he's a crazy old bastard. I mean, really, if man wasn't supposed to discover nuclear power or live off our natural resources, then we wouldn't have! You and I both know, as scientists, that the benefits of any of those discoveries far exceed any detriments. We are doing valuable work, work that could change and benefit the whole world. We have to do this. This is your life, Amy. And this is my life, too."

"I know, Stephan, but, what about the others? Our colleagues...shouldn't we let them know or bring them along? I don't feel right doing something behind everyone's back like this."

"I thought of that, but if we wait to find out what the others think of this idea – it'll be too late. Athans, Baruti, and Conte are old school, rational thinkers, they would never approve of taking the lifeboat. I don't need to mention Dr. Duiker and where he would stand on the issue. That only leaves Stuart, but I don't know about him. I know you two have a past, but he seems too self-serving and angry to be trusted. He could turn on us and let the others in on it. Hell, he could even tell the Captain. No, I think we need to act alone, just you and me. To the others, desperate times *don't* call for desperate measures. No, to them desperate times call for analytical thinking. But we don't have time to think rational or analytical. Besides, if we told them of our plan, they would surely ban us from this mission – permanently. Athans would make sure we'd be off the project. Our funding would be cut, and we'd probably be thrown out of the university and blacklisted in our respective fields forever."

"And you *don't* think that would happen if we stole a lifeboat?" asked Amy.

The reality of what Amy had said became apparent to Stephan. His demeanour shifted from that of a respected scientist to that of a child - one who was told that he couldn't watch anymore television, and that he had to go to bed. He slapped his open hand against the side of the lifeboat in anger.

"This is bullshit!" Stephan yelled up to the sky, only to collapse to his knees as if he were a puppet whose strings had just been cut.

The pair was silent. Neither knew what to do or say. Amy looked at Stephan kneeling on the ground and she felt sorry for him. She knew that Stephan was right. The only way either of them were going to get to St. Helena in time, was to make use of this lifeboat.

Stephan leaned up against the fibreglass of Savior 5 and began rhythmically banging his head against its side. Amy looked back to the sea, trying to catch a glimpse of St. Helena with her naked eye. Her efforts would prove fruitless once again.

The wind blew heavy again, muting the sound of Stephan Woodley knocking his head against the rescue boat. White capped waves bounced off the side of the disabled mother ship. All surrounding noises were enough distraction that neither Stephan nor Amy heard the side hatch door on Savior 5 open. Nor did either one notice a man slowly climbing from the lifeboat.

Amy finally decided that she would take part in Stephan's plan, but it was too late. As she turned to tell Stephan that they should take the boat and that she was prepared to suffer all consequences of their actions, Amy saw the stranger who had emerged from the lifeboat.

Standing before her was a young Caucasian man. His clothes were dishevelled, his steel blue eyes looked tired, his tanned complexion was weathered and his entire being seemed frightened and beaten.

"Omigod!" said Amy.

Stephan looked up at Amy to see what startled her, only to have the butt of a gun smash into his face. His world turned black.

9

The sound of water breaching the hull could be heard before Captain Grey entered the engine control room. As he slowly entered the engine room with Ruiz and Cody close behind, he could see a small spray shooting into the air. The water appeared to be coming from the hull near the back of bulkhead number three. The water sprayed mercilessly into the engine room and carelessly bounced off the steel plating protecting portions of main engine number two.

"Ruiz, close off bulkhead number three!" commanded Captain Grey.

"Yes sir, right away," responded Ruiz as he set to compartmentalize the bulkhead. By the push of a single button on the engine room console, a watertight door sealed off the leaking portion of the ship.

"Closed, sir. But sir, when I came to find you that breach wasn't there. That wasn't the problem! There was another breach in the hull by bulkhead number one. I've already closed that compartment off."

The rushing sound of the water continued to reverberate through the engine control room as the bulkhead filled with seawater. The Captain listened as bulkhead three knocked and pinged with water rushing in. Within twenty minutes, the compartment would be totally filled with water. The pressure within the compartment would be equalized to the ocean, but the Reiziger would be carrying a heavier than normal payload with the water trapped within her hull. However, the Captain knew the Reiziger would remain stable and afloat, even with two bulkheads completely full.

"What the hell happened here, Mr. Ruiz?" said Captain Grey.

"I'm not sure, sir. I was doing some pressure testing on the pumps when I saw the first breach. I tried to take a closer look but there was too much water. It looked as if the water was coming in beside the intake-cooling system, but I can't say for certain. I'm wondering if it could possibly be an old weak point going back to Captain Klaustzman's days. You know, from the Reiziger's accident in Morocco?"

"No, I don't think so Mr. Ruiz. When the Reiziger's previous captain Mr. Klaustzman ran her aground, she suffered a tear across the thwart side. That damage was extensively repaired. No, this seems to be something different. But I don't know why. And you say you didn't notice that number three was in breach?"

"No, Captain. It must have happened sometime after. But sir, there's another problem. I don't know why, but for some reason we're running hot. Even with the engines off, the pumps seem to be overheating. I can't bring their temperature down, yet everything else seems to be in check."

"Who gave you the order to cut the engines in the first place Mr. Ruiz?" said the Captain.

"Nobody sir, I didn't kill the engines. I thought Officer Bailey shut them from the command center bridge. I was in the mess hall with you when they ceased."

"Perhaps he did. I don't know. I didn't really think to ask when that went down. I'm sorry Alan, it's been a hell of a day."

Captain Grey looked around the engine room. He looked for any sign of anything out of the ordinary.

Was it possible a saboteur had come in here and caused damage? Just about now *anything* was possible.

"Have you left this room at all, Ruiz?"

"Only when I came to get you, sir. Other than that, I've been here since our meeting this morning."

"What the hell is going on? Where are the Baileys?" the Captain asked. He was hoping for an answer from Ruiz, but instead, Ruiz stood there looking just as puzzled as the Captain.

Cody was standing near the main control lever for the clutch that drove the props. She was sniffing at the lever and wagging her tail.

"What's got you, old girl?" Captain Grey asked to his dog.

Cody barked a response back to her master that he would never understand. She then lay down on the cold metal flooring as her master looked at her. The Captain envied Cody. The life of a dog seemed so simple to him. No worries, no concerns, no cares. He smiled at her.

"Life of a dog," he said, "You're one lucky pooch."

"Sir, what should we do?" Ruiz interrupted the Captain.

Grey snapped back to the task at hand. Without speaking he began to check the engine's gauges and readouts one by one. Finally, he acknowledged Ruiz and answered his question. "Mr. Ruiz, stay here and purge the remaining water from this room. Get the engines primed, back online and ready to fire. Monitor the temperature and pressure. Keep the screws at an even turn, but with no mobility once you're online. I don't want to proceed just yet, so don't engage the clutch. Not until we find out where the Baileys are. Our communications are broken at the moment, as you know, so once you are up and running, just wait for myself or Second Officer Medupé to return with the next command. Is that clear, Mr. Ruiz?"

"Yes, sir."

"Come on, Cody."

* * *

"Omigod - is he dead?" cried Amy.

"Naw, he ain't dead, Red. He's just having a nap," replied the young man holding the gun, the same gun that just crashed into Stephan's face.

He spoke in a flippant tone, characteristic of someone strung out on drugs or someone who just didn't care about anything. The truth was he didn't really know if he had killed Stephan Woodley. If he had, it was too late, so there was no point worrying about it.

Amy was in shock; fearful for her own life. She was torn: she wanted to help Stephan and make sure he was alright, but she couldn't - the man who just knocked out Stephan was pointing the gun directly at her.

She had never seen a man hit so hard in the face, and she couldn't recall seeing that much blood ever. Even for a biologist who has worked around tissues and fluids for most of her life, Amy found the sight of the blood quite disturbing.

Amy turned her attention back to the man with the gun.

"Why did you do that? Who are you and what do you want from us?"

"Never mind. I've got my reasons. And as for you, you're my ticket out of here, Red. Come on."

Before Amy could run away, he grabbed her by her auburn ponytail and directed her to walk while he kept his pistol trained to the back of her head.

"No, please...stop! I don't want to die. Ow...that hurts...please...stop...What about Stephan? He needs help, please!" cried Amy.

"I said move," the gunman yelled as he smacked Amy across the back of the head with his pistol. He didn't hit her hard enough to knock her out, but just hard enough to let her know that he meant business.

Amy wasn't expecting the hit. She was slightly dazed from the blow. Instead of following the gunman's commands, she felt her legs become weak. Her mind wandered from the moment as she marvelled how strange she suddenly felt. The pain in her head suddenly became insignificant. She almost expected her sympathetic nervous response to kick into fight or flight mode, but instead she drifted away in her thoughts.

Amy forgot about the gun to her head, or her mission to reach St. Helena. She was no longer on the Reiziger. Instead, she was having thoughts of home. She reverted back to her childhood. There she was, in Zeeland, North Dakota, the impoverished farming community in the middle of nowhere, middle-America.

Zeeland had once meant the world to Amy. It was the place of her birth, the place of her childhood; the place where her life had begun and ended...it was also the place where she planned to return to die someday.

Amy's eyes filled with tears as she thought of her mother, twenty-seven year old Dee Woodley, who died when Amy was only four.

It was a warm and beautiful North Dakota summer day, almost two years after her father left her mother, brother and Amy to fend for themselves. Dee was busy hanging laundry while Amy sat playing nearby in the sandbox with her brother.

Dee was young, beautiful, and strong, much like Amy at her current twenty-seven years. Amy could see her mother's face with such clarity. She could remember her smile as though it was only yesterday. What a beautiful smile she had. It was the same smile she was giving to Amy while she was hanging the laundry on the clothesline, when, as quickly as she smiled, Dee had a massive aneurism and died instantly. In a flash, her mother was dead. All that remained was her mother's smile; an image forever captured into Amy's mind.

After Dee's passing, Amy and her brother Stephan were sent to live with their aunt and uncle Jules and Billy Masterson, up in Billings, Montana.

Transported to a bigger city, the siblings slowly adjusted to their new surroundings.

Jules and Billy didn't have children of their own, which afforded Stephan and Amy a proper education, proper nutrition, and a stable home life.

Over the years, Amy had a harder and harder time remembering her mother's face, but now, at this moment, it was so clear in her mind's eye. Dee was there smiling at Amy.

Amy snapped out of her dream state and looked back at Stephan unconscious on the ground beside Savior 5. She could now see how much he looked like their mother. She understood why family friends and relatives had made that reference as he grew up. Stephan seemed to have the exact same smile on his face that Dee had the moment she died.

"Please be okay, Stephan. You're all I have," Amy whispered.

The gunman pushed Amy again, "Don't worry about him, Red. He'll wake up with a big headache, but he'll be fine. If I were you, I'd just worry about myself, not your boyfriend. Now move!"

As the gunman repeatedly pushed Amy from behind forcing her to walk away, she froze. His tactics weren't working. Very slowly he released his grip on her ponytail. Suddenly, Amy felt the cold steel of the gun pressing against the base of her skull.

"I said move," he whispered close to her ear.

"He's not my boyfriend, you son of a bitch!" Amy yelled back to her assailant. "He's my brother! And if he dies, I swear to God, I'll kill you."

The gunman grabbed Amy by the shoulder and spun her around to see her face. She was crying, but didn't raise a hand to wipe away the tears. She didn't want to show her fear, not to this bastard.

Amy could see her assailant's eyes widen and his lips unfurl as he watched her cry. Moments ago, this man with a gun was ready to kill her, yet now he seemed somewhat concerned. Was he? Or was he psychotic and had no emotion? Maybe he was going to kill her regardless. All she could do was stand waiting to find out what his intentions were.

The gunman slowly pointed the gun at Amy's face and cocked the hammer, but he didn't fire. He just stood there looking at her for a minute. Then he moved the gun away, disengaged the hammer and tucked the weapon into the back of his pants. He warned Amy not to move as he knelt down and checked on Stephan.

He didn't speak a word while he turned Stephan onto his side into a recovery position. Placing two fingers under Stephan's neck, he checked the unconscious man for a pulse. He gave a little nod to himself, and then proceeded to rip a small piece of Stephan's shirt to hold over Stephan's bleeding eye and nose.

"Here - hold this!" he said to Amy.

Amy dropped to her knees and gently pressed the cloth against Stephan's eye and nose while gently stroking his cheek.

"Is he going to be okay?" Amy asked.

"Like I said - he'll be fine. He'll come around soon enough. He'd be safe here, but I can't take that chance. I don't have time to explain, but if you love your brother, you'll listen to me, Red. I'll grab his head and arms, you grab his legs, and we're going to put him into the life boat. You understand?"

Amy nodded.

As planned, the gunman opened the door to Savior 5 and the pair, as carefully as possible, placed the unconscious Stephan Woodley inside. It wasn't easy to carry the dead weight of the man, but the pair managed. Once Stephan was safely hidden inside, the gunman locked the door to the lifeboat from the out-side and put the key into his pocket.

"You have the key? Why do we have to lock him in there?" exclaimed Amy.

"How else do you think I managed to hide out in there? And, I can't risk him coming around and jumping me, now can I?"

Amy accepted the gunman's explanation, but she knew her brother better than anyone else did. Stephan had never been a courageous person. When he woke up, he wouldn't be look-ing for a fight. He'd keep hidden for his own personal safety. Stephan wasn't entirely timid, but he wasn't a fighter either.

"You the one who let the life rafts go." Amy said.

"Had to, Red. I couldn't take any chances."

She couldn't believe it. She stood face to face with the man responsible for single-handedly ruining her chances at complet-ing her research.

"And you destroyed the communications?"

The gunman shot her a look, "Communications? No, Red. Why would I do that? Are you telling me that the ship has no communications?"

"No, none."

"Now that I know that piece of information, I need to find out who did it, and why. But I have a pretty good idea. Most importantly though...is we need to get this ship moving. I'm sorry about your brother, but I will need you to accompany me to the command center."

He produced his gun, pointing it once again at Amy.

"Don't think we're friends, not one bit, Red. This is life and death. Move!"

10

Captain Grey decided he would swing by his cabin before heading back to the command center. It was after leaving the engine room that he felt that need to get his gun. In all the years that Captain Grey had commanded the Reiziger, he had never felt the need to carry his gun. However, over the past nine hours, he was becoming uneasy with the events that were unfolding aboard his ship. Captain Grey wanted to take all the necessary precautions, especially if he came face to face with who-ever was wreaking havoc.

The captain bypassed the main mess hall that was now empty and trotted down the flight of stairs leading to his cabin. Cody followed him step for step.

Entering through the steel frame archway down from the exterior of the ship, the Captain ran down three more steps before taking a left and heading down a short passageway. The passageway led to a single door at the end of the hall. The metal door was painted a pale orange, and on the door hung a bronze name plate reading: 'Captain D.S. Grey'.

Captain Grey fished his key from a ring tucked securely in his front pants pocket. He slid the key into the lock and turned the tumbler of the deadbolt. Immediately Devon Schuyler Grey knew that something was wrong - the tumbler was already in the open position.

Captain Grey positioned his hand in front of Cody to warn her of the potential danger and to stay put. Cody continued to wag her tail at him. He realized that even though Cody was a great companion, but she had never experienced any real danger with him as her master. Sure, she could be frightened, but any real danger she had experienced in her lifetime came well before she met her master.

Cody could read Captain Grey's body language and quickly sensed that something was wrong. Someone had been in the Captain's quarters, and for all they knew, that someone could still be there now.

"Cody, stay girl. Don't move. Lay down."

The obedient canine stopped wagging her tail, gently whimpered yet ultimately listened to her master. She lay down on the cold steel floor and placed her head upon her paws.

"Good girl."

Captain Grey slowly and gently opened the large steel door to his quarters. The latch to the door handle clicked as he released it from his grip.

The lights were on. The covers of his bed were tossed about. Pages of paper had been tossed from his desk onto the floor. The mirror above his sink was smashed, and a trail of blood-stained footprints led to the bathroom. He hadn't noticed the bloody footprints when he came to his door, but looking back at the door and down the hallway, he could now see they were in fact there. Cody was lying right next to a pair of the prints.

Captain Grey called Cody to come inside. He realized his nerves were raw and he needed the security of his companion nearby, whether it could frighten her or not. He looked around the room to see if anything else was out of place. The room was a disaster; it was hard to tell if anything was amiss because *every-thing* appeared to be out of place. Then his eyes caught it. The key cabinet on the wall, normally locked, was ajar. This particular cabinet held the keys to every lockable door, switch, or device aboard the Reiziger.

Captain Grey wondered how the cabinet could have got open. At first glance, it was obvious that the cabinet wasn't damaged, tampered with or pried; the cabinet must have been opened by key. And the only two people that have the master key to open this cabinet: the Captain and the First Officer, Tom Bailey.

Looking into the cabinet, he noticed that of the fifty plus keys normally there, only about twenty remained.

"My God, Cody. Tom is the saboteur," he said in a disappointed tone.

Then a muffled sound came from the bathroom.

Captain Grey quickly pulled out his keys once again and fumbled to find the one he was looking for. He found it. He turned over his mattress revealing a shiny metal footlocker. Fortunately, nobody but the Captain knew about this footlocker. Inserting the key with a quivering hand, he opened it. Inside the footlocker were a few magazines on marine life, a picture of his daughter at her graduation, and the item he needed, his Walther P5 - 9mm German made pistol.

Grabbing a preloaded clip also from the footlocker, he loaded the gun, checked it for readiness, and flicked the safety to the 'off' position - something he'd definitely never done before today. But today...everything was different.

Captain Grey cautiously entered the bathroom where the bloody footprints travelled. Once inside, he left the door ajar and motioned to Cody to stay put in the bedroom. She obeyed. There was not much space to hide inside the bathroom - it was too small.

There was a toilet, a magazine rack beside it, a small sink opposite the toilet and a shower directly across from the two. The curtain to the shower was drawn.

Captain Grey approached the curtain slowly. He raised his gun, keeping it pointed directly in front of him. He reached for the dark brown curtain and pulled it back. There, lying on the tile floor in a pool of blood was Tom Bailey.

"Oh my God, Tom," Captain Grey yelled as he carefully flicked the safety back on to his gun and placed it upon the corner of the sink before reaching for his First Officer.

"Tom! Tom! Answer me!"

Tom didn't answer. Captain Grey grabbed Tom's wrist and checked for a pulse. There was a pulse, but it was weak. Tom's skin was clammy, gray and mottled. He appeared to be bleeding from the mouth and head.

"I'm going to get you some help, Tom. Just hang in there buddy. Can you hear me, Tom? It's Devon."

Captain Grey lifted Tom's eyelids to check his eyes, but Tom's gaze was frightening. His pupils didn't dilate when exposed to the light of the room – a sure sign of brain damage.

"Tom, I'm going to leave you here and get help. I know you can hear me, so don't worry, I'll be right back."

Captain Grey rushed from the bathroom grabbing the CB off the wall inside his cabin by the entrance door. Just then he remembered that it wouldn't work. He checked anyway. Click. Click. Click.

"Shit," he yelled, as he threw the receiver against the wall.

"Cody, stay here. I need you to stay girl. Stay here and watch over Tom. I'll be right back."

Captain Grey left his room and closed the door behind him to ensure that Cody would remain inside. It was best for Tom and best for her. He needed to find Dr. Baruti immediately.

11

The Pemba Koningin continued on a steady pace towards the Reiziger. Within an hour, the cutter was expected reach the paralyzed Reiziger.

"Mr. Asunda, report!" called Carlito over his CB radio.

"Twenty-two knots, sir," replied a voice.

Carlito checked his gauges and computer readouts from the console with flashing lights in front of him. Still holding the CB radio, he clicked through again. "Mr. Asunda, why the hell are we only running at twenty-two knots when I specifically asked you for full speed?"

Lefu could overhear Carlito's conversation from outside the command center and decided to enter.

"What's the problem now, Carlito?"

"Nothing. Hang on. Mr. Asunda - answer my question. Why are we not running at full speed as you were asked?"

"Sorry, sir," responded the voice again. "There's a problem here sir. Engine two is overheating quite badly. Oil pressure is running up and I've had to tune her down to keep her online. If I push her all the way, we could lose her."

"I could see that from my readouts up here. Figure out the problem and report back to me at once," Carlito said releasing his hold on the CB key. "You see the shit I have to work with?" he asked looking at Lefu.

Settling into the nearby captain's chair, Lefu removed his sunglasses and positioned them across the back of his bald head. He kicked his heels onto the main console of the command center.

"So, you have troubles, hey Carlito? Let me ask you something, do you know what a 'perfect pink' is?"

Carlito looked back at Lefu, confused by the question. He figured Lefu was beginning a conversation that could end in trouble. The Italian captain pulled out a handkerchief and wiped his brow.

"You heard Mr. Asunda, the engine is overheating. What the hell do you want me to do? The Reiziger still isn't moving...don't worry, we'll be on top of them..."

Lefu cut him off.

"I asked you if you know what a 'perfect pink' is."

Carlito started to bite his finger and squinted at Lefu trying to think of an answer to his question.

"No, I don't...but I guess you're going to tell me."

"A perfect pink is the rarest type of diamond in the world, almost completely flawless. In the right light, the diamond picks up a pink hue. It is the most sought after, the most prized, and of course the most valuable. I myself have only ever seen one."

Carlito didn't move - he just kept looking at Lefu.

Lefu pulled his gun from his side holster and released its clip. He moved so fluidly. He placed the gun on the main console and removed the bullets from the magazine: one, two, three, four, and five. Lefu thought he had more bullets but then realized he had wasted a few killing Ramon Diez earlier in the day. 'Five left, just enough,' he thought. Realizing that Carlito was still watching him, Lefu shrugged to himself.

"Would you believe, Carlito, that only a month ago, a single 'perfect pink' sold at auction for nearly fifteen million dollars. Hard to believe, I know. But it's true. That's why we're here, my friend. You see, Ramon Diez and his partner – a man named

Joost Kees, stole a 'perfect pink' from my boss just last week. And it just so happens that the 'perfect pink' they stole is unrefined, still in its natural state, a rough stone if you will."

Carlito shrugged at Lefu, "So?"

Lefu shot Carlito a look that let him know that he wasn't finished talking. "That means that the stone they stole is most likely worth nearly thirty million dollars."

Lefu slowly pressed the bullets back into the magazine clip one by one.

"Now, the reason I'm telling you this is simple. If I don't find Joost and that diamond, it'll be my head. And if it's my head..." Lefu said as he put the loaded clip back into the gun and pointed it directly at Carlito. "Then it's your head, too."

Carlito gasped and brought up his arm in a defensive motion, shielding himself from the gun pointed at him.

"I'll get us there. We'll get your diamond, my friend. I promise," he clicked the key on the CB radio again. "Asunda, I don't give a shit about the damn engine...you hear me? You put us to full throttle. Now! Now, I said!"

A double click sound came back across the CB radio. The message was received. Within two minutes, the Pemba Koningin lunged forward with extra power and cruised faster across the Atlantic.

Lefu grinned as he lowered his gun from Carlito and put it back into his holster.

"The power of persuasion, I love it. Don't you, Carlito?"

"Yeah, it's fantastic." Carlito said dropping himself into a chair.

"And, Carlito, if I feel this ship slow down again, take this as a warning my friend, I will blow your damn head off. But remember – just as things were back at Koton-Karifi prison - it's just business."

12

Doctor Baruti was just about to have a late afternoon nap when a knock came at the door. The early morning excitement had most of the passengers trying to catch up on lost sleep; Baruti figured he should do the same.

When he answered his cabin door, the last thing he expected to see was Captain Grey panting on the other side. The Captain was dripping in sweat and his face was red, quite understandable considering how he had just ran the entire length of the Reiziger to get to Dr. Baruti's cabin. "Captain, my God. Come in," Dr. Baruti exclaimed.

"No. Quick - grab your medical bag, resuscitation kit, whatever. I've found Tom Bailey; he's in bad shape and needs your help right away. Hurry up!"

Doctor Baruti jumped at the shaking news. Scrambling about his small room, he gathered up his advanced first aid kit, and a narrow suitcase labelled 'oxygen'.

"Captain, is he conscious? Where did you find him?"

"He's inside my quarters, just inside the shower. He's looking pretty beat up and he's not responding."

Baruti and the Captain raced from the doctor's cabin and quickly made their way to the Captain's quarters. The doctor was speedy for a man in his sixties, although Captain Grey still found that he had to wait for the slightly overweight man around every turn.

"Please, Doctor, let me give you a hand." Captain Grey said as he took the first-aid kit and oxygen from the doctor.

The doctor obliged, but unfortunately it didn't help quicken the pace much. Beside Savior 5, Captain Grey stopped again to wait for the doctor to catch up.

Along the ground beside the lifeboat, Captain Grey noticed a small trace of blood. Nothing compared to the large quantity he had found earlier in the morning by the vacant life raft bays, but enough to take notice. Captain Grey quickly bent down to examine the blood. There was a small puddle and a few scattered spots of blood. It hadn't had the chance to coagulate yet, so this was fresh blood. Just then, Doctor Baruti caught up with him.

"What is it?"

"More blood," said Captain Grey.

"My God, what is happening on this ship?"

"I don't know, Doctor, but we'll have to come back to investigate this later. Right now, we need to check on Tom. Follow me."

Captain Grey continued to lead Baruti to his quarters, reaching the metal archway leading from the outside of the ship to the interior corridor. He looked back to make sure that the doctor saw him heading inside. Baruti nodded and waved a hand to the captain that he was coming.

Once inside the passageway, Captain Grey took notice of the bloody footprints on the floor leading directly to his cabin. He thought it strange that he didn't notice them when he came through earlier. Regardless, there they were in front of him, as plain as day. He did notice something different this time around though. Grey put down the first aid and oxygen kit and knelt to the floor for a closer look. There he could see what he was hoping wasn't true - there were two distinctly different sets of footprints, not just one. Clearly, Tom Bailey wasn't alone when he went to the Captain's quarters.

"What is it?" asked Baruti as he rounded the corner into the passageway.

"I'm not sure, Doctor. We'll figure it out later. Come on, let's get to Tom first."

The pair arrived at the pale orange door to the captain's quarters and found it closed just as the captain had left it. Captain Grey tried the door - it was still locked. Good, he thought. Fishing out his key, he opened the door and there was Cody, standing and waiting with her tail wagging. He patted her on the head and showed his approval for her obedience. Doctor Baruti slowly entered the room behind the captain making sure to keep a safe distance from Cody, as he was still slightly fearful of the dog.

"Don't worry, Doctor, she wouldn't hurt anyone."

"I'd rather not be the first!" Baruti said.

"Cody, go lay down. Let the doctor come through."

The malamute responded to her master's request and jumped up onto the captain's tossed mattress and bedding. She lay down. This room was nothing new to Cody; she had always been allowed to sleep alongside her master. To her, the bed was just as much hers. Cody preferred this bed to her blanket bed in the command center, though the cabin room in its current state frightened her. She curled up and rested her head across her paws, watching her master and the doctor closely.

Doctor Baruti took comfort in having the large dog out of his way. Still intimidated though, he side-stepped along the edge of the room towards the open bathroom door.

"What happened in here?" Baruti asked.

"I don't know. I think someone was looking for something. Quick, in here, you must check out Tom. I'll bring the kits."

Captain Grey grabbed the first aid and oxygen again and the pair entered into the bathroom. The shower curtain was closed; Captain Grey couldn't remember if he left it that way. Doctor Baruti covered his mouth with his hand as he pulled back the curtain to reveal Tom Bailey.

There was blood everywhere. From where Tom's body lay, a spray of blood decorated partially up the side of the wall from behind his head. A large bloodied and blackened hole was present near his temple. Tom Bailey was dead. Somebody had shot him while he lay there unconscious.

Doctor Baruti dropped to his knees and frantically checked Tom for a pulse. As anticipated, he found none. He then checked over Tom's body for any other signs of trauma.

Captain Grey watched the doctor in total disbelief at what had happened; he dropped the emergency kits to the floor. The small bathroom turned deathly quiet - so quiet that the buzz of electricity could be heard pumping into the light fixture above the sink. Cody nosed her way into the room. She wasn't comfortable with the quiet. Grey patted his leg and Cody came close for reassurance.

As the Captain knelt down to nuzzle his dog, his hand brushed his side and felt the void where his gun should have been. Realizing that it wasn't there, he began to panic. In his mind, he frantically retraced his steps. He looked at his watch - only twenty minutes at most had passed since he found Tom and retrieved his pistol from the footlocker. Okay, rewind, thought Grey. What happened? He remembered loading the gun, following the footprints into the bathroom, finding Tom, and then going to get the doctor. At some point, he must have put the gun down, but where? Then he remembered. It was on the sink counter. The Captain jumped up to check the sink counter. It was bare; the gun was gone.

Captain Grey slowly dropped back down to his knees behind Dr. Baruti. Cody nuzzled her head under Grey's chin to comfort him, but he was in a daze. He gently pushed her face away.

Somebody killed Tom, but how...and why? Whoever did it would have needed a key to get into this room. Only two people had a key to this room, the same two people also had the key to the key cabinet: the Captain himself and Tom Bailey. As well, whoever entered here to kill Tom would have had to know that the Captain had left. Once they were in here, apparently they didn't care even if Cody was present.

Grey realized that this *somebody* would have to have known Cody quite well, to know her calm nature. Sure, Cody appeared to be a force to be reckoned with: a fair sized dog with a loud bark and some fierce looking teeth, but in reality, it was quite the opposite. She was timid and afraid of humans. Only a few people were aware of that.

"Captain, I'm so sorry about Tom. There was nothing we could have done. But I think there's something you should see," Baruti said, tilting Tom's body forward from the wall.

Captain Grey looked over to the doctor and then looked over to his dead First Officer. Doctor Baruti had Tom doubled over, exposing the dead officer's back. Grey had never seen anything like it before. Large red circles ran down the entire length of Tom's back.

"Doctor, what the hell is that?"

"I don't know. And look here..." Baruti said pointing to that backside of Tom's head.

"It looks like he suffered a severe head trauma before being shot...feels as if his skull is fractured in a few places."

"How do you know that was before being shot?"

"The blood," said Baruti, "When he was shot, his heart would have stopped pumping blood almost immediately, but as you can see...here...there is a lot of blood from this area."

"Then why would somebody shoot him?"

"I don't know, Captain."

Captain Grey was beginning to feel weak from examining Tom's body so he backed away. "I don't get it doctor. When I found him, he was in bad shape - but alive. I didn't notice his head, but I didn't look too close. I just left him with Cody to watch over him. When we came back...my gun is missing...and...I left it right there on the counter. And now Tom's dead."

Doctor Baruti gave the Captain a puzzled and frightened glance.

"Now you know damn well it wasn't me, Doctor. Please tell me you believe me..."

"I do, Captain," said Baruti.

"Thank you. What I can't figure out is why someone would kill a man who is so badly injured?"

"Mercy killing?" suggested Baruti.

Captain Grey brought his eyes to meet Doctor Baruti's. "Are you saying he was going to die anyway?"

"I would say so. I don't know what these markings on his back are from, but his injuries alone...I would say that most probably would have died from them anyway, very fast. To be honest, Captain, the head injury alone, I was surprised to hear you say you found him alive. Half of his skull is pushed in, there was no way for him to survive this trauma...I've seen it before...I know."

"Then why pray tell would somebody shoot him?"

Doctor Baruti watched as Captain Grey rubbed his fingers across his mouth. The Captain had tears running down his face.

"I think that someone didn't want to take a chance that Tom would survive – they wanted him dead." Baruti said, realizing what he had just said. He felt sick.

The pair sat in silence on the cold bathroom floor beside Tom's body. They looked around the room for a sign, a clue as to who had been in here. Nothing could be found. Cody paced quietly on the opposite side of the bathroom. She too was uneasy.

After a couple of minutes, Captain Grey got up and went to his sleeping quarters, grabbed a blanket and brought it back to the bathroom. Grey crouched next to Baruti and began to whisper to the doctor, as if somebody might be listening to their conversation. "Let's cover him up. Leave him here. Draw the curtains again. Make no mention of this to anyone, Doctor. We'll gather the passengers and crew again. See if anybody is acting strange."

"I'd really like to do a more thorough investigation on Tom's wounds if I may. To find out what may have caused these injuries."

"Not right now. We have a murderer on board. For all we know everyone's safety is at risk. No Doctor, leave Tom. You can check him later...you have my word. Right now, we need to find out what's going on and who is responsible for this."

"But whoever is responsible – they have your gun. Do you have another?"

"No."

"Then what are we going to do if we find out who it is?"

Captain Grey hadn't thought of that. Not much good finding a killer holding a gun if you have nothing to defend yourself with.

"Tranquilizer gun!" Captain Grey said as he snapped his fingers in the air. "There is one in the command center in the small office at the back. It's not much protection head to head against a pistol, but the tranquilizer is powerful...enough to subdue a large shark or sea lion. It would be effective against a human."

The captain got to his feet. "Doctor, I need you to head to the engine room. Tell Mr. Ruiz to fire the engines and engage the clutch. Tell him to get us moving right away. I'll go get the tranquilizer gun. Don't stop for anyone. Nobody whatsoever - your team or my crew, it doesn't matter. Just get to Mr. Ruiz and get the ship going. I'll lock up here and bring Cody with me."

Doctor Baruti nodded and left the captain's quarters, leaving the first aid kit and oxygen behind on the floor.

Captain Grey straightened his shirt, smoothed back his hair and put on another one of his captain's caps that hung from a hook on the wall just by his bed. Leaving his quarters with Cody in tow, he locked the door behind him.

"Who did this girl? I need you to show me," the Captain said to Cody. She simply wagged her tail and barked.

13

The hum of the engine room was deafening. Dr. Baruti stumbled down the metal stairs and entered the stuffy room, already reeling from the noise. He called out for Mr. Ruiz as he continued into the room ducking his head along the passageway toward the back of the ship.

The walls of the engine room were painted a bright white. Pipes ran the entire length of the walls and travelled in all directions in and out of the engine room. Huge valves, water tanks, control boxes and panels were positioned in every corner of the room. 'A very tight space,' thought Baruti.

Heading down a small set of steps, he saw the main computer console with its flashing red, green, and yellow buttons. There he found Alan Ruiz sitting with his back to Baruti. His body was motionless. His face was pressed into the Plexiglas cover of the main console. His arms dangled lifelessly from his sides.

"Mr. Ruiz?" called Baruti.

Ruiz didn't respond to the doctor. He looked dead.

"Ruiz?" the doctor called again, this time putting his hand on the engineer's shoulder. Ruiz jumped in his seat; he had been sleeping.

"Oh my God, you scared me, Doctor," Ruiz said, as he adjusted his eye patch and wiped a slight trace of drool from his lips.

"I'm sorry, Mr. Ruiz. The Captain requested that I come to you right away. He wants you to get the ship moving. Um...fire the engines...and turn the prop?"

Ruiz smiled at the doctor. He knew what the captain was asking of him, even though the doctor's instructions were a little bit vague.

"Okay, okay. I understand. It's about time. I'll be glad to get going again. Excuse me, doctor."

Ruiz stepped around the doctor. He went to a different control box on the other side of the room and flipped a switch. Then he came back to the main console he had been sitting at and lifted a safety cover that protected a large green button. As he pressed the button, the hum of the engines turned into a roar. Numbers and dials on the gauges of the console sprang to life giving readouts that the doctor couldn't understand, but he knew the engines were throttling up as the sound became more deafening.

Ruiz grabbed a pair of headphones hanging from a hook and handed them to the doctor. Baruti nodded and said thank you, but neither man could hear their own voices.

Baruti watched the engineer check the gauges, nodding to himself as he went along. Ruiz then took a clipboard from the console and entered information on the pages. He checked his watch then added some more information. Finally, the engineer reached for a large lever located on the far end of the console and gave it a slow, gentle pull, then a harder pull, and then an even harder pull. The lever wouldn't move past the halfway point.

Ruiz released the lever, reset it to its starting point, and then tried to pull it down again. Same as before, it only moved to the halfway point.

Baruti could see the frustration mounting on the engineer's face. He leaned close and yelled to Ruiz, "What's the problem?"

Ruiz looked back at Baruti with frustration, "The clutch is stuck - I can't get the props to engage."

"Is there a bypass?" Baruti asked. Ruiz shot him another look, this time with a look that said, 'You stick to what you know, and I'll stick to what I know.'

Ruiz pushed past the doctor and pressed a few more buttons on the main console, checked a few more gauges, and kicked a panel below the console just for good measure. The engineer then went back to the large lever and tried it again. Same result, it wouldn't move.

Ruiz kicked a couple more times at the exterior of the panel and although he couldn't be heard, Baruti could tell by watching his lips move that Ruiz was cursing loudly.

Ruiz waved a hand, beckoning the doctor to come closer. He leaned in close to Baruti and lifted off one of the doctor's headphones.

"Tell the Captain that the screws are locked."

"What?" asked Baruti.

"Tell the Captain the screws are locked. Something is preventing the clutch from disengaging. He'll know what that means."

Baruti nodded to the engineer, handed over his headphones, and left the room. Once up the small flight of stairs, he turned and looked back down to the engineer. Ruiz was rubbing his head in frustration trying to figure out what the problem was. Baruti realized that the ship was in dire trouble when he saw Ruiz grab a hammer from a nearby bench and throw it across the engine room. The hammer bounced off a steel column and vanished to the steel floor below the engine room.

"God help us," Baruti said, but nobody could hear him.

14

Amy didn't know what to expect. She certainly wasn't expecting to be taken back at gunpoint to her cabin, but that's exactly where her captor was directing her. Her mind raced with the thought of this young brute getting her into the cabin and then having his way with her. She debated taking him to a different cabin, perhaps to one of her colleagues. Of course, she reconsidered. That would be a mistake. If she brought him to a different cabin, he would surely kill its occupant and then her. No, her only option was to oblige him - go where he wanted to go and then use her wits to keep herself alive.

As they reached her cabin door, Amy and the gunman heard the sound of the engines rumbling again. The gunman smiled briefly. Meanwhile, Amy had completely forgotten that she was even aboard a ship. She didn't return a smile to the gunman. She simply opened the door to her cabin and stopped. She didn't move. Instead, she decided to take a look around. Amy realized that once inside her cabin, she may never see the light of day again.

The midday sun was beating hard against the Reiziger. The sky was mostly clear. Once large white clouds had now been reduced to fine white ribbons in the blue sky, evaporating in the heat of the day. The ocean air was invigorating, fresh and comforting to Amy. The Reiziger itself appeared clean, safe and sturdy - the same way it was when she boarded the ship a few days earlier. Amy turned her head to the left and looked into the distance, hopeful to see St. Helena with the naked eye, but she couldn't. She closed her eyes. Aside from the rumbling of the ship, there was no other sound. No birds chirped. No waves splashed. All was quiet.

"Come on, Red. Get inside before someone sees," the gunman said.

She thought of running. However, the notion of a bullet to the back of the head was too frightening...and too real. So she turned, bowed her head, and entered the cabin. The gunman followed her inside and locked the door behind them.

The cabin seemed even smaller than it was. It felt like a strange and unfamiliar place. Amy couldn't remember this being her room, but it was.

Her bed sat unmade since she had awoken so early in the morning. The cupboard door where she bumped her head remained open, and a light in the bathroom still on. A small chair sat in the corner of the cabin beside a small dresser. The gunman sat down in the chair and told Amy to sit on the bed.

"You're probably thinking I'm going to rape you," he said with a snicker, while kicking off his boots.

"I don't know what to think." Amy quivered as she sat uncomfortably on the bed.

"No, Red. You're a pretty girl alright, but I'm not here for kicks, if you know what I mean?"

"Then what do you want?" Amy said, clasping her hands trying to keep them from shaking.

The gunman pulled off his shirt revealing a slim, tanned and muscular frame. "I just need to get to a safe haven, Red. But first, I want to get cleaned up and have a drink. You got anything here?"

Amy shook her head.

"Well, can you at least get me a cloth with warm water?" The gunman said pointing to the bathroom with his gun.

He wasn't going to turn his back on her, she knew it. Amy got up from the bed, went to the bathroom, ran some hot water and soaked a facecloth for him. Bringing it back, she noticed that he had put the pistol on the dresser. Amy handed him the cloth.

He smiled and nodded to Amy as she sat back down on the bed. Taking the cloth, he ran it across his forehead, the back of his neck, across his chest and under his arms. He then threw the cloth on the floor beside himself and put his shirt back on.

"A few days in that container and I'm starting to ripen," he said, laughing.

Amy watched her captor laugh. His teeth were bright and straight. A dimple formed in the middle of his cheek. Until now, she hadn't noticed how handsome he was.

"You're not a murderer, are you?" Amy asked.

The gunman looked at Amy with his piercing blue eyes. "No, Red. I've never killed anybody before in my life."

"Then what are you doing on this ship? Why did you hurt my brother?"

"Wrong place, wrong time," he replied nonchalantly, "I don't want to hurt anyone, but if someone gets in my way – I will!"

"Why are you here though? I realize you're a stowaway, but do you even know where we're going?"

"No. But that's the hard part, Red. I need to get away from some people...some very bad people. So I jump on this ship, and I go wherever it takes me. Problem is...this ship stops, and now I'm in trouble. Because as sure as the moon is in the sky, I know those bad people are looking for me – they're coming. I have a feeling. So, it doesn't matter where we're going, but if we don't get moving soon, they're going to find this ship. And trust me; they're the real bad guys – they're not like me. These guys...*they* are murderers. And to get to me, they'd kill everyone aboard this ship."

Amy's face turned white with horror. "So you're saying that you being on this ship could get everyone killed, and you're telling me you're not a murderer?"

The gunman shot her a 'how dare you say that' glare.

"How many people are on this ship?" he asked, changing the subject as he began to put his boots back on.

"I think maybe...I don't know...I'm here with a team of seven and there are maybe eight or ten crewmembers, so fifteen, maybe seventeen. I'm not one hundred percent sure."

"What do you mean 'team'? What are you doing?"

"We're going to...we *were* going to St. Helena to do scientific research. That was until somebody released the life rafts. The captain figures it's one of us, so he stopped the ship until he finds out who is guilty. But as it turns out, he's looking in the wrong places - it was you."

"I had no choice there, Red. If I didn't get rid of those rafts, there was always the chance that if I was found, I could be sent adrift as a stowaway. I couldn't take that chance."

"What about the life boat? Why didn't you get rid of that, too?"

"I was going to, but then you and your brother came along."
"So, how did you get the keys to the life boat?"

The gunman began to laugh again. "God, you ask a lot of questions, don't you?"

"I'm a scientist, that's my job." Amy replied with a spice in her voice. As she started to give him a smile, she quickly pulled it back realizing that she didn't want to soften to her captor.

"Well, if you must know, I found the keys. I was sneaking around the side of the ship looking for a new place to hide when I came across what appeared to be a puddle of blood. And right there beside the blood was this key, a single key that said 'Savior 5'. Sounds far-fetched, but it's the truth," he said as he fished the key from his pocket and held it in front of Amy's eyes. "I don't know where the blood came from, and I don't want to know. I just want to get the hell out of here. And that's where you come in."

"Me!" asked Amy, "What am I going to do? The captain has made it clear to everyone that we're not going anywhere until he gets answers as to who released the life rafts."

"You heard the engines fire up again, Red. I think you and I both know we're going to get moving again soon. And you are going to make sure we do."

"How am I going to make sure we get moving?" Amy said.

"Simple, Red. You're going to be my hostage. If he doesn't get this ship moving...then I think I might turn from being a man who's never killed anyone, to a full blown murderer. You never know. I'm sorry, Red. But desperate times call for desperate measures...I'm sure you've heard that one before."

Amy began to bite at her fingernails, all the while looking at her assailant. "What's your name?" she asked him.

"Joost...my name is Joost," he responded, not sure why she was asking.

"Joost, never heard that name before," Amy said.

"Afrikaans, Red."

"It's nice. I like it. It doesn't sound like a murderer's name. I'm Amy," she said. "And I don't think you would kill anyone, Joost. You may be acting out as a desperate man, I don't doubt that. But I don't think you would actually kill someone if you never have before. You have human emotion, I've seen it. You felt bad for hurting Stephan. You're not in the habit of hurting any-one, are you?"

Amy thought if she kept her assailant talking, she may be able to disarm him, if only mentally. She pretended she was playing psychologist. If she kept him talking, she could get him to settle... hopefully.

Joost's smile faded quickly as he snapped at her, "Don't think you know me! I may have never hurt people before, but I will if I have to. This isn't a game. This *is* life and death. My life and death, and I won't let anything stand in the way when it comes to my life." Joost grabbed the gun again but kept it pointed to the floor.

"Why are these bad guys looking for you?" Amy asked, hoping to continue the disarming line of questioning.

Joost exhaled deeply, rubbed a hand across his forehead and lowered his eyes. "They want something from me...something of great value...something they say I stole."

Amy stared her assailant; his head bowed down. Then Amy asked in a very quiet voice.

"Well, did you? I mean, what could you possibly steal that would be so important to come after you? Do they think you took money, or drugs, or someone's girlfriend?" Amy realized she was pushing too hard and backed off.

Joost wasn't impressed, but he still answered, "They think I stole a diamond, Red." He was still calling her that name. "And this diamond is worth a lot of money, worth more than this ship and everything aboard it. But we found it...so it's ours. Unfortunately, some people think it belongs to them, so they want it."

Amy's mouth was open, but she couldn't make a word come out. Joost was aware of what she intended to ask.

"And no, I didn't steal it! So I'm not going to give something to somebody who it doesn't belong to. It's mine, and I'm keeping it. And if that means I have to start killing people to keep it...I will."

Joost stood up and waved the gun at Amy directing her to stand as well. Joost was fed up with question and answer period; it was time to move.

"What do you mean we? No, where are we going?" Amy asked.

"Come on, Red. No more questions. We're going to get the ship moving. We're going to see your captain. I pray for your sake that he listens...I wouldn't want you to be the first person I've ever killed."

15

Captain Grey knew, as did everyone else on board, that the ships engines were online again. He felt the rumble beneath his feet as he made his way toward the command center. The ship had a hum deep within its steel frame once again.

Inside the command center, Winston Deedat was still busy trying to fix the broken communication controls while his work partner Nelson Blomkamp was in the corner of the room picking up the last piece of furniture.

Cody took her place in the corner of the room on her tidied up blanket bed. She took a little bit longer to settle considering her bed had been disturbed, but eventually she managed to lie down.

"Gentlemen, status report," the Captain said.

Deedat pointed to the pressure gauges mounted on the wall directly to his left.

"As far as I can see, Captain, the engines are online. Oil pressure is not quite satisfactory and aft bulkhead one and three are closed. I can't see much else, sir."

"That's fine," replied the Captain. "And, might I add - you're correct. Thank you. Where is Officer Medupé?"

"We haven't seen him since we came back from cleaning up the 'urgent matter'. After you left with Ruiz to the engine room, he stuck around for a while, and then just left. He didn't say where he was going." Blomkamp said.

"I think he said he was going to talk to Dr. Baruti about the blood spill," Deedat said.

Captain Grey shook his head, "I was with Dr. Baruti only ten minutes ago. He wasn't with him."

Just as Captain Grey finished his sentence, Dr. Baruti entered the command center red faced and out of breath once again. Cody jumped up when the doctor came into the room. Baruti put one hand on his thigh as he bent over trying to catch his breath. He raised his other hand up towards Cody in a defensive stop motion. Cody quickly settled again once she saw the familiar face. She was getting used to this old man.

"Oh, thank God, pup. I can't handle any more excitement. Not right now. Captain, I just came from the engine room. Ruiz wants me to tell you that he can't turn the screws. And that the clutch won't disengage. He tried a few times, but it just won't go," Baruti panted.

Captain Grey shifted his attention to a large lever on side of the command console. This one looked very similar to the one Baruti just saw Ruiz struggling with in the engine room. The Captain pulled the lever towards himself. Unlike the lever in the engine room, this one didn't move at all. He tried repeatedly to pull the lever, it wouldn't move an inch. Frustrated, the captain kicked at the lever.

Stone faced, Captain Grey slowly turned from the men in the command center and went into a small room located behind the control room. Once inside, he locked the door behind him. Quickly scanning the room, he found what he was looking for. On the bottom shelf of one of the wall cabinets, were two large metal boxes. The Captain grabbed both boxes and opened the first one labelled 'TG'. Inside was the tranquilizer gun. He loaded it with a dart, closed the box and put it back on the shelf. He tucked the gun under his belt at the back of his pants. Then, he then opened the other box. It contained a flare gun. He loaded the gun, unlocked the door and walked outside the small room. He walked unassuming from the command center, headed out onto the main deck, and fired a single shot into the air.

The other three men hurried behind Captain Grey out of the command center and watched as the bright red tracer fell slowly from the blue sky. Cody remained on her bed within the command center.

"Oh My God, Captain, what is going on?" Deedat asked.

The Captain didn't reply.

"I don't know, Winston, but I think we're in trouble," whispered Blomkamp.

Captain Grey didn't speak, but simply went back inside the command center and threw the discharged flare gun onto the broken console.

"Blomkamp, are you fully trained on the operations for ROK?" yelled the Captain.

"Yes, sir."

"Suit up then; we're sending her down. If there's a snag on the screws, you're going to have to free them."

"Screws?" asked Baruti.

"The props, Doctor. Something is wrong with the props, and we can't disengage the clutch. Without the props, we can't move."

* * *

Carlito was the first to spot the flaming red ball dropping from the sky in the distance.

"Lefu, do you see it?" Carlito pointed and yelled from the command center to the men on the lower deck.

Percy, Jako, and Lefu all looked up toward the sky. Lefu leapt from his seat and ran up to the command center.

"What does it mean?" Lefu asked Carlito as he entered.

"I believe it's the Reiziger. They must be in trouble. I'm not why, but you don't send a flare if you're only experiencing mild difficulties. My guess is they are in serious trouble...perhaps mechanical or perhaps somebody aboard is badly hurt. Either way, they're not moving and we'll be on them shortly."

"How much longer do you figure until we're there?" Lefu demanded.

"Half to three quarters of an hour. Here, look!" Carlito replied handing Lefu a pair of binoculars.

Lefu grabbed the binoculars with his large black hands and looked into distance to where the flare originated. There, still miniature, but there – sat the Reiziger like a mirage, floating on a magic carpet of water.

"Doesn't look like you had to work hard for your triple payment after all...did you?" Lefu said.

"A deal is a deal, my friend, I get you to them, and you pay me. That was the arrangement." Carlito smiled.

"Your greed is going to get you into deep trouble one day, Carlito."

* * *

Joost grabbed Amy by the arm and held her back. "Stop! Look, up there!" he said.

Amy looked up and saw the red flare arcing across the sky while a cloud of smoke dissipated in the air above the ship. The pair realized that the flare emanated from aboard the Reiziger.

"What does that mean?" Amy asked with a quiver in her voice.

"Quickly! Back to your cabin," ordered Joost. "The ship is in distress. Something is wrong."

Joost tucked his gun into his belt and grabbed Amy by the forearm. He directed her to turn around and head back to her cabin. Amy didn't resist her captor. She followed him step for step back to her cabin. Oddly enough, she seemed to be helping Joost keep hidden from sight: slightly ducking, pausing around corners, and keeping a watchful eye on the surroundings.

Once the pair reached her cabin, Amy opened the door and went inside ahead of Joost. She wasn't as scared as she was the last time they entered her room. Joost followed inside and locked the door behind.

"Where's the rest of your team?" Joost asked as he leaned his back against the door.

"They're in the cabins along this same passageway, the next few doors down. Why?" Amy asked, as she sat into the chair Joost earlier occupied.

Just as Amy was about to relax back into the chair, almost feeling comfortable with her captor, she jumped as Joost raced past her, across the room to the cabin window. Pulling up the blinds, he peered outside.

Gentle waves continued to caress the side of the motionless ship. Looking to the distance, he couldn't see anything but water.

"You mentioned you were going to a place called St. Helena, what kind of research are you doing there?" Joost asked, turning to Amy. There was a fear in his eyes and Amy could see it.

"Biological research...my team is here to study the effects of extreme environments on different species," Amy said cautiously.

"Why St. Helena? I'm not familiar with it."

Amy eyes lit up. With everything that had happened in the last few hours, she'd almost forgotten about why she was aboard the ship in the first place.

"A volcanic eruption!" Amy said enthusiastically. "The island of St. Helena is set to experience a volcanic eruption in the next few days. We wanted to be nearby to study the immediate effects on different life forms. Why?" Amy was puzzled, yet excited that someone beside her immediate peers was interested.

Joost let the blinds go and sat down on the edge of the bed. "Well, Red. I was hoping to get to Brazil or Argentina for a safe haven, but..." He trailed off.

Joost put his head into his hands and rocked back and forth. Amy watched the young man in silence. She could see that his desperation was beginning to take a toll on him. Joost ran his large hands through his medium length hair. Letting out a sigh, he flopped back on the bed and starred at the ceiling.

Amy no longer felt like a victim to Joost. She realized that he too was a victim. Looking at him, she reconsidered his story of the trouble that was looking for him - and she believed him. She thought of how only recently he had hurt her brother, but how he also redeemed himself by offering assistance after the fact. She knew that she could forgive him. She knew she needed to forgive him. He wasn't a bad person. He was simply a desperate person.

The pair sat in silence the room. The minutes passed by like hours. Amy was exhausted. Then, unexpectedly, a knock came at the cabin door.

Joost jumped up swung his gun around wildly.

"No! Here, hide in the bathroom...I'll get rid of whoever it is. Put that away, please," Amy whispered.

Joost's eyes met Amy's. He couldn't understand why she would offer to get rid of whoever was at the door, but he didn't have time to figure it out. He knew that if she gave him away, he would be forced to kill her – as well as whoever was at the door.

Joost hid in the bathroom, leaving the door slightly ajar to keep a watchful eye on Amy. Unfortunately, from where Amy stood at the door, he was only able to see the back of her legs. Amy leaned back ready to answer the door and waved Joost back into the bathroom. He pulled the bathroom door closed a few more inches but kept it open just enough to see Amy.

Amy unlocked and opened the cabin door. Standing on the other side were two of her colleagues, Doctor Conte and Doctor Athans. The pair had their arms crossed in unison and both wore silly smiles on their faces.

"Dr. Conte, Dr. Athans, hello, what can I do for you?" Amy asked calmly.

Joost continued to peek through the small opening he'd left for himself in the door. Again, all he could see was Amy's back and legs. He could hear the voice of a man and a woman on the other side of the door. Both had strong South African accents.

"Have you been in here this whole time? I didn't think you would be one to listen to the Captain," laughed the male voice.

"She must be working..." said the female voice.

"Maybe she's writing him an apology letter," added the male voice.

Amy laughed softly to the voices. "No, I'm just resting. I'm still a little tired from this morning and my head's not feeling just right. I'm going to go back to bed and rest for a while."

"No problem, dear, just wanted to let you know that we're going to get the team together. Dr. Baruti asked us to run some tests on a blood sample and..." the male voice said, as Amy cut him off.

"Not right now, please...I have a bad headache. I'll catch up with you later."

"Ms. Masterson, this is very important, Dr. Baruti has brought something to our attention and it would be best if you took a look at..." said the female voice.

"I'm sorry - I'll have to talk to you later. Thank you," Amy pleaded.

Joost felt his hair stand up on the back of his neck as the pores on his head opened up. A warm bead of sweat began to form across his forehead. He couldn't see Amy's hands or face. He didn't know if she was warning the pair at the door of his presence. He didn't know if he could trust her. Joost had trusted people before, and it usually ended badly. He closed his eyes and thought of Ramon Diez, wondering if he was okay.

Not able to keep it together any longer, Joost burst out from the bathroom - gun drawn. It was at that same moment that Amy finished closing her cabin door. She looked back at him surprised and slightly shocked. "I said I'd get rid of them," she said.

Joost said nothing. He lowered his gun and walked across the cabin. Instead of lying back on the bed, he chose the chair again. Placing the gun on the table beside him, he looked up at Amy who was still standing by the door.

"Why?" he asked.

"Why?" Amy paused. "I don't know. I guess it's because...I want to believe you."

For the past few weeks, Joost had been on the run, constantly in hiding, keeping a low profile, and avoiding human contact. He had been under so much stress that he felt like he could explode. Looking at Amy, he could feel the tension begin to unwind. Unusual circumstances had brought them to where they were now. Here he sat, looking at this young woman; a pretty, young woman who had just protected him. He wasn't used to that. It didn't feel right, but it <u>did</u> just happen...and he felt relieved.

"Thank you," Joost said. "I don't want to hurt anyone. You're right. You know that don't you, Amy?"

"I know," Amy said, realizing Joost had just used her given name. "I know that you're not a bad guy. I just had a feeling about you. But what should we do now?"

Joost noticed she had just referred to the two of them as 'we'. He tapped his fingers gently across his lips as he spoke. "First off, I want you to know that you can trust me, too."

"I believe I can," Amy said.

Joost grabbed his gun and offered it to Amy. "Here, take it!"

Amy wasn't sure what Joost was doing. Was this some sort of trick? Cautiously, she reached her hand out and took the gun from Joost. The thought of pointing the pistol back at him crossed her mind. She was in the position of power now. Amy looked at Joost as he put his hands behind his head and leaned back in the chair. Amy realized that he was waiting to see what she would do.

Amy bit her lip gently and placed the gun on the bedside table.

"I want you to trust me too," she said.

Joost smiled and nodded.

Amy smiled back.

"The gun isn't loaded," he said.

Amy's jaw dropped. "You bastard!" she yelled.

"But I'm glad to see that you trust me. I know we can work together." Joost began to chuckle.

"You bastard!" she said again. "You cut my head with that goddamn thing. You hit me!"

"I'm sorry. Could we please start again?" he asked while flashing a pleading look.

Amy was only mildly disgruntled that she'd been taken for a ride, but was happy to see that Joost was coming clean with her. If he was telling the truth about the gun and the diamond, then he must have been telling the truth about the 'bad men' coming for him.

Amy looked at Joost and rubbed her head where he had struck her. The area didn't hurt anymore.

"I'm sorry about that." he said.

Amy nodded.

"Look, I think we should get back to the life boat and get the hell off this ship, if not for the sake of your experiments, then for the sake of your life. I have a bad feeling that if we stay here, things are not going to end well. There is only one small problem – what about your brother?"

"He's all I've ever had in life and I won't leave him behind. I wouldn't even be on this ship if not for him. He's my security. I couldn't have made this trip without him. He has to come with us, he can be trusted. There is no other way I would go."

Joost nodded. "Okay, then let's..."

He was cut off mid-sentence when the Reiziger heaved. Amy fell across the bed, while Joost braced himself in the chair. It felt as if a huge wave had just knocked against the side of the ship causing it to rise up into the air. Joost and Amy looked at each other in disbelief.

"What the hell was that?" Joost said.

"I don't know." Amy said as she scrambled from the bed to look out the porthole window. Joost followed right before her.

Maybe it was too late. Maybe the volcano at Saint Helena was already beginning to erupt.

"I don't see any waves..." she said.

16

Doctor Baruti checked Blomkamp's blood pressure and then removed the cuff to allow the deckhand to get his right arm into the dry suit. The doctor wrote down the pertinent data into his journal and walked away as he continued to jot in his book.

Blomkamp was left to get his arm into the suit by himself and he seemed to be having some trouble. Deedat saw his partner struggling with the suit and helped him to get into the rest of it properly. Once he was fully inside the suit, Blomkamp smacked the sides of his thighs and waddled around in a circle pretending to be a penguin. The two crewmembers laughed at Blomkamp's ridiculous sense of humor.

"Looks like you're ready for a diet buddy," Deedat commented with a snicker.

"You want to do this? I can't say I'm happy to be dressed like this, that's for sure. I don't know why the captain asked me to do this anyway - you're the underwater professional." Blomkamp replied.

"Ah, seniority rules, Nelson. Always remember that, my friend," Deedat said.

While the two men were having a laugh with one another, Captain Grey was busy readying the ROK submersible vessel for a dive. He checked that the underwater vessel was in proper working order: the seals were tight, the batteries were charged, the lighting was operational, the oxygen supply tanks were full, and the control arms were operational. After checking the critical components of the submersible, Captain Grey made double sure to adjust the cable attached to the submersible's top. The clamp and cable was the lifeline to the submersible, and were required for insertion and retraction into the ocean below.

As the Captain was finishing up his inspection of ROK, he ducked his head inside the containment control chamber where he came across a handheld short wave walkie-talkie.

"Mr. Deedat!" the Captain called, poking his head back out of the chamber. "I've found a walkie-talkie inside ROK. Looks like it's a battery powered one, independent of our main CB control. Does it have a partner?"

Deedat smacked Blomkamp on the back and ran off towards the Captain.

"Yes, sir. Ruiz put a couple of these units in the submersibles a few months ago. Just so we could talk 'off-air', while doing pressure-testing."

Captain Grey shot him a slight look of disapproval, but he was glad to come across a secondary form of communications. Deedat climbed up the side of MIG IV submersible and opened the hatch to its containment control chamber.

"The other one is in here." Deedat yelled to Captain Grey as he turned on the walkie-talkie and spoke into it. "Testing, one, two, three. Hello Captain Grey. Come in."

"I hear you loud and clear, Winston. It would have been nice to know about these units a few hours ago."

"Sorry, Captain, I forgot we even had them," Deedat replied sheepishly.

Captain Grey placed the walkie-talkie back inside the ROK submersible and proceeded to check the Reiziger's crane arm for its functionality. It worked fine. You could always count on Canadians to make a quality product.

Doctor Baruti finished writing in his journal and watched the men work at a feverish pace to get the submersible ready for deployment. Just then, Dr. Athans and Dr. Conte approached from behind Baruti.

"What are they doing?" asked Athans, startling Baruti.

"Oh, hello there. There seems to be a bit of trouble with the screws, they are going to check it out," replied Baruti.

"Screws?" Conte asked.

"I'm sorry, Doctor. That means the props in marine language. I have to say, I've learned quite a bit from these able seamen over the past couple of days."

Conte nodded. "Doctor, could you come to the lab with us for a moment. There's something you need to see."

Doctor Baruti looked at his colleagues. Right away, he knew it had something to do with the blood sample he had given them to examine. "Could it wait for a few minutes?" Baruti said.

"I really wish you would come right away, Doctor. We found something rather puzzling," Athans suggested.

Doctor Baruti looked at the two doctors. Both had concerned looks on their faces, and nodded to Baruti that it was imperative that he come at once.

"Okay. Let me finish checking over this crewmember and then we'll go."

Doctor Baruti followed up his examination of Blomkamp as the young deckhand was readying himself for his mission in the submersible. Baruti took his temperature, examined his skin condition and color, shone a light across his pupils for dilation response and snapped his fingers next to Blomkamp's ears, checking his hearing. Again, he noted the results in his journal. "You look good Nelson, off you go. Be safe, young man." Baruti said.

"You'll be sure to get me a copy of your report, Doctor?" Captain Grey said.

"Most definitely," Baruti said, "Now, if you'll excuse me, Captain, I have to go to the lab to check something, if that's okay with you?"

"Yes, please do. I appreciate your help, Doctor... normally Tom would perform all medical..." the Captain stopped.

Baruti didn't say anything. He knew what the Captain was thinking.

Nelson Blomkamp then entered ROK and began to flick switches and knobs while he waited for Captain Grey and Deedat to lower him into the Atlantic.

The trio of scientists didn't leave right away. Instead, they watched as Captain Grey began to manoeuvre the large crane, carefully lifting and lowering the ROK submersible with Blomkamp inside. Up the large steel bathysphere went, over the side of the Reiziger. Once the ROK touched into the water, the cable's umbilical clamp was released and the ROK plunged underwater sending a crescendo of bubbles and whitecaps to the surface.

"You're all clear," Deedat said into the walkie-talkie.

"Ten-four," Blomkamp replied. "Propulsion control on and working fine. I'm going to do a three-sixty inspection just below surface before heading to the screws. I'll radio in when I get there."

"Sounds good. Just remember to take it easy," Deedat said.

"Yes, Mom!"

Baruti felt a sense of relief seeing the submersible was successfully released. He knew that the Reiziger was on its way to being repaired and functional once again. He smiled briefly before following his colleagues as they quietly left the main deck and headed to the lab.

* * *

Amy and Joost couldn't understand what had happened. No tsunami approached, and the waves didn't even seem out of the ordinary. The sudden rocking of the Reiziger was a mystery.

Joost slumped back in the chair and began looking at the floor. His eyes were tracing the patterns on the carpeted floor. He looked as though he was in a trance as he attempted to count the Reiziger logos printed on the wool material.

"Joost?" Amy called.

Joost didn't respond to Amy; he was deep in thought at the moment.

"Joost!" Amy called out again, finally startling her former captor. He looked up at her expressionless.

"We should go and check on Stephan."

Joost just shook his head. "Look, I realize he's your brother and you're worried, but we left him in a reasonable state. If we try to head to the Savior right now, we could be spotted. Even worse, if we take Stephan from the capsule, and someone sees us – they'll know that we've been inside, and that we have a key. Neither you nor I would get away from this ship after that. No, we have to just sit back, and wait until its dark."

Amy knew that Joost was right, but she couldn't stop thinking of her brother. He was alone, inside of a lifeboat capsule – waking up with a terrible headache and not knowing where he was. The thought horrified Amy; she felt claustrophobic for her brother. But as Joost said, if they went to the Savior right now, they risked being seen, and that would most likely jeopardize their opportunity to get away later.

She threw herself onto her bed, pulling one of the pillows over her face. Amy tried to relax but couldn't; she tossed the pillow aside and looked at Joost. He was falling asleep in the chair. '*Can I trust him?*' she thought to herself. She still wasn't sure if she could, but she didn't have much choice. She closed her eyes as she thought about the events of that day. Within minutes, she was asleep.

* * *

"What are you slowing down for, you son-of-a-bitch?" Lefu yelled at Carlito.

"We have to. I can't exactly pull up alongside of another ship going twenty-two knots. I'll fly right past them."

Carlito shook his head at Lefu while he busied the controls - flipping switches and pressing buttons. Carlito grabbed his CB and clicked the key, "Mr. Asunda, slow and steady twenty-five percent."

"Twenty-five percent, yes Mr. Carlito," the voice responded.

Moments later, the loud rumble of the Pemba Koningin cut out. The vibrations aboard ship subsided. Audibility returned to a normal level.

"They've seen us by now I'm sure," Carlito said.

"That's okay, I thought of that," replied Lefu. "Remember, they sent out a distress flare not long ago. And we're going to use that to our advantage. That's why we're here - to offer assistance. Once we're aboard, then we'll take over."

Lefu turned to his thugs who were standing nearby.

"Percy, no guns when we board; we don't want to give ourselves away too early. Jako, you stay here. I'll take the engineer, Mr. Asunda with us. When we get over there, don't do anything, Percy – don't speak, don't act - just follow my lead."

The men nodded their heads and Percy began to arm himself with a small caliber pistol and a knife, strategically placed in such a way they were concealed. Lefu watched him.

"I'm not going empty handed," Percy said, as he grabbed for another pistol.

Lefu reached out and grabbed Percy's giant wrist. "No. I said don't do anything. This is a research ship. They probably don't even have *one* gun aboard. There's no need for us all to be armed to the teeth. You don't need one. Do you understand?"
Percy nodded to Lefu, though it was obvious he wasn't happy about it.

* * *

Dr. Athans flicked on the lights inside the research lab while Dr. Conte and Dr. Baruti followed behind.

The research lab was painted bright white with an accent of blue along the trim at the top and bottom of the walls, paying homage to the Reiziger itself by mimicking the ships exterior.

Various charts and graphs hung on every wall: a periodic table here, a conversion chart there; along the center of the large back wall was a life size picture of Albert Einstein sticking out his tongue.

A few tables were set up throughout the room. One had a Bunsen burner; another had a platform shaker with several dyes and beakers carefully positioned next to it. A large table was along the back wall, and at the center station sat a row of microscopes. The scientists gathered around a single electron microscope already fitted with a slide for viewing.

"Go ahead, Doctor," Conte said to Baruti.

Baruti removed his glasses to look into the microscope. He already knew that he was going to be looking at the blood sample he handed to his colleagues earlier in the day.

"I think you'll be quite shocked when you see it, Doctor." Dr. Athans said, "Dr. Conte and I examined the sample with great care, but as you know, our biological background is limited at best. All that we could ascertain is that the blood is most definitely human, which of course doesn't bode well for whomever it came from. If there was as much blood as you said, then that person is surely dead – or very near death without medical intervention. However, something else was present within the sample - something that has us puzzled. Something we need your help with."

"Is that what I think it is?" Baruti asked with his eyes fixed to the microscope.

Dr. Baruti pulled back from the microscope and looked at his friends. "It can't be!"

"If you're referring to the secondary molecular structure present within the sample, then yes," replied Conte. "It appears to be an independent polymer chain, but we can't identify it. A seismologist and a geologist can only do so much, Doctor. We tried to contact Ms. Masterson, but she said she was too tired to help and dismissed us quite readily," Athans said.

"Amy? That's strange. I wonder why she would do such a thing. That young girl lives and breathes research. I'm surprised!" Baruti sat down and put his glasses back on.

"What can you tell us, Doctor?" asked Athans.

Baruti took his time to think of an answer that would satisfy his colleagues. He pulled a handkerchief from his back pocket and wiped his forehead where a cold sweat had begun to form. He couldn't give an answer to the two scientists that would reveal too much. He couldn't mention Tom Bailey, he couldn't mention the missing gun, and he couldn't mention much about what he saw under the microscope.

"As you might know, there are very few places we're going to find what I believe we're looking at – this one particular type of polymer chain – appears to be Chitin. At least I'd say so. I could do more tests, but I've seen this structure enough times to know. It's a derivative of glucose – it's actually a monosaccharide, but regardless. It is very common in plant and animal life. Which is reasonable in this particular environment as Chitin is found on crustaceans like crab or lobster. The other place Chitin is found is on the tentacles and beaks of cephalopods like octopus or squid. But why it was found mixed with human blood – I can't..." Doctor Baruti paused.

He thought about the large red marks across Tom Bailey's back. At first sight, he couldn't explain what they were, but now it began to make sense. Tom's other injuries played into the equation: the broken bones and severely fractured skull.

"Oh, my God." he whispered.

"What? What is it?" asked Conte. "Why would there be Chitin mixed with this blood sample?"

Doctor Baruti's lips quivered and he looked as though he was about to cry when he looked up to his counterparts. "I need to see the Captain, immediately!"

17

The horn from the Pemba Koningin sounded as it approached the Reiziger only a short distance away.

"Captain, a ship is here. They must have seen the distress flare. We're going to be okay!" Deedat cheered.

Captain Grey raised his hand to block the sun out of his eyes. The glare from the late afternoon sun in the east sat almost perfectly above the Pemba Koningin. Once his vision adjusted, he got a good look at the ship approaching and was delighted to see the South African flag flying high above its main. The captain smiled as he watched the ship slowly maneuver parallel to the Reiziger about a hundred yards away.

Captain Grey felt the weight of the day lift from him. The life rafts, the damage to the bridge, the breach in the hull. All these things seemed insignificant at the moment. Although, the thought of Tom Bailey still haunted the Captain. He tried not to think about him right now. Fortunately, with a ship at their rescue, the Captain could radio for help, unload his passengers and crew, and wait for assistance to arrive and investigate the matter. He smiled.

"Winston, come in," a voice called across the walkie-talkie.

"Go ahead, Nelson. What is it?" Deedat replied.

"I can see the hull of another ship...looks like they're going to pull beside us. Is everything okay?"

"It's a South African ship; they received our distress flare signal. Hopefully they'll help. Don't worry about them. Have you seen any problem with the screws?"

"You're not going to believe this. I can hardly believe it myself. I've never seen anything like this in my life. Both screws are completely entangled with what looks to be a bunch of tentacles. Might even be a complete squid or octopus wrapped up in here; I can't tell. It's huge. Really long tentacles - they'd have to come from one big mother of an octopus or squid. Like I said, I've never seen anything like this."

Captain Grey overheard the conversation and asked for the walkie-talkie from Deedat.

"Is there any way you can use the ROK's arms to untangle the mess?" Captain Grey asked.

"Oh shit, Captain, they're probably wrapped around the screws a few times over. I mean, honestly, I was just telling Deedat, it could be a whole octopus wrapped in these things. Maybe two! It's hard to tell."

"Can it be fixed?" the Captain repeated.

"I'll try, Captain. I'll use the arms to try and pull the pieces off that I can grab without banging into the ship. You're going to feel a pull here and there if they don't come off easily."

"That's fine. Just keep working at it and check in every ten minutes. You hear me? Every ten minutes."

"Yes, sir," replied Blomkamp.

Captain Grey double clicked the receiver of the walkie-talkie and handed it back to Deedat. Just then, Officer Medupé appeared on the deck.

"Mr. Medupé!" Captain Grey exclaimed. "Where the hell have you been? You've been gone without reporting in for well over an hour."

Medupé looked surprised at the Captain. Protocol never required him to check in with the Captain every hour or less. It never required him to check in at all.

"I was doing my job, sir, with all due respect. Our regular communications are down – so how was I supposed to..."

Captain Grey cut him off, "And what exactly would your job be at this moment, Mr. Medupé? Considering we are missing two members of our crew, our life rafts are gone, the bridge of the command center is destroyed, we have a breach in our hull, and we can't get the goddamn ship moving...please tell me, what exactly would you be doing that is so important?"

Captain Grey was furious. As he spoke, his hands waved in the air frantically. Medupé had seen the Captain angry once earlier today in the mess hall, but this was much more extreme.

Medupé tried to calm the Captain by remaining composed.

"I was doing my job as safety and security officer of this ship. I was looking for any signs of the Bailey brothers and at the same time I was ensuring that all other aspects of the ship were in check. I'm sorry, Sir, I didn't think I was required to stay with you and the rest of the crew. I honestly thought you'd rather that I try to help in the capacity I was hired for."

Captain Grey glared at Medupé through angry eyes. He didn't speak a word. The Captain tried to silently scrutinize Medupé, but he was interrupted.

The horn of the Pemba Koningin blew loudly once again. Deedat, Medupé and the Captain turned their attention to the ship positioned alongside the Reiziger a hundred yard away. A few people could be seen waving from the main deck of the other ship. Deedat and the Captain returned the welcoming gesture.

"I also wanted to report that I saw a ship approaching," Medupé said.

"Duly noted, Mr. Medupé," Captain Grey said, still cross with his officer.

The crew on the Reiziger watched as the figures aboard the other ship lowered from the side what looked like an outboard Zodiac. Then they fastened an accommodation ladder over the side of the ship. Slowly, three people descended the ladder and climbed into the small inflatable. The Reiziger had a permanent steel access ladder attached to both starboard and port side of its body with a mooring post attached at either base so an accommodation ladder wasn't necessary to drop over her sides - she was ready to accept her rescuers.

"Mr. Deedat, please find Fenyang. Make sure he has something ready to serve to our guests," Captain Grey said.

"They're on a pretty big ship, sir. What if they've already eaten?" Deedat asked.

Captain Grey exploded, "Well, I haven't eaten. Our passengers haven't eaten. It's almost tea, so please...tell Fenyang to have something prepared. Thank you, Mr. Deedat."

The normally smiling deckhand handed Captain Grey the walkie-talkie and walked away. He wasn't smiling anymore.

"Why do you have to talk to the crew like that, Captain? If you are mad with me, then be mad with me...but please..." Medupé tried to reason with Grey.

Captain Grey ignored Medupé and called for Blomkamp over the walkie-talkie. "How are you making out, Nelson?"

Five seconds, ten seconds...thirty seconds...no reply.

"Mr. Blomkamp, this is the Captain. Come in, over."

Five seconds, ten seconds...then a voice, "Sorry Captain, I must have accidentally turned the volume down...what were you saying?"

"How are the repairs coming along?" Captain Grey repeated with a frustrated tone.

"It's a bit of a rat's nest down here, sir. I'm trying my best, but this stuff is really tangled in there."

"Keep checking in, every ten minutes, Mr. Blomkamp...and keep your volume up!"

The Captain double-clicked his receiver and clipped it onto his belt buckle. It was then he was reminded that he still had the tranquilizer gun on his person. 'Shit,' he thought. It was concealed, but not completely. Not wanting to seem a threat to his rescuers, Captain Grey wandered away from Medupé and towards the MIG IV submersible vessel. Pretending to be doing something of importance, he opened the hatch and placed the tranquilizer gun inside, just on the seat. He closed the door and glanced over his shoulder to see if Medupé was watching him. He didn't seem to be.

Returning to Medupé, Captain Grey watched as the rescue boat slowly pulled up to the Reiziger. The small craft did a tail kick towards the rail ladder and mooring post of the Reiziger as it gently nudged the side of the big ship.

The waves of the Atlantic, although almost unnoticed aboard the Reiziger, tossed the smaller boat with zeal.

Aboard the tiny Zodiac inflatable were three men; two very large black men, and an older Caucasian man. The older man was driving the Zodiac as one of the black men moored the boat to the Reiziger. The other black man, the one with a bald head and sunglasses; just watched the other two. He was giving directions to the two men with gestures and verbal commands, but Captain Grey couldn't hear them from this distance. However, Grey was correct to assume that this man was the one in charge.

As the boat pulled up alongside the Reiziger, Dr. Baruti reappeared on the main deck with Dr. Conte and Dr. Athans at his heels. The trio immediately noticed the other ship sitting parallel to the Reiziger. The three scientists headed straight for Captain Grey. Dr. Baruti was holding something in his hand.

"Captain Grey!" called Dr. Baruti. "I need to talk to you immediately, sir."

"Yes, of course, Doctor. Give me a minute, please."

Captain Grey looked away from the doctor as he gestured to the men over the side of the ship. Dr. Baruti and his colleagues looked over the side of the Reiziger and saw the two large black men climbing the outer stair rails to the main deck. The doctor couldn't wait.

"Captain, we must assemble the crew and passengers immediately. I also recommend that Mr. Blomkamp come topside at once!" Baruti urged.

Medupé, eavesdropping, raised an eyebrow and decided to intervene. "What is the concern, Doctor? Perhaps, I can assist."

Captain Grey, although quick to dismiss the doctor at first, heard his Officer make an offer. Quickly shooting a look to Medupé, he leaned back from the rail and snapped his fingers at his Second Officer.

"No! Whatever information the doctor has, it is for me - the Captain - first and foremost! Miguel, return to your security detail and checking the ship, that's an order!" Captain Grey yelled.

Dr. Baruti and the other scientists realized that the Captain had just disrespected his Officer by using his first name. They all looked at one another awkwardly as the mood on the deck briefly became uncomfortable.

This was the first time in years that the Captain had addressed Medupé by his first name. Medupé felt it was intentional, unconventional, demeaning and rude – especially in front of passengers. 'What the hell did I do wrong?' Medupé thought. He pursed his lips ready to fire back at the Captain for making him feel like a child. Instead, he respected his rank and simply nodded and walked away.

As Medupé marched off in the direction of the command center, Deedat rejoined the group, returning from the mess hall.

"Fenyang says food will be ready in twenty minutes, Sir," he said with a satisfied smile.

"Okay, good. I want you to take the walkie-talkie again, and stay here. I've informed Nelson that I want him to check in every ten minutes. You stay in radio contact, and if anything is of concern, bring him up at once."

Deedat saluted. As Captain Grey finished giving his orders, Baruti jumped in right away, "Captain, please, you must bring Mr. Blomkamp up immediately."

"What is it, Doctor?" Captain Grey turned to the doctor and gently pulled him away from the small group. "I don't want to panic anybody right now; we have a rescue boat here," the Captain said in a whisper as he leaned in close to Baruti.

"Captain," Baruti began, almost scared to speak, "I've checked the blood sample from the spill we found earlier...and it suggests that there was something else mixed with the blood."

Captain Grey looked at the doctor confused. "Mixed with the blood? What do you mean?"

"I found traces of Chitin."

The Captain shrugged. He had heard the name before, but didn't know what it really was. Baruti continued.

"It's a long chain polymer – a derivative of glucose. This stuff is found in lots of places: the cell walls of fungi, or even the exoskeletons of crabs and lobsters. At first I thought of those animals...but them having possibly introduced the Chitin to the sample...it didn't make sense."

Captain Grey leaned in even closer to Baruti. "What do you think then, Doctor?"

"Well, the other place you would find Chitin would be on cephalopods, like squid or octopus. Chitin is found on their beaks or even on the ends of their tentacle suckers, like little teeth. It made me think of Tom Bailey. He had those red marks on his body, remember? I didn't know what they were at first, but now it makes sense. It is possible – but bear in mind this is just a theory right now, but it is possible that Tom and Drew were attacked on deck by a giant squid or octopi."

Captain Grey's eyes stared blankly at the doctor. He couldn't believe what he was hearing.

"I need to check Tom's body to confirm this, Captain. But more importantly, I don't think you should have a man in the water. If a creature like that is out there, your crewmember could be in real danger."

Captain Grey pulled off his hat and wiped his brow.

"If what you're saying is possible, and that is what happened to Drew and Tom, then I want to know. I need to know. But Doctor, think about it - we can't alarm the passengers and crew right now. Tom is lying dead in my quarters and it's not because of some damn giant squid. Somebody aboard this ship shot and killed him, remember? If we say that a giant squid is attacking us, everybody will want to know how we came to this conclusion. And you can't get to that conclusion without mentioning Tom."

Doctor Baruti nodded.

Captain Grey realized his new guests would be on deck any minute now. He reached into his pocket and grabbed his key ring. He shuffled through the keys, unclipped the single key for his quarters, and handed it to Baruti. "Do what you have to do, Doctor...but do it alone."

"Yes sir...but what about Blomkamp?"

The Captain thought for a moment. "Doctor, if it *was* a giant squid or octopi, I have a feeling its dead. Right now Nelson is working on removing large amounts of tentacles from the screws. Looks like it got wrapped up in them."

"Pray he doesn't find anything else. I still suggest you bring him up," Baruti said.

"I will. I promise. Just let me welcome this rescue team then I will bring him up."

Doctor Baruti nodded but then jumped suddenly as Cody sprang to her feet and began to snarl.

"Hello there!" Lefu exclaimed as he climbed over the side of the Reiziger. "I understand you are in need as assistance."

18

Amy woke when a knock came at her door. She was slightly disoriented, but realized soon enough that she was still aboard the Reiziger. The knock at the door was hard and deliberate, yet sounded like a random pattern as if someone was kicking instead of knocking.

"Joost," Amy whispered into the darkened room, "you have to hide again. Joost? Did you hear me? Someone is at the door."

Amy's looked to the chair where Joost had been sitting. He wasn't there. She got out of bed, flicked on a light and quickly scanned her cabin. The knocking continued. Joost was nowhere to be found inside the cabin. 'Damn,' Amy thought, 'He must have gone outside and now he's locked out.'

Her mind raced. This could her one chance to get away from Joost, but she wasn't sure if she wanted to. The young stowaway had offered her the chance to get off the Reiziger; he was going to coordinate the escape. However, he had shown aggression before – albeit in the face of desperation, but nonetheless – aggression. 'Would he do it again?' she wondered as the image of Stephan beaten and bloodied crossed her mind.

The knocking at the door grew stronger. Amy knew that if she left him out there, he would eventually find a way in, and he surely would be angry for her betrayal. He wouldn't think twice about hurting her – not to mention what he may do to Stephan? If she left Joost outside at risk of being discovered by someone else, he might go back to the Savior and hurt Stephan just to spite her.

Amy went to her cabin door and then noticed it wasn't locked. She opened the door. There stood her brother, Stephan. His face was bloodied and swollen, his shirt torn, and his overall appearance not good.

"Oh my God, Stephan...why didn't you just open the door? Get in here. Holy shit. Are you okay? How did you get here? Here, sit down."

Stephan was still unsteady from the blow to the head. He entered the cabin and sat in the chair his attacker sat in less than an hour ago.

"Amy, slow down. Tell me, what happened?" Stephan said.

Amy was in the bathroom running a towel under some warm water. She brought it back to Stephan and helped him clean the dried blood from around his face.

"You were attacked, buddy. We both were. But you're okay now."

"Who attacked us? I can't remember. I just know that I woke up in a daze. Someone was calling my name, and I felt like I was floating, and then I was completely awake."

"Where did you wake up?"

"I was on the main deck, right beside the life boat."

"You were beside it?" Amy pressed, "You mean in it?"

"No, I was beside it. I was on the ground. Why was I there?"

Amy figured her brother possibly suffered a concussion and his memory was a bit fuzzy.

"What do you remember last?" she asked.

Stephan stopped Amy as she questioned him. He badly needed a drink of water. Amy obliged as she filled her toothbrush rinse cup with water from the bathroom sink. Stephan reached for the glass, realizing it was a toothbrush cup, but he didn't care.

He just rolled his eyes at Amy and drank it down. At least his sense of humor didn't seem to be compromised.

"The last thing...the very last thing I remember was...we were all gathered in the mess hall for a meeting or something. Yes, that's it. The Captain was giving us the story of why we couldn't go to St. Helena. And then..."

Stephan sat with a blank look on his face. He stopped speaking and began to trace his fingers along the sides of the chair.

"Stephan, a lot has happened since then," Amy began to worry about the memory loss. It really was a severe hit to the face. Maybe he had some permanent damage. She searched her own memory-banks to try to come up with something to jog his.

"Do you remember the binoculars?" she asked.

Stephan looked at his sister slightly confused. It was clear that he couldn't remember.

"Your bag," she said. "Inside your carry bag you had a pair of binoculars. You found them by the blood. That's what you told me...or what about the lifeboat? Going to St. Helena?"

Stephan just shook his head. He didn't remember. And if he didn't remember the binoculars, the blood or St. Helena, he clearly wouldn't remember the man with the gun that did this to him.

"Maybe you should have a lie down; you've got a bit of a concussion. You need to rest. Here."

She helped her brother from the chair and moved him to the bed. She threw his lanky legs up on the end of the bed and then pulled the covers up just past his waist.

"Now, I'm going to get Dr. Baruti to come and look at you. I'll be right back, so you just close your eyes and rest until I get back...okay?"

Stephan nodded as Amy took away the towel. She ran it under some cold water from the bathroom, brought it back and placed it across his forehead. She gently kissed his cheek and told him to sleep. Amy then threw on a light pullover as she went to the door, before she even left her cabin, Stephan was already asleep.

Amy needed to find Joost. As much as he was a stranger to her, he was her only hope.

He must have slipped away while she was sleeping, she thought. He must have gone back to the Savior and taken Stephan out. Maybe he was planning on leaving without Amy, not holding his part of the bargain...maybe he was going to betray her and the deal they had struck.

Regardless, her brother was alive, and she knew that he was going to be okay. Unfortunately or fortunately, he didn't remember anything about the possibility of fleeing to St. Helena with the life boat. He also didn't remember Joost hitting him in the face. That was probably for the best.

As Amy walked from her cabin, the afternoon sun was beginning to set. Amy couldn't believe it was already that late in the day. She hadn't eaten. Amy crossed onto the main deck and watched the glorious red and orange orb begin its decent from the horizon. She figured about maybe one more hour until it set - just enough time to find Joost and make an escape in the life raft.

Looking across the main deck, nobody was around, but Amy saw something strange. Something she hadn't expected to see. Sitting across the water from the Reiziger was a very large, black and gray ship. The ship wasn't moving; it just sat there. Amy remembered the flare that someone had sent up; perhaps this was help. Her heart began to race with excitement.

Keeping herself hidden in the shadows of the command center, Amy manoeuvred across the deck of the Reiziger to get a closer look at the foreign ship anchored in the distance. She stopped as she reached the MIG IV submersible. Anticipation turned to fear; something wasn't quite right.

Amy peered over the guardrail of the Reiziger. Looking down, she noticed the small Zodiac boat harnessed to the side of the stairs. Turning her attention back to the large ship, she noticed the flag flying from its main. It was a South African flag.

"Omigod," Amy said, realizing that this ship potentially could possibly be carrying the group of 'really bad men' Joost had warned her about. 'What if this was the group of men that would kill anybody aboard to find Joost and his diamond,' she thought. What could she do? Should she warn the Captain? Tell him about the stowaway named Joost? Should she warn everybody that this other ship could be full of bad people? It may already be too late; with the empty zodiac sitting below, it was apparent that some of their crew were already aboard the Reiziger.

Amy knees grew weak as she leaned close to the submersible. Her face pressed up against the glass front window of the MIG IV. By chance, she looked inside, and saw something on the seat. This something gave her a feeling of hope. She checked the main hatch door to the submersible - it was open. She opened it, reached in, and grabbed the tranquilizer gun.

19

Dr. Athans and Dr. Conte sat at one of the round tables near the back of the mess hall. Stuart Radcliff and Dr. Uuka Duiker sat directly across from them at the next table, while a larger group gathered at the captain's main table in the center of the room. At this table sat Lefu, Percy, Mr. Asunda, Deedat and Captain Grey. Fenyang stood behind his workstation at the ready to serve up some food, while Cody gnawed on an old soup bone in the corner of the room.

Captain Grey explained to his new guests the problems they had encountered, including the breach in the hull, and the trouble they were having disengaging the clutch for the props. He vaguely touched on the fact that the Reiziger was experiencing communication problems of sorts, without going into detail of how someone had ruined the command center. The Captain also conveniently left out the details of the missing life rafts and the body of Tom Bailey. This was information that he felt could jeopardize any budding relationship they were forming.

"Sounds like you're having one hell of a day, Captain," laughed Lefu.

Everyone at the main table laughed at Lefu's comment.

"I'll say. I'm just glad that someone got our distress signal. Please...have something to eat." The Captain stood up. "Please, everyone, have some food."

The room came alive as the scientists, crew, and their newfound friends took in a wonderfully cooked, hot meal. The conversation throughout the supper was full of laughter and smiles.

"Okay, I understand Doctor Baruti said he had some work to do...and that explains him not being here. But has anyone seen Amy or Stephan?" Stuart Radcliff asked the scientist members seated at the two tables in the rear.

Doctor Athans cleared things up explaining to the other scientists that he and Dr. Conte were recently in contact with Amy, and that she was having a rest. Nobody knew the whereabouts of Stephan Woodley. Nobody considered checking his cabin, but it was possible that he too was sleeping. Everyone accepted the explanation and went on discussing their pending mission.

Lefu informed his table of why his ship was this far out to sea. He told an elaborate story of how the Pemba Koningin was on a merchant mission heading to Ensenada, Argentina. There, the crew would gather and bring back various grains to the starving areas in southern and central Africa. He told his hosts how Captain Carlito wished to remain on the Pemba with a couple of deckhands, while Mr. Asunda, the chief engineer, and Percy would accompany Lefu to check out what was wrong with this ship that had sent up a flare.

Captain Grey was too overjoyed to see that somebody had come to their aid and he didn't see any reason to doubt Lefu's story – nor did he look very hard. Had he looked harder, he would have realized that a ship the size of the Pemba Koningin couldn't carry nearly as much grain as a container style ship; it wasn't designed for such purpose. Unfortunately, the obvious was never questioned.

"Could I offer you a drink?" Captain Grey asked as he held up a full bottle of wine.

Percy almost began to accept when Lefu cut him off. "No, Captain, thank you," Lefu said.

Percy seemed put out, but didn't dispute with Lefu. Instead, he sat quietly with his hands folded.

"Mr. Asunda, how about you?" the Captain offered.

"No, he's fine too," Lefu said, gently patting Asunda on the head.

Mr. Asunda too, didn't dispute with Lefu.

"Please, Captain, we shouldn't waste any more time," Lefu smiled, "we are merely here to serve you. The sun is beginning to fade on us, and I'd hate to work in the complete darkness of night. No, I say let's check the progress of your man underside and see if we can get your mighty ship moving again. Agreed?"

"Agreed," Captain Grey said with a smile.

Captain Grey stood up from the table. Cody noticed her master stood up and quickly dropped the soup bone and went to attend his side. Cody kept her two different colored eyes fixed on Lefu. She didn't growl, but she wasn't wagging her tail either.

As Lefu stood up, Mr. Asunda and Percy followed suit. Cody gently lunged backward in a defensive stance from the trio. Captain Grey laughed and patted her side letting her know that everything was okay - that these people were here to help. Cody didn't seem to take solace from her master. She never took her eyes off of the three men, especially Lefu.

The scientists remained seated in the mess hall continuing their meals, while Fenyang worked feverishly cleaning plates and dishes. As the group left the mess hall, Lefu asked in a nonchalant manner, "So, how many people are aboard this ship, Captain?"

* * *

Amy reached the Savior without being noticed, or at least as far as she could tell. She didn't come across anybody during her travels, so that was a good start.

At the Savior, she found that the door was locked, just as it was when she and Joost left Stephan inside. Joost must have come back, unlocked the door, removed Stephan, and then locked the door again. She knocked on the door a couple of times. There was no response. Getting frustrated, she banged her hand on the side of the fibreglass vessel thinking that perhaps Joost had crawled inside and maybe was asleep. She knocked a few more times. Still, no one answered.

Checking around, she noticed a large steel I-beam that supported the Savior in place. At the base of the steel beam, where it was harnessed to the main deck appeared to be an opening. Amy took a closer look. She ran her hand along the outside of the beam toward its base. She realized that the hollow point was exactly that, a hollow in the beam. Almost like a tiny cubby hole. Although it wasn't intended to be one – it was one. A simple design flaw that offered Amy opportunity. She took the tranquilizer gun and tucked it inside the cubby. She gave a glance back at the Savior; the door was still closed. Checking over her shoulder; no one was around. Amy pulled out her lipstick from her front pocket and marked a small star on the beam at eye level. Just then, she heard a voice.

* * *

Doctor Baruti followed down the passageway toward the Captain's quarters. He was taking a closer look at the footprints of blood leading to and from the cabin. Indeed, there were two distinctly different footprints marking the passageway. Once he reached the door, the doctor knocked and waited. There was no answer. He then put the key into the lock and opened the door.

The room looked exactly as he and the Captain had left it; the bed was tossed about, and the footlocker was sitting on the floor with its lid open. The bloodstains on the floor had dried up and were somewhat faded, but nonetheless still present.

The doctor entered the bathroom and found a pair of legs protruding from underneath a blanket cover. He pulled back the blanket and found Tom Bailey, still dead...just as he was before.

Baruti knelt down once again tilted the body of the officer forward and lifted his shirt. There as plain as day were the red marks he had trouble explaining, but now, they seemed to make sense. The red marks were huge red circles. They began at Tom's left hip and continued all the way to his right ear, crossing over his shoulder blade, which was severely broken.

Dr. Baruti wondered if Tom's broken skull may have been sustained by being slammed against the ship. It was hard to tell, but it wasn't an unreasonable thought.

Going about his business in a professional manner, the doctor took out a small razor from his medical kit and cut a portion of Tom Bailey's back flesh, removing a section of one of the red circles. He put the sample into a small plastic container, sealed the lid, and put all the items back into his kit again.

Gently placing the body of Tom back against the wall, the doctor then re-covered the corpse with the blanket, said a prayer for the departed and closed the curtain.

20

The air began to cool as the day faded. The sky was covered with an array of white cumulous clouds splashed against a blood red background. The waves of the ocean responded to the presence of the clouds and began to act up; kicking off white caps left and right, bouncing the Reiziger gently back and forth upon the surface of the water.

Captain Grey, Lefu, Percy, and Mr. Asunda stood on the main deck close to the location where they first met less than an hour earlier. Deedat sat nearby at the MIG IV submersible holding the walkie-talkie.

Every ten minutes Deedat and Blomkamp made radio contact. Deedat informed the Captain that Blomkamp's progress was coming along fine, and that all work should be done within the next half hour.

"Maybe only an hour or so of sun left Lefu, what do you want to do? Should I go back and tell Carlito that we are staying the night?" Mr. Asunda asked.

"Yes, go tell *our* crew that our friends here are in need of our assistance and that Jako should bring the tools necessary to help them." Lefu said with a sinister smile.

Of course, by tools, Lefu meant for Jako to bring the guns, but only Percy and Mr. Asunda understood that message.

"As well, Mr. Asunda...I would prefer if everyone came over to the Reiziger, please pass that message along. The more help they can get over here, the better."

Mr. Asunda nodded and headed off to the waiting Zodiac. He unhooked it from the side of the Reiziger with a bit of difficulty as he bounced with the waves. Once unhooked from the ship, he started the engines of the Zodiac and went back to the motionless Pemba Koningin.

"Winston, are you there?" Blomkamp's voice came across the walkie-talkie.

"Right here," answered Deedat. "What's up?"

"I just saw a small boat leaving the Reiziger. What's going on?"

"Nothing, they are just going to get their crew and come over to see if they can help."

"Good, I think we're going to need a little bit here."

"Why, what's the problem?"

"It looks like that breach in the hull, is...well...it's looking like it's a lot worse from this side. We might want to let the Captain know we should weld this bitch up before we engage the screws again."

"The Captain said the breach is sealed from inside the bulkhead in the engine room."

"I know, but this looks quite nasty from down here. I'd say it might be worth patching up before we go. There's too much chance it could branch into another chamber in the hull if we leave it."

"It's that bad, hey? Okay, I'll tell the Captain."

Deedat double clicked the walkie-talkie and proceeded to tell Captain Grey of Blomkamp's findings. Captain Grey agreed that the crew should take advantage of fixing the breach in the hull before proceeding back to Cape Town, but advised Deedat to bring Blomkamp topside for now. The remaining entanglement of the props and repairs to the hull could wait until the rescue team came back.

Blomkamp received the message from Deedat and promptly stopped his work. Travelling gingerly to the side of the Reiziger, he took the ROK submersible to the surface where it was hooked up to its umbilical cable and hoisted back onto the main deck.

"Whew! It gets frickin' hot in there," Blomkamp said as he finally emerged from the ROK fifteen minutes later.

"How's the oxygen level?" Captain Grey asked, while helping Blomkamp from the vessel.

"Seventy percent, sir."

"Okay, Nelson. Good job."

Captain Grey then introduced Blomkamp to the rescuers. Blomkamp looked at the two large black men, nodded his head to them, and shook their hands.

"Why don't you take off your gear, and head to the mess," the Captain said, "Fenyang has some food prepared and waiting."

Smacking his belly, Blomkamp quickly unzipped his wetsuit, kicked off the gear and left it in a heap beside the ROK. He looked at the Captain after realizing his unprofessional actions in front of guests. Captain Grey just waved him off. Blomkamp nodded to the Captain, smiled and jogged off.

"Thanks Captain...oh and hey, nice meeting you," he yelled back to Percy and Lefu.

* * *

"Hello my dear," a voice said. Amy recognized it right away as she spun around startled. It was the voice of Second Officer Medupé.

"Is there anything I can do for you?" he asked.

"Oh, hello again, Mr. Medupé," Amy said, again forgetting to pay the respect deserved of a man in his position. "I was just wandering around, not much to do when the ship isn't moving."

Amy smiled, and Medupé returned the gesture. His returned smile felt oddly cold. Earlier in the day when the pair had their conversation on the bow of the ship, Amy had felt a bond with Medupé. A trust. A closeness. Right now, she felt a distance.

"Are you okay, my dear?" Medupé asked.

Amy realized it was her own doing. Medupé wasn't the problem...he wasn't acting weird...she was. She was the one who had concealed the saboteur of the lifeboat; she was the one and only person who even knew about the stowaway, she also knew that later tonight she was going to steal this very life boat she was standing next to. No, Amy convinced herself that Medupé was fine - she was the problem.

"I'm so sorry, Mr. Medupé. I've had such a horrible day and night, and I'm so tired and hungry. Of course, I'm upset with the chance of my work being cancelled. It's just, well, it's all a bit overwhelming," she said knowing it was partly a lie.

Medupé nodded. Without saying a word, Medupé slowly walked around Amy and put his hand on the side of the Savior lifeboat. He smoothed his large tanned hand across the side of its door, and then held the handle and gave it a tug. It didn't open.

Amy watched Medupé as he checked the vessel. Biting the side of her lip, she looked around to see if anybody else was nearby. There was nobody, they were alone.

The sun was beaming its final rays of the day as the surrounding sky took on the look of death - blood red and endless.

"What were you looking for, my dear?" Medupé asked.

Amy looked at him in shock. "I wasn't looking for anything, why would you ask that?"

"Please, Ms. Masterson, you and I both know you were banging on the side of this vessel. I could hear it as I came this way from the command center. What exactly are you looking for?"

Amy looked sharply at Medupé. The man, who she trusted to express her inner feelings to earlier in the day, now took on a sombre appearance. The same man who she presumed to be an understanding and peaceful person glared at her with evil in his eyes.

"I wasn't looking for anything," she lied again. "I'll admit, when you heard me banging...yes, I hit the life boat here. But that's only because I am so frustrated with being stuck on this ship. All I want to do is get to St. Helena."

Amy pointed off into the distance. "Look, if you look hard, you can see it. It's right over there."

Medupé didn't look away from Amy. He just stood there in silence staring at her.

"I understand your anguish my dear, but is there anything else you want to tell me?"

"No."

Amy began to fidget her hands. She realized quickly that her body language could be giving away that she was lying, so she stuffed her hands into her jean pockets. Medupé didn't say a word. He just continued to smile at her and then went back to feeling his hand along the outside of the Savior lifeboat as if by some strange osmosis he would be able to discover something. He found nothing.

"Well, I guess I should be going now. Stupid me, I haven't had supper yet. Like I said, I'm kind of hungry," Amy said.

"Oh, I understand. Please let me again escort you." Medupé held out his arm as he had only done earlier that day. This time Amy wasn't as receptive.

"Thanks, but actually...I'm going to head back to my cabin first and change and, and, and..." Amy stuttered, "And, I'm going to get Stephan. He told me to get him when I was going to head to the mess hall. So, thank you, but I'll be okay."

"Very well," Medupé withdrew his arm, "I'll see you there."

Amy smiled at Medupé and quickly walked away toward her cabin. She looked back once, only to see that Medupé was watching her as she left. Once she turned the corner toward the cabins of the inner main deck, she ran.

"Omigod, Omigod, Omigod," she repeated quietly to herself as she went back to her cabin to find Stephan.

21

Doctor Baruti entered the lab and flicked on the overhead lights once again. The room was warm, quiet, and inviting - just the way he liked his lab to be. If he didn't know he was on a ship, he would have presumed he was in the same lab he worked in at the university back in Cape Town.

Proceeding to the microscope table, he pulled out his kit and withdrew the container holding the sample from Tom Bailey's back. He grabbed the necessary stains and slides and set them on the counter beside him. Using a razor and a pair of tweezers, he gently scraped the flesh along the bumpy, red exterior. Small flakes of skin brushed off onto the razor blade. Briefly lifting his glasses to examine the razor's contents, he nodded to himself that his sample was sufficient.

He then pulled out another razor blade and a glass microscope slide. He scraped one blade against the other letting the blade with the skin flakes drop its contents gently onto the glass slide. Then he added a single drop of purple stain to the flakes.

Placing a thin glass cover over the slide, he placed it into the microscope holder and gave it a viewing.

Baruti examined the sample for a few minutes. He then pulled out a small book from his kit and flipped through its pages. Once again, he checked the sample. Finally, he sat down in a chair, took off his glasses and wiped his forearm across his tired eyes. After a moment, he reached into his kit again and pulled out a calculator, pen, paper, and ruler. He drew a picture on the paper, measured it, and then started to punch numbers into the calculator. Once finished, he didn't believe what he was seeing, so he did the calculations once again. They came back the same. The results were not what he wanted to see, but the results didn't lie.

* * *

"Fifteen aboard, well that's an adequate manifest. We only have a six member crew," Lefu joked with the Captain.

"Seven of them are passengers," said Captain Grey. "They hired this vessel to do their explorations; we are just going where they want."

"Oh really?" said Lefu acting surprised. "What are they doing if you don't mind me asking?"

"I believe it has to do with microscopic organisms, animals, some biology and volcanic eruptions. I really don't know much about it," laughed Captain Grey. "But I get paid to take them where they want to go. That's my job."

"Yes, I understand completely. I get paid to make these voyages to gather and deliver food to starving countries, but I'd do it free. It really makes me feel good to help other people. I even feel good about helping someone like you in your time of need," Lefu said trying to appear sincere.

From out of the shadows appeared Ruiz. He'd been working, hidden in the engine room for so long that the Captain forgot about him. The Captain had forgotten that he told him to wait for his next orders. Thankfully, Ruiz got tired of waiting and decided to come looking for the Captain.

"Ruiz, I am so sorry," Captain Grey exclaimed, "I didn't mean to leave you there unattended, but with the communications problems and all, and - I'm sorry. We've been dealing with the screws; we've almost got them ready to turn. Oh, I'm sorry."

Captain Grey then turned to Lefu. "Lefu, this is Alan Ruiz, our engineer. Mr. Ruiz this is Lefu and Percy from the Pemba Koningin over there. These men are here to help us."

Ruiz held out his hand and gave a shake to Percy and then to Lefu.

"Nice to meet you both," he said.

Ruiz then turned back to the Captain and made a gesture indicating he wanted to talk in private.

"Please excuse me, gentlemen," the Captain said. With Ruiz at his side, the pair walked just out of earshot from their guests. "What is it?"

"Captain, I don't want to alarm you again. I know it's been a hell of a day, but I didn't come up here because you forgot to come and get me. I came here to tell you that I've had to close off another bulkhead...we have another breach. Number two has a leak."

The Captain pulled off his cap and with one hand swung it by his side narrowly missing the head of Cody who was, as always, standing next to him.

"My god," exclaimed the Captain. "What the hell is going on?"

"I don't know, sir."

"Okay, here's what we're going to do. Ruiz, you can weld, right?"

"I'm not that good sir, not for repairs. I can do simple fabrication when necessary, but I wouldn't suggest using me for anything serious. Not for repairing a breach in the hull. No sir, not me."

"What about Deedat or Blomkamp?"

"I don't think so, sir. I believe our best welder is Tom."

Captain Grey looked to Cody and apologized to her for almost knocking her with his hat. He shook his head. Of course, it made sense that Tom was his best welder. Tom was his best everything – that's why he was the First Officer. But none of that mattered anymore. Only the Captain, Doctor Baruti, and someone else on board knew – Tom was dead.

"Mr. Lefu," the Captain turned and yelled toward his new friend. Ruiz and the Captain walked towards him. "Please tell me that one of your crew is a proficient hyperbaric welder."

"A welder? What, with your capable crew, you don't have a welder? What's the problem?" Lefu laughed.

Captain Grey explained the situation to Lefu. How it was imperative that they fix the breach while removing the snag of tentacles before the Reiziger would be operational again. He also let Lefu know that they did have the equipment available, but unfortunately, the first officer Tom Bailey, who happened to be the ship's welder, was very sick at the moment.

Lefu took his time thinking about the Captain's request. He almost felt it was time to pull out guns, put an end to the charade, and take everyone hostage...but then something occurred to him. Instead, Lefu assured the Captain and Ruiz that his own captain, Mr. Enzo Carlito was a not only a great captain, but also a very crafty man, and surely a skilled welder.

"Here they are now," Lefu said, "I'll ask him."

Just then, Mr. Asunda, Mr. Hogg, Jako and Carlito climbed over the rail of the main deck. Jako was carrying a backpack that looked heavy. As he and the others found firm ground on the deck, Jako put the backpack down. Cody noticed the new strangers on board and began to snarl.

"Easy girl," Captain Grey said not wanting to frighten the guests.

As the Pemba Koningin men made their way onto the main deck, Lefu slyly greeted them with a smile and did informal introductions to the Reiziger crew. He then pulled Carlito aside, grabbed the back of his neck and whispered in his ear.

"Listen to me Carlito, this ship has a breach underside, and you're going to repair it. I know you can weld, so don't bullshit me. A have a new plan. When we're done here, we'll find Joost and the diamond – and then we're going to take this ship."

Carlito's face lit up with a dirty smile.

"So it's in our best interest to make sure it's fixed properly. Got it?" Lefu said.

Carlito nodded, laughed and spoke a little too loud, "No problem. I've always wanted a ship of my own."

Unsure if the Reiziger crew overheard the shady Italian captain, Lefu released Carlito's neck and yelled to the crowd, "And here, everyone, is our fine captain himself, Mr. Enzo Carlito. I've told him of the problem and he would be happy to fix your ship."

"Fantastic, thank you very much gentlemen," Captain Grey said, shaking Carlito's grubby little hand.

"So, you have all the necessary gear?" asked Carlito.

"We do, Mr. Carlito, but I see you brought some of your own," the Captain said referring to the backpack Jako brought on board.

"No welding gear in here, just wrenches and stuff," Jako said, giving the backpack a little kick.

Captain Grey nodded, even though he thought it strange to bring wrenches aboard, he didn't question Jako.

"Okay, well, Mr. Ruiz and I will fetch the welding gear and get you ready to head underside shortly, Mr. Carlito. And we'll have the ROK submersible down there with you cleaning up the screws."

"What's wrong with the screws?" Carlito asked.

"An octopus was trying to hitch a free ride," Ruiz laughed. The men thought the comment was funny and everyone joined in on the laugh.

Just then, Doctor Baruti came around the corner looking for the Captain. The poor old doctor once again looked as though he had just run a marathon.

"Everyone," the Captain exclaimed, "this is Doctor Baruti, one of the finest physicians in all of South Africa. Doctor, these are our friends, here to help us get the Reiziger back in action."

Baruti nodded and smiled sheepishly at the crew of the Pemba Koningin. He wasn't in the mood for niceties at the moment, "Captain, could I speak with you?" Baruti said as he slowly walked away from the crowd.

"Yes, of course, one second. Ruiz, please head to the mess and grab some food before Fenyang cleans up for the night. While there, tell Blomkamp and Deedat that we're taking ROK down again. Captain Carlito from the Pemba Koningin is going to assist. When you're done there, come back and we'll grab the welding gear. Go now, hurry!"

Ruiz acknowledged the captain with a salute and exited the main deck. As he left, Captain Grey followed Baruti away from the crowd toward the MIG IV so not to be heard. "What is it?" asked Captain Grey.

"Captain, I have some bad news. I took a sample from Tom's body and did an analysis. The same Chitin we found in the blood appears to be the same found on Tom's body. That means Tom and Drew most surely were attacked by a giant squid or octopi. It is the only reasonable explanation for Tom's injuries. I'm almost one hundred percent sure of this."

Captain Grey stood speechless. He looked back to the crew of the Pemba Koningin standing on the deck. They were in good spirits, laughing and joking with one another. The Captain didn't want to upset the mood of his rescuers.

"Further to that, I tested the blood sample again, and compared it to Tom's. And I can say without a doubt that the blood we found was *not* Tom's. My assumption is that it was Drew's. If it was, he is surely dead too - it was too much blood loss."

The Captain didn't know what to say. His eyes began to well with tears.

Baruti continued, "I also did some measurements of the marks on Tom's body. I measured the size of the rings, found their diameter and created a model of where within the tentacle they were in relationship to its placement on this cephalopod itself. I assumed that, because the ring sizes diminished as they moved up Tom's back towards his neck, that the largest ring near Tom's hip was the one closest to the cephalopod itself. Using this information I figured that this creature would be at least forty or fifty feet in length. At least that is what I thought...but I was wrong. The tentacles are used for grabbing, and the Chitin ridged suckers are mostly prevalent toward the creature's outmost extremities, they are almost non-existent toward the body and mantel of the creature. Captain, with a cephalopod such as a squid, the tentacles are usually three times the size and length of the creature itself. So, if you further extrapolate the data as I did, and to try and determine how large of a creature that your men were dealing with, well...I have a guess. But no such creature has ever been recorded."

Captain Grey's mind began to wander. He had to fix the Reiziger, but with the Doctor's newfound information, he was hesitant to put anyone in the water again. "How big, Doctor?"

Baruti realized what the Captain was thinking. "Captain, you can't put anyone in the water again. It's suicide!"

"Just tell me how big this thing might be." Captain Grey demanded.

"You've already lost two men, Captain. Please, dear God. Don't even consider this!"

Captain Grey grabbed the doctor by the shoulders and leaned in close, giving him a slight shake. "I asked – how big?"

As Captain Grey released Baruti, the doctor began to quiver as he lowered his eyes to the ground. He kept shaking his head. "Captain, this creature could be over one hundred feet long."

22

"What the hell are you talking about? You made a deal with a goddamn maniac?" Stephan yelled.

"No, it's not like that, I told you. He's a man needing safe passage. He isn't a bad man. I really don't believe he is. When he came out of the Savior, we surprised him. He didn't know what to do. And he genuinely felt bad for hurting you," Amy pleaded.

Stephan sat on the edge of Amy's bed still holding the damp cloth against his forehead. The orbital region of his eyes had turned a slight purple-black in color, while his nose looked distorted and swollen. It was easy to tell that his nose was indeed broken. Fortunately, since his nap, his memory was beginning to come back.

"So let me get this straight. He wants us to go with him to St. Helena? Amy, think about it. Why does he need us? He could just go to St. Helena by himself. You said you've already told him where it is..."

"I suppose he could, but I don't think he'd get away without our help anymore."

"Why?" Stephan asked.

"I think Medupé is suspicious. When I went looking for Joost while you were sleeping, Mr. Medupé found me, and he was acting weird."

"You were probably acting weird. You told me you were banging ship property with your fists. So, of course he's going to act weird; he's the ship's security officer. Think about it, Amy, you're on a ship that's not moving. You mentioned to him last night that you want to get to St. Helena no matter what...and then he sees you hanging out by the only way off this ship, and you're banging the crap out of it. Yeah, Amy, I think he is watching you, and he'll be watching the Savior. Shit, I hate to say it, but your new best friend, the jewel thief, is stuck here with the rest of us."

"Don't yell at me." Amy said as she sat on the edge of her bed and pouted.

"Well, what do you want me to do? My head hurts and this is all a little too much to handle right now." Stephan yelled, just as a knock came at the door.

Amy looked at Stephan. Fear raced through her eyes, as she mouthed to her brother, "What should we do?"

"Answer it," Stephan said a little louder than a whisper.

"We can't," she whispered back.

"Why not? You already said that this guy Joost was not a bad guy, so open the door; prove it."

Amy quickly told Stephan about the men that were looking for Joost and how this could be the exact same men who were on the ship right now.

Stephan didn't get the whole story, but he heard enough to cause concern. He began to pace around the small cabin moving his fingers around as if he were counting. He pointed a finger briefly at Amy, shook it with a disappointing nature, and then went back to pacing. He didn't speak.

Amy shot her brother a look that let him know he wasn't being very helpful.

Maybe they'll just go away, she thought.

Then, someone knocked on the door again.

What if it was Medupé? Perhaps, he wanted to question Amy more about why she was hanging around the lifeboat. What if it was the 'bad men' from the rescue ship...what if they've come looking for Joost. What if they were looking for a perfect pink diamond and they'd kill anyone with information about it.

Amy put the thoughts out of her head. She straightened herself up, brushed back her auburn hair by hand and pushed her glasses up on her nose. Reaching out, she put a hand on the doorknob. Stephan noticed what Amy was doing and quickly hid himself in the bathroom.

Amy opened the door. On the other side of the door was none of her fears. Instead, there stood a very tired looking old man with a smile on his face. It was Doctor Duiker.

In his aged hand, he held a brass cane with a black rubber stopper at its base. His stance was somewhat tilted to the left and his body hunched forward revealing severe scoliosis of his spine. His wispy white hair blew gently in the outside air as he stood at the doorway. Amy just stared at him. After a few seconds, he asked in his deep, raspy voice, "May I come in?"

* * *

Captain Grey and Baruti stood with the crowd on the main deck, exchanges pleasantries. After a few minutes, Captain Grey excused himself from the group and went to the engine room bringing along Ruiz and Cody. The Captain told his guests that he needed to assess the current situation of the breach while at the same time, retrieve the welding gear. Dr. Baruti also departed the main deck to retreat to his cabin. He said that he wanted to confer with his colleagues on the status of their voyage. Blomkamp and Deedat had yet to return from the mess deck.

With no one from the Reiziger's around, the Pemba Koningin crew began to discuss their plan of attack.

"Why is Carlito fixing their ship? I thought we were looking for this Joost character. We find him, get the diamond, and get out. What is this bullshit?" Jako asked.

"Easy Jako," Lefu warned. "I've already explained everything to Carlito, and this is part of the new plan. All you and Percy need to worry about is searching this ship. But play it very casual. Don't provoke anyone, and don't raise any suspicion as to what you're doing. If anyone asks what you're looking for...make something up, and don't create suspicion. It is your job to find Joost... that is your only concern. Is that understood?"

Jako nodded.

"Did you bring the gear?"

"Yes," Jako said, opening his backpack revealing a small cache of weapons including a few Glock 9mm's, a Heckler, a Koch MP5 and ample ammunition.

"Take a pistol and hide it. Leave the rest of it here." Lefu said.

The men each grabbed their weapon of choice and quickly hid them on their persons. Jako then zipped the backpack closed and looked to Mr. Asunda, "Don't let anyone touch this bag, you got it?" Jako said.

Mr. Asunda assured Jako that he would guard it with his life.

Just as Jako and Percy left the main deck, Blomkamp and Deedat returned from the mess hall. Moments later, Captain Grey, Ruiz and Cody returned from the engine room. Ruiz had a bag slung over his shoulder and was pushing a cart full of all the necessary tools for the welding job: flux core metal wire, long lines of welding cables and a specialized underwater welding mask.

Ruiz stopped next to Carlito and handed him the bag from his shoulder. Inside the bag were a wetsuit and some pink flippers. "I'm sorry, that's all we have," said Ruiz.

Carlito grabbed the flippers from the bag and held them up in disgust. "You've got to be kidding me!"

"It's not a fashion show, Carlito," Lefu laughed and everybody else joined in.

"Oh come on. This is ridiculous. I don't see any of you suiting up and doing this work," Carlito began to yell. "This is bullshit!"

Captain Grey tried to calm the fiery small Italian, "I'll tell you what Captain Carlito - you get this ship stitched up, and when we get back to Cape Town, I promise to buy you a pair the color of your choice."

23

D r. Duiker entered Amy's cabin with a slow, methodic gate. Amy encouraged him to have a seat in the chair near the end of the bed and the doctor obliged, very happy to sit down. She offered him some water, but he politely declined. Instead, he rested both of his wrinkled hands firmly on top of his cane and smiled at Amy. "You can tell Mr. Woodley to come out now, I won't hurt him."

Amy briefly tried to act naive to the doctor's remark, but the old doctor grabbed his cane and tapped on the wall separating the bathroom from the bedroom cabin. "Come out, Stephan, unless you're doing something in there. I'd like to talk with both of you."

The bathroom door slowly opened and Stephan emerged. Amy shrugged at her brother, referring to how the doctor knew he was in there.

"Hello, Dr. Duiker." Stephan said as he walked into the main room of the cabin.

"Your face, Stephan! My goodness! Are you all right?" the doctor asked.

"I think my nose is broken, but I'll survive."

"I'd say it's broken for sure. Would you like me to take a look?"

Stephan waved off the doctor, "No, I'm fine. Thank you."

"Please, both of you have a seat. It's much too hard for a man of my age to be looking upward while talking. Please, sit on the bed," the doctor said as he patted the edge of the bed.

Amy and Stephan sat down beside each other and watched the doctor.

"Very dark in here." said Dr. Duiker, "May I open the blinds?"

Amy leaned over towards the porthole and pulled the blinds up for the doctor, saving him the trouble.

Daylight was almost completely gone. Just enough natural light streamed into the room, making it seem more spacious, even though it wasn't. Doctor Duiker smiled as he looked out the porthole window for a moment. "I think that's the one thing I'll miss the most..." he began and then stopped.

Reaching into his outer shirt pocket, Dr. Duiker retrieved a soft white linen handkerchief and dabbed the corner of his eyes.

"Are you okay, Doctor?" Amy asked.

"I'm fine, my dear. An old man like me has nothing to feel bad about. I've lived a very full life. I've lived it by the rules of the Good Book, and have never had to fear anything. God is always there for me. I never question His motives."

Stephan and Amy looked at each other concerned for the old doctor - when another knock came at the door.

"Omigod!" Amy said, getting up from the bed to answer the door. Strangely, she didn't hesitate to open the door this time around, but she couldn't explain why to herself.

When she turned the knob and opened the door, on the other side was yet another surprise; it was Doctor Baruti.

Amy smiled politely and invited him inside, opening the door wide enough to expose the company within her cabin. Baruti was happy to see three familiar faces, but politely declined her invitation. Instead he requested that they all meet in the lab in ten minutes. Stephan, Amy, and Dr. Duiker thanked the doctor and said they would be along shortly.

After Baruti left, Amy locked the door and sat down on the bed again.

"Baruti. What a good man." Doctor Duiker said. "We'll go meet up with him in a minute. But I want to talk to the two of you before we do. So, first things first, I guess you're wondering how I knew you were here, Stephan."

Stephan nodded yes.

Using his cane, the old doctor pointed to the air grate positioned high on the wall beside the bed. "It's not like I was eavesdropping," he laughed, "but sound travels through these thin walls quite easily."

Amy put a hand to her mouth. She knew Dr. Duiker was stationed in the cabin beside hers, but was shocked to think that the old doctor would put the effort into listening to a conversation in the room next to his.

"Doctor!" she exclaimed.

"Oh, no my dear, It's not what you're thinking. I assure you, I wasn't trying to listen...the sound just carries through these walls effortlessly. I even had the unfortunate luxury of listening to Mr. Radcliff in his room by himself the night before. His cabin is next to mine on the opposite side. I didn't want to hear, but I couldn't prevent it either."

"So, did you hear everything that Stephan and I were talking about?"

"Not just you and Stephan," Duiker said as he shook his head and smiled.

"What do you mean, Doctor?" Stephan asked.

Doctor Duiker pointed his cane at Amy.

"I also overheard young Amy here talking with a young chap - the man who spoke about a diamond."

Amy couldn't believe it what Dr. Duiker was saying.

"You heard...everything?"

"Yes, but don't worry, Ms. Masterson. It is not my place to report you to Dr. Athans or Dr. Conte. No, I understand your motives. You want to get to St. Helena; I understand that. I also understand that the man with the diamond wants nothing more than to get off this ship. I heard his story, and I too believe him." The doctor dabbed his eyes once again, and then put the handkerchief back into his pocket. "I heard your plan. At first, I was a bit shocked, but something made me realize that if you and your brother didn't help this young man get away, that everybody on board this ship may be in danger. I don't know if you've noticed, but there is another ship here. It's sitting not far from us." The doctor paused, "It's a safe bet that this ship carries the men looking for the man with the diamond, which can mean only one thing."

"What?" Stephan asked, jumping from the bed.

"Please sit down, Mr. Woodley," the doctor waved him back down. "I have something to show both of you."

Doctor Duiker patted the air with his hand telling the two scientists to relax. As they did, Duiker reached into his coat pocket and fumbled inside for a moment, finally he pulled out his hand as a closed fist. He extended his closed fist toward Amy and Stephan. Realizing he wanted to show them something, the pair leaned in close. As they leaned in to see what the doctor had hidden, Dr. Duiker slowly opened his hand and revealed nothing more than his empty palm.

"I don't get it," Stephan said.

"You are not meant to see it," Dr. Duiker replied.

Amy sat up straight and scratched her head. "Please, Doctor... no riddles, what are we supposed to be looking at?"

"You already know what you are looking at. What I carry in my hand is merely faith."

"You hand is empty, Doctor." Stephan said, visibly upset at the doctor.

"Please, let me explain," said Dr. Duiker. "You cannot see faith, but it exists."

Amy and Stephan didn't nod or respond in any way. They just sat with their eyes focused on the doctor.

"Just because you cannot see it, does not mean it is not there. You cannot see faith. You didn't see the diamond this man spoke of Ms. Masterson, yet you believed him. You believed his story.

That *itself* is faith in character. He told you that he was being hunted, he was the victim, and together you would help each other to reach a goal. That is faith in your fellow man. You and your brother believe that you can take the lifeboat, set sail and achieve your scientific pursuits. Your goals will be achieved. That is faith in self." The doctor laughed. "I am amazed at the amount of faith that you have, but obviously neither of you are aware of it."

The doctor paused and repositioned himself in the chair. "Please believe me; I'm of the mind that everything in life happens for a reason. We may never know that reason, but nonetheless, there is a reason. We cannot see it, we cannot feel it, we cannot touch it, but there is a reason. Good or bad, there is a reason. When something happens, it is the will of God. I believe in that and so should you. You should embrace your faith."

"What are you trying to say, Doctor? That we should take the boat and go to St. Helena?" Amy asked.

Amy and the doctor's eyes met.

"I mentioned earlier that if I am not to see St. Helena on this voyage, then that is by design. I truly believe that when I boarded this ship that was my purpose, my goal, but I realize now that was not my purpose. Perhaps it is your purpose, by design, it is meant for you. Everything is telling you it is your purpose, your goal. If you have faith in reaching your goal, as well as faith in yourself, in others, and in your fellow man. Then, maybe for you, it *is* the right choice."

"What about the others on the ship? Stephan and I thought of telling the others to come along. Should we?" Amy asked.

"I cannot tell you what is the right thing to do my dear, nor am I going to tell you what is wrong. If you feel it is necessary to tell the others, then you will. If you feel that if you tell the others, it would jeopardize your chances, then you will not tell them. That choice is yours. It is not my choice, and therefore, I will not interfere in the design of what He has planned for the rest of us."

"What do you mean 'planned'? What do you think is happening on this ship?" Stephan interjected. "Why so quick to assume that this other ship is here for this guy with the diamond. Isn't it possible that they are just a passing ship that wants to help?"

The doctor woefully shook his head. "I would like to believe they were, Stephan. But Mr. Kees saw them when he found me. He knows who they are, they *are* indeed the men."

"Him? Mr. Kees? Who are you talking about?" Amy asked.

The old doctor realized he slipped up and gave a gentle smile as though he were Santa being caught eating cookies on Christmas Eve. "Mr. Kees? Oh, you've know him... He is the young man you know as, Joost."

Amy's eyes lit up.

"We met by chance, my dear. You see, he came looking for your cabin and instead found mine. Slightly my fault I suppose. He was returning to your cabin when he saw the approaching ship. Realizing it was the men who were looking for him, he tried to navigate back to your room just as I was stepping out from mine. Well, needless to say, I startled him. So he grabbed me, took me into my cabin, and held me hostage...albeit very briefly and not at all forcefully. I told him that I already knew his story by my unintentional eavesdropping. He assured me that he meant no harm. But he also warned that the approaching ship was indeed the 'very bad men' he spoke of."

Stephan stood up. "Did you ask him where he got the diamond? Maybe this guy is just a criminal. We can't exactly help a criminal. We should tell the Captain. Maybe these guys looking for him aren't bad guys. Maybe they're undercover police or..."

"Where is he?" Amy asked, interrupting Stephan's questions.

Stephan shot Amy a look and continued at the doctor. "Or if these guys are bad, shouldn't we warn everyone on board. Shouldn't we get everyone to safety?"

Stephan was very excited.

"Stephan, Stop!" Amy yelled.

"Please...please...both of you. If you believe that is what you should do, then you will." Dr. Duiker said calmly. "That is why I am telling you about faith. Personally, I believe this young man and his story of how he came into possession of the diamond.

These men are going to harm him if they find him so he needs to get away. If these men don't find him, they may assume that they've made a mistake and leave the Reiziger and the rest of us alone. I don't know. Believe what you wish."

"Stephan," Amy began, "The doctor is right. Joost needs our help. And it's the only way we can..."

"Well, where is he?" Stephan said, cutting her off this time. "I want to meet the guy that bashed my face in when I wasn't looking."

"Calm down, Stephan, I already told you. We startled him and..." Amy pleaded.

"Okay, okay...let me meet him first and then I'll decide if I want to help him. So where is he, Doc?" Stephan asked.

"He is safe for now. As a matter of fact, he is probably listening to our every word."

Doctor Duiker, Amy and Stephan looked up in unison at the grate covering the ventilation duct high on the wall. No one spoke – it was understood. Joost was in Dr. Duiker's cabin next door.

The doctor turned his attention back to the porthole once again. The sky had faded to a grey black.

"It is no longer my purpose to reach St. Helena. I believe my purpose now was to guide you. And I am satisfied that I have."

Turning back to Stephan and Amy, Dr. Duiker reached his hand out to them. The same hand he held out to them moments earlier. "Take my hand," he said.

Amy and Stephan reached out together and touched the old man's wrinkled, soft hand.

"You have my faith," he said. "Now use yours."

24

The ROK submersible sat ready on the main deck of the ship next to the MIG IV and a strange metal cage that had been brought out from storage.

The ROK and MIG IV were identical twins. They had the same manufacturer, with the same purpose of use - marine exploration and research. Their biggest drawback seemed to be their hideous design. The two submersible units looked like two large metal marbles with feeble metal arms protruding from their sides, similar to a weeble-wobble toy with claws. To add to their unsightly appearance, a large steel ring sat atop their head like an upright halo. This was where each vessel would attach a cable harnessed in an umbilical manner to the Reiziger for insertion and retrieval. Just below their rounded bellies sat two battery operated props, capable of multidirectional pivoting, allowing the submersibles to manoeuvre in various directions.

"Ugly, yet very functional," Captain Grey said to the crowd as he knocked on the ROK's steel exterior.

Peering through the large front window of ROK was the face of Nelson Blomkamp. He was suited up and prepared for his second attempt at clearing off the tentacles from the props. He looked out to Deedat, Captain Grey, and the remaining members of the Pemba Koningin. He gave everyone the thumbs up.

Captain Grey ran the controls to the crane arm, lifting the ROK from a long cable attached to its top. Grey delicately manoeuvred the ROK above the side rails of the ship and carefully lowered the vessel to the Atlantic below.

Once the ROK touched down on the surface of the water, Blomkamp turned on the powerful halogens mounted just above the ROK's base platform. Instantly, the sea glowed with a clear greenish blue for yards in the distance.

With the ROK positioned below, Captain Grey used the other crane arm to lift up the unusual looking cage box sitting next to the MIG IV. Inside the metal cage was Captain Enzo Carlito, fully suited in a wetsuit, SCUBA tank with a specialized underwater welding helmet, and of course - his pink flippers.

On the floor of the cage was a mobile wire feed arc welder, spare steel plating and all the required cables and tools for the job he was about to undertake.

Carlito held tight to the bars of the cage as he was lifted over the side of the Reiziger towards the waiting ROK submersible below. Once the cage entered the water next to the ROK, the Captain stopped the crane controls to allow the two units to connect.

The ROK used its powerful, yet strange looking appendages to grab hold of one of the bars of the cage containing Carlito. Once a secure hold on the unit was made, the cage was held fast by the ROK and could be steered in any direction the ROK was going to travel.

Blomkamp came across the walkie-talkie, "We're good to go!"

"Ten-four," replied the Captain.

Keeping the ROK and the cage tethered to the ship for extra security, the Captain fed out the two cable lines at a slow and steady pace. Within moments, the two units drifted below the surface of the ocean, where they disappeared into darkness below the Reiziger.

"How long do you think this will take, Captain?" Lefu asked.

"I'm not sure; it really depends on how good of a welder Carlito is. ROK has two and a half hours of air and Carlito has four half-hour bottles, so hopefully they can get it done in that time. In the meantime, why don't you and your men grab yourselves a coffee or tea? I'm going to head up to the command center and finish some work. Mr. Deedat will maintain the status of our men from here."

"Thank you, but I'll stay here. So will these two," Lefu said, making reference to Mr. Hogg and Mr. Asunda. "Percy and Jako have already gone to get us all something to drink. They'll be back soon."

"Very well, then. Come on Cody," Captain Grey said as he patted his leg. Cody sprung from the floor and joined her master at his side. "I'll see you gentlemen soon."

Handing the walkie-talkie to Deedat, Captain Grey and his dog left for the command center.

"This is the ROK. Come in. Over!" A voice came across the walkie-talkie.

"Hey, Nelson, what's going on?" Deedat replied.

"Oh, hey, Winston. Stop feeds on the cables. We're in position."

Deedat stopped the crane from feeding more cable line over to the ROK and the steel cage.

"There you go, buddy!" Deedat called back over the walkie-talkie.

"Perfect, okay, Captain Carlito has emerged from the cage. He's hooked up the two-twenty volt and a personal tether to the ROK, attached his ground to a point off the keel, and is ready to start welding. I've got a good shot of light on the problem area. It doesn't look too bad. The openings are maybe four inches across, but there are several of them. They're kind of weird looking. Almost more like rust...but we should be able to plate it up if needed."

"Okay, good. You keep me posted on your progress. Same as we did before, ten minute check-ins."

"Yes Dad," Blomkamp laughed back over the radio.

Deedat sat down on a step beside the MIG IV holding the walkie-talkie. Pulling out a pack of cigarettes from his pocket, he flipped open the packet and offered it to Lefu and his men. "Want one?"

"No thank you," Lefu said as he reached into his shirt pocket and pulled out a fresh cigar. "I only smoke the best."

The men laughed and carried on quite amicably for a few minutes. They talked about life on the sea; they spoke of soccer, and their homeland of Africa.

All was quiet and peaceful on deck of the Reiziger. The stars emerged across the darkened night sky and cast a beautiful light across the waves.

As the men sat enjoying the night, Percy and Jako reappeared. Lefu looked to his minions for an answer, but the two shook their heads in a negative.

Lefu stood up with anger in his eyes. He leaned towards the guardrail of the Reiziger and flicked his unfinished cigar overboard. He watched it fall to the black water below, and then disappear.

Deedat's walkie-talkie sounded just as the ship lurched forcefully.

"Carlito...I mean...Deedat...holy shit...Deedat...oh my god..." Blomkamp's voice cried out over the handheld radio.

"What is it? Nelson. Come in," Deedat pleaded into the little black handheld radio.

"Deedat?" The voice broke up over the radio.

"Nelson? Come in. Nelson? What is happening down there? Nelson, come in, over."

"Oh my! – What? - Deedat!" Nelson Blomkamp screamed into the walkie-talkie, causing it to crackle with distortion. "Pull us up... pull me up. Now! For the love of God, pull us up...right now!"

Deedat jumped to his feet and grabbed the crane controls. Lefu and his crew were frozen by the voice that just cried out through the walkie-talkie. The five men from the Pemba Koningin leaned over the edge of the Reiziger watching the cable feeds that disappeared into the blackness below. The cables simultaneously pulled tight as Deedat began to reel the ROK and the steel cage back up.

Slowly, the edges below the Reiziger began to brighten with a green hue as the lights of the ROK were coming closer to the surface of the water.

"There he is!" Lefu called out.

Deedat continued to recoil the cables tethered to the ROK and the cage. The tension created from the pull seemed to drag the Reiziger towards its side. Suddenly, the tension gave way on both cable lines and recoiled back into the crane at a faster pace. Deedat reeled in the cables as fast as the crane arm would allow, but soon, it was obvious to him what had happened. Neither cable was attached to the cage or the ROK any longer. When the final portion of cables reached the top of the crane arm, they were nothing more than frayed ends.

"Holy shit, can you see them?" Deedat yelled to the Pemba Koningin crew as he too ran over to the edge of the ship. As Deedat looked over, he saw what everyone else was looking at.

The ROK was sitting just below the surface of the water, unable to bring herself topside any further without the assistance of a tether.

"Deedat...what is going on?" Blomkamp cried over the radio. "Bring me up!"

"Nelson, listen to me. The cable has snapped. We're going to have to reattach it to you."

"No, I've got to get out of here, right now. Carlito's dead. He's gone. The Goddamn thing just ate him right in front of me. Get me out of here now!" Blomkamp pleaded with his friend.

"Ate him? What is he talking about?" Mr. Asunda asked.

"Shut up," Deedat said, waving him off. "Nelson, listen to me. You're safer inside the ROK. Whatever is happening down there, the only thing we can do is reconnect you and pull you and the ROK up together...safely."

"Hurry! You have to get me out of here!"

"Lefu, can you get one of your men to reconnect the ROK? I'll attach a new hook, lower the cable, and give lots of slack...all they have to do is hook it to the top ring," Deedat asked.

Lefu quickly appointed Mr. Asunda as the unwilling man who would perform the task. Reluctant as he was with the proposition, he knew that he didn't have a say in the matter; Lefu didn't tolerate insubordination.

Deedat instructed Mr. Hogg to summon Captain Grey from the command center while Mr. Asunda prepared to climb down the side of the ship. Mr. Hogg looked to Lefu for direction, but Lefu didn't take notice of him, although, Mr. Asunda did manage to catch Hogg's eye, and waved his hand to Hogg with a candid motion. Nobody caught the signal, but Mr. Hogg knew exactly what it meant, as he set off for the command center as requested.

Mr. Asunda hesitantly climbed over the side rail of the Reiziger and proceeded down the welded ladder rungs. Once he was close enough to the ROK, Deedat lowered a fresh length of cable newly fashioned with a snap hook on its end.

With one hand and one foot securely hooked onto the ladder rungs, Mr. Asunda grabbed the dangling cable with his free hand and tried his best to reach the ROK. The cable was very heavy, but he managed to keep a firm hold onto it. Unfortunately, the ROK was still too far underwater, and Mr. Asunda couldn't hook onto the vessel without jumping into the ocean; something he wanted to avoid after hearing Blomkamp's cries over the radio.

"Closer, the submersible needs to be closer," Mr. Asunda yelled up to the men on deck.

"Tell him closer! Asunda can't hook on! Your man needs to be closer," Lefu yelled at Deedat. The deckhand nodded back.

"Nelson, you need to position the ROK closer to the ship. Look up through your window. Mr. Asunda is there to harness you. You've just got to get a bit closer to him."

"Okay," a very shaky voice came back over the walkie-talkie.

The ROK moved slowly and methodically toward the side of the Reiziger. Once it was positioned close enough, it began to gently knock against the side of the ship. The ROK then exposed through the surface of the water as much as it possibly could by using a downward thrust of its props. It was just enough. Mr. Asunda reached over, clamped the new cable hook onto the ring on the top of the ROK and cheered his accomplishments.

Water splashed Asunda in the face, but he was relieved to have done the job that he didn't take much notice of the water.

Mr. Asunda looked up the side of the ship and yelled up to the men, "Okay, I've got him. Pull him up."

"Pull him up, he's hooked," Lefu relayed to Deedat.

Deedat again engaged the crane as it slowly began to recoil the cable feed. The tension was instant, and he smiled.

Mr. Asunda watched as the giant steel marble slowly resurfaced from the cold Atlantic waters. As the ROK moved towards him at a safe distance, he saw the ROK's arm still holding onto what was left of the metal cage. It looked as if the steel itself was melted; only twisted portions of its bars remained intact. Inside, all of the welding materials and Captain Enzo Carlito were gone.

Blomkamp came into focus in front of Mr. Asunda as the ROK was going past him. Through the large front window, Blomkamp smiled at the man that had just saved his life, and gave him the thumbs up. Mr. Asunda smiled back, but then his eyes opened wide, filled with the darkest of fear.

Blomkamp briefly saw the pink flash across ROK's large window before he lost sight of the outside world. Loud crashes and bangs rattled throughout the interior of the ROK. The air seemed to be pressing in from rivet points and breaking glass as small traces of water began to spray in. Blomkamp had been shaken violently inside the ROK and banged his head on the interior wall of the vessel.

"Pull him up, pull him up!" Mr. Asunda screamed as he scrambled up the ladder rungs, his eyes fixated on the horror unfolding before him.

It was no use. Within seconds, the ROK was in the clutches of what appeared a large tentacle reaching from the blackness below the Reiziger.

Deedat set the recoil speed of the crane arm gear to full throttle. A tug of war ensued between the crane and the ROK, which was being held fast. The back and forth battle caused the Reiziger to lilt heavily to the starboard side.

"What the hell is going on?" Deedat yelled at the men watching from the rail.

Finally, the cable snapped. The built up pressure from the tug of war that just took place sent the cable flying upward and over the side rail of the ship. Everybody who was watching the events unfold saw the cable coming at them and ran for safety, all except Percy.

When the cable came down, it was unforgiving. It struck Percy on the side of the head and shoulder with a brutal whipping force. The huge man fell to the ground in a limp, bloody heap. The men on deck watched as Percy's body went into a rapid spasm and then tense up. The Reiziger began to sway back and forth.

"Percy!" Lefu screamed.

Jako and Lefu ran to their friend and held onto him as his body began a decerebrise response. Deedat stood by the crane, stunned as he watched Percy twitching and bleeding.

Over the side of the Reiziger, Mr. Asunda continued to watch the lights of the ROK as they disappeared into the abyss - taking Blomkamp along.

Deedat's walkie-talkie sounded. The connection was weak and crackled, "Deedat...help me...help me...Deedat? Oh my GOD – DEEDAT!" Blomkamp's voice cried out, and then silence.

Deedat fumbled with the walkie-talkie as his friend's voice beckoned for help. In his state of panic, he dropped the walkie-talkie to the deck and it broke to pieces. He knelt down and scrambled to pick up the pieces, but it was ruined.

Deedat quickly ran to the edge of the ship and yelled over the side, "Nelson!"

As he reached the top of the ladder rail, Mr. Asunda met Deedat face to face. "He's gone."

25

Stuart Radcliff, Dr. Athans, and Conte all sat quietly in the lab where they had been asked to meet by Dr. Baruti. Stuart tapped rhythmically with a pencil on the side of a Petri dish, while Dr. Athans was slowly nodding off in his chair. He was startled awake when the ship heaved, as if a large wave passed below.

"Whoa, that was a weird feeling," Athans said.

Stuart snapped his pencil in two; clearly frustrated to be waiting again. "What are we waiting for, Doctor Baruti? Can't we just get on with it? I'm really tired. This has been a horrible day."

Dr. Baruti gave Stuart a look as if to say 'you have no idea', but instead waved off the young scientist, telling him to relax. Checking his watch, Baruti realized it had been twenty minutes since he went by Amy's cabin. It was rude and out of character for her to make her colleagues wait this long. Just then, the door to the lab opened and in walked Stephan, Dr. Duiker and Amy.

"Finally," Stuart muttered.

"Your face, Stephan. Are you okay?" Dr. Athans asked.

"I'm fine, Doctor. I tripped. I'll be alright though. It's just a broken nose. Please go ahead, Dr. Baruti."

Stephan, Amy and Dr. Duiker proceeded to sit as all eyes turned to Dr. Baruti.

The doctor took a deep breath and began. "The mission is off. I spoke with the Captain in great detail about the matter, and considering the troubles beleaguering the ship at present, he feels it is in our best interest to head back to Cape Town at once."

The scientists groaned sounds of disappointment.

"As we speak, the Captain has procured help of able seamen from a nearby rescue ship and they're working to fix the problems aboard, but once the problem is remedied, we'll be heading home. I know we've all been waiting a long time for this mission, but it's out of my hands. There's nothing further we can do."

Amy felt her insides begin to turn. She knew there was something they <u>could</u> do. She could tell her friends about the lifeboat and how everybody could continue the mission aboard it. She knew she *could* tell them, it was just a case of whether or not she should. She looked to Stephan and Dr. Duiker to see if they would give her a sign as to if she should say something, but neither did. Amy felt completely alone.

Doctor Conte spoke up, "What about this other ship you mentioned Doctor? Perhaps we could get aboard that vessel, radio our benefactor to pay them for transport to complete our mission..."

Baruti hesitated, pondering the suggestion.

"I hadn't thought of that," he said. "You know that might not be a bad idea. I've met their crew and they seem like decent men. You're right, if we could convince them to assist us, they would be compensated quite handsomely."

"Yeah, screw the Reiziger. This ship has been nothing but a nightmare since the moment we left Cape Town. We've had alarms, leaks, bad food, and a moody captain. I'm sick of it. I say we go and ask the rescue crew right away." Stuart said.

The room began to buzz with chatter amongst some of the members, when Dr. Duiker stood up and spoke; his deep raspy voice stopped the commotion. "No!" he said, with a warning in his tone, but also a hidden anger.

All eyes turned to Dr. Duiker.

"What do you mean 'No'?" Stuart retorted towards the old doctor, "This mission is costing hundreds of thousands of rand already. Even *if* we get the money back, we'll never get another chance to work St. Helena when she's due to erupt! Who knows when the next volcano is set to erupt? Especially one in a suitable environment that we require to do our work; it could be years... or even decades! We need to act now!"

"No!" Dr. Duiker barked again.

Only Amy and Stephan knew Doctor Duiker's reasoning for denying Stuart and the other scientists the opportunity to ask the other crew for assistance. The doctor didn't reveal his reasoning to the others. He knew that he might come off as a crazy old man if he explained that the rescue crew could be a group of 'bad men' chasing down a stowaway. Even if Amy and Stephan backed him up, and the others accepted his claim, it could create fear, and that fear could turn into chaos.

Dr. Duiker seemed torn in front of his colleagues. Stephan and Amy were equally torn, but they weren't the ones putting a stop to Stuart's persistent demands. Dr. Duiker took this challenge on himself. His face seemed expressionless while his hands trembled at his sides. Amy could see that the good doctor's faith was being tested.

"I want you all to know that we are scientists first and foremost. We look for answers to science, not to God's will," Duiker began before Stuart cut him off.

"Oh, cut the crap about faith and what's right and wrong, Doctor. I came here to do some very important work. And because our benefactor chose the wrong ship for us to travel on, we're going to suffer for it. Well – I for one won't suffer for it. I'm going to achieve my goals. I've been researching for this expedition for three years solid, and I'm not going to just piss it away! To hell with God's will – did you hear me? Yeah, I said it! And I don't care what you think. So, I'm going to ask the other crew if they can help. Does anyone have a problem with that besides this crazy old man?"

"I do," said Dr. Baruti as he sat at a table rubbing his forehead. He was too tired to fight anymore. He'd seen too much for one day. He just wanted to go home and leave this bad voyage behind him. "I think we should carefully consider what Dr. Duiker is saying. Perhaps we should just let the mission go. It is probably for the best. Too many things have set us back, and even now, there would be no guarantee that our goals could be met, even with assistance from another ship. No, I say we chalk this trip up to bad luck, and proceed at a later date."

Baruti didn't tell his colleagues about the blood, Tom and Drew, the Chitin or even the fact that somebody on board was a murderer. There was no possible way to explain those things.

Stuart quickly disregarded Baruti. "Okay, fine, so Dr. Baruti is out, and Dr. Duiker is out. Who thinks we should ask the other crew...a show of hands?"

"Stop it!" said Dr. Athans, as he slammed his hand down hard on the table. "That is enough, Mr. Radcliff. This is not a democracy...so sit down! This is my mission. I hand-picked each of you for this mission, and I will not tolerate infighting or decision making on when or how we proceed. That is entirely up to me."

Stuart shamefully looked over at the doctor. He knew the doctor was right. Amy knew the doctor was right. Everyone in the room knew the doctor was right. Regardless of how much time and effort each scientist had invested into the operation, it was ultimately Dr. Athans' mission, and therefore his call on what they would do.

Amy bit her lip as she began to second-guess her plan with Stephan and Joost to take the lifeboat. If they took the boat, and did their research, what purpose would it serve other than a boost to her own self-serving ego? As Doctor Athans had just clearly stated, this wasn't her mission; it was only her expertise that was required. She couldn't force the mission to happen, and maybe she shouldn't try.

"So what do you propose?" Stephan spoke up.

"I see we have only one choice here, my friends. We did not make that choice, but we must accept it. And I agree with Dr. Duiker and Dr. Baruti. It is probably best if we..."

Dr. Athans was cut off mid-sentence when the door to the lab burst open.

"They're in here! Quick! Bring him in." Deedat said as he held the door ajar with his heel.

Struggling to get past Deedat, Jako and Lefu entered the lab carrying the bloodied and twitching body of their associate Percy.

"Oh my God, what happened?" cried Dr. Baruti.

"Quick! Get him up on this table," Dr. Athans said, clearing off the largest table near the back of the room.

Dr. Duiker snapped his fingers at Amy.

"Amy, go to the medical supply room and get some clean towels, gauze, a blanket, oxygen...bring everything you can!" he said. "Stephan you help her. Go, quickly!"

"I'll go find the Captain," said Deedat.

"Here, take a lab coat. Stop the bleeding," Dr. Conte said, grabbing a nearby smock and handing it to Dr. Baruti.

The lab itself was not designed as a trauma center, but under the immediate circumstances, it would have to do; it was clean, bright and quiet.

Amy and Stephan exited the lab together as Lefu and Jako placed their friend on the cleared table at the back of the room. Then they both took a step back and stood staring at their friend suffering.

Dr. Baruti grabbed the lab coat from Dr. Conte and elbowed his way past Jako, who was frozen at the sight of his friend.

"Please, let me though," asked Baruti.

Percy's head was tilted backwards and twitching uncontrollably. His hands twisted inwards as if they were broken at the wrists and his feet pointed straight. His breathing was shallow, but present, while his eyes were swollen shut. A large gash gaped open on the left side of his head revealing his skull. His left ear was missing, sloughed off into a pile of flesh beside what remained of his left shoulder. The shoulder itself had been pulverized into his left ribcage.

Dr. Baruti placed his hands across his mouth and almost began to cry, but held back. He pressed the clean white lab coat against Percy's head as everyone watched in horror as it almost instantly turned a dark crimson.

Baruti had seen injuries similar to Percy's during his time in residency at the University. For a moment, Dr. Baruti froze and didn't know what to do other than to hold the lab coat firmly in place. Fortunately, his training took over, as he began to go through the motions of examining the patient. "Dr. Athans," he directed, keep pressure here. Doctor Athans took over holding the coat while Baruti continued a primary exam of the patient.

As he did so, Baruti couldn't stop thinking of a young man he tended to at Baragwaneth Hospital during the Soweto Uprising of 1976. Back then, a young black student was intentionally dropped from a school building by the African military for simply being in the wrong place at the wrong time. The young man wasn't part of any protests of the Uprising, but the military didn't care. The local government captured him and made an example of him to the onlookers below. When he hit the ground, his face smacked the corner of an open underground well. The steel grate of the well ripped his face apart and shattered his shoulder. Even with Dr. Baruti's specialized care, the young man quickly died of his injuries. That young man happened to be Dr. Baruti's son, Lee.

"Do something, for crying out loud," Lefu demanded.

"Where the hell are the medical supplies?" Baruti yelled back, checking over his shoulder and noticing that everyone was frozen watching him.

Baruti continued to check over Percy. He desperately wanted to help, but he knew it was useless. Percy was in decerebrise response. Within moments, Percy would likely go into full cardiac arrest and die. If by miracle that didn't happen the doctor knew that Percy's posturing was a definitive sign of severe brain damage.

When Dr. Baruti attended to his son in 1976, Lee had presented the exact same signs. Even then, as he worked feverishly to save his son, he knew it was futile.

Baruti gently pressed two fingers to Percy's throat trying to get a read on his carotid pulse. Just as he did, the large black man's body arched up with a great heave, and then fell back to the table...dead.

The room was silent. Dr. Athans knew what had just happened and stopped applying pressure to Percy's wounds. Dr. Baruti kept his fingers pressed to Percy's throat, but there was no pulse. A moment passed, and then finally, he drew his hand away, removed his glasses and began to cry. "I'm sorry, Lee," he whispered to himself.

26

Deedat almost bowled over Officer Medupé as he came around the corner toward the command center. Medupé was startled and shoved the smaller Deedat to the ground in a defensive response to the man running at him.

"What the hell?" Deedat exclaimed as he slammed his back against the nearby wall.

"I'm sorry, Deedat. I didn't see you coming. You scared me. I apologize," Medupé offered a hand to help Deedat up from the ground.

Deedat grabbed Medupé's hand and pulled himself up from the ground. Medupé's hand felt sweaty and cold. Once he was up, Deedat withdrew his hand and rubbed the sore spot on his back where he had just landed.

"What are you doing hiding in the shadows? Man, I didn't see you." Deedat asked.

"I was just coming from...I was coming to see how you and our new guest were making out with the repairs to the ship. I wasn't hiding, I can assure you. So, how did you gentlemen make out? Is the ship ready to depart once again?"

"My God, Medupé. It's horrible. We've lost the ROK and Blomkamp. I don't know what happened. I didn't see it! Something pulled him from the tether, and the next thing I knew, he was gone. And we don't know what's happened to the captain from the other ship – the cage he was in was ripped open...and then Percy, one of the crew from the other ship was hit by a cable and he's in really bad shape. They're tending to him right now in the lab. There's blood everywhere! I have to tell Captain Grey what's happened...and...and...and..."

"Slow down, Mr. Deedat," Medupé ordered. "Now tell me again – what happened to Mr. Blomkamp?"

"I don't know," Deedat began to cry, "one minute he's screaming for help saying that Carlito is dead, and the next I've got him safe, and then," Deedat raised his shoulders and shook his head.

"And then?"

"I don't know, I didn't see it! That engineer from the other ship, Mr. Asunda, he saw something, and the next thing I know Nelson is yelling for help over the radio, but in the next breath, he's gone. The ROK is gone. They're all gone. We have to tell the Captain."

"Okay, here's what you must do. Get the Captain and bring him to the lab with the others. I'll head there right now and see how they're making out with the injured man. Go, right away. I'll meet you there."

Deedat paid respect to Medupé with a quick salute and then ran off once again in search for the Captain.

* * *

Amy and Stephan stood outside a door with a large red cross painted upon it and below the cross in white lettering it read: 'First Aid.'

Stephan opened the door and flicked on the light.

It was a standard first aid room. Wall cabinets were filled with bandages, gauze, creams, and wipes. On one wall of the small room hung a picture of human anatomy, the opposite wall had a picture calendar of naked ladies dressed as nurses.

"Nice!" Stephan said pointing to the calendar.

"Very cute," Amy said, obviously not amused. "What did they say we were looking for?"

"Blankets, and the oxygen tank, and...I don't know. What are we doing here anyways? You saw that guy they brought into the lab, he was messed up. I don't think he's going to make it. And did you notice, as they carried him into the lab, that big bald one? Did you see inside his jacket as he walked past?"

"No, what? What did you see, Stephan?"

"He had a gun, Amy. It was the butt of a gun, I'm sure. It was tucked inside his jacket. I'm sure that's what I saw. The doctor and your friend Joost were right. These guys are the 'bad guys', and I think if we don't get out of here right away, we're in big trouble."

Amy took some time to register what her brother was saying, but she eventually clued into what it was. If they returned to the lab with the materials they were asked to get, they could find themselves trapped in a room with a couple of men armed and ready to hurt people. Maybe Dr. Duiker was right. Maybe sending Stephan and Amy to retrieve the items from first aid room was his attempt at helping them get away.

"Everything happens for a reason!" she exclaimed.

"What? What are you saying?" Stephan asked.

"I'm saying this wasn't a mistake. Us being here right now and it being Dr. Duiker who sent us here for the first aid materials... he meant to do that. He got us away from the danger. It's as he said – everything happens for a reason. I get it. And this has nothing to do with our research on St. Helena. This is about us surviving. Quick Stephan, leave everything. Let's go. We must find Joost and get the hell off this ship."

Stephan dropped the blanket he had just picked up and tossed a few rolls of gauze he'd stuffed into his pockets into the sink.

"But what about the others? They're trapped in that lab with some bad people. We can't just leave them."

"That's not up to us, Stephan. There comes a point where you can't save everyone. Sometimes all you can save is yourself. And if we go back to the lab, it could be the end for all of us. If we try to get away now, we've got a chance. We won't get this chance again. But if we're going to leave, we have to do it now."

"Okay, but how are we going to find Joost? He's the one with the keys to the Savior."

"I have a feeling I know exactly where he is, come on!"

The pair didn't even bother to turn off the lights to the first aid room; they just hurried out, looked around to make sure no one saw them, and headed straight for Dr. Duiker's cabin.

* * *

Cody was asleep on her blanket bed in the corner of the command center when Deedat ran in. His entrance startled the malamute and she began to bark.

"Easy girl," Captain Grey said without even checking who had just barged into the center. The Captain was lost in deep thought. He was sitting at the main console, staring through the forward windows of the ship into the black nothingness beyond. His face was expressionless, his eyes tired and weary.

Deedat's composure went from flustered to that of concern. He'd never seen the captain in such a state. The man looked catatonic, broken and somewhat like a zombie.

"Captain?" Deedat called softly. He called again three more times before he finally got a response.

"Yes, Mr. Deedat. How can I help you?" the Captain replied in a monotone voice.

"Sir, I have some bad news. You must come at once, sir. Officer Medupé and the others are at the lab. One of the men from the rescue crew has been badly hurt."

"Injured? I'm sure one of the doctors can help him. How did the repairs go, Mr. Deedat?" Captain Grey asked, still staring out the glass windows.

"Sir, I think we've failed. It is a nightmare. Captain Carlito and Blomkamp are gone. The ROK is gone. Everything is gone," Deedat began to cry again.

As Deedat slowly crumbled to his knees while crying, Ruiz entered the command center. Cody lifted her head, recognized the engineer, and lay back down. Ruiz saw Deedat on the ground beside the Captain. Again, Captain Grey didn't acknowledge someone entering the command center. Instead, he continued to stare into the darkness of the night, as a single tear ran down his face.

"Captain," called Ruiz.

Both Deedat and the Captain broke from their trance at the sound of Ruiz's voice. They turned to him almost in unison. Their faces searching his for a sign of hope and good news, he brought them none.

"Captain, the breach is expanding. Bulkheads five and six are beginning to take on water. I've closed their chambers, but now the thwart side is in breach. Captain, we're flooding fast and I can't contain it." Ruiz said.

Captain Grey stared blankly at Ruiz for a moment. The moment seemed to last an eternity. Finally, he smiled and began to laugh.

Deedat couldn't believe what he was hearing. The Captain was laughing? Really? He looked back at Ruiz and held out his hand to be helped up. Ruiz obliged.

"Captain, we're sinking. Did you hear me? We're sinking!"

"I think he's cracking," Deedat said quietly to Ruiz.

"And I think you're bleeding, buddy." Ruiz said to Deedat as he held out his hand - the hand he just helped Deedat up with. Ruiz's hand was smeared with fresh blood.

"I'm not bleeding, at least I don't think I am," Deedat said, checking his hand. It too was covered in a brownish-red blood.

"Holy shit!" Deedat exclaimed.

He felt around to his back with his other hand. Turning back towards Ruiz, he asked the engineer to see if he was bleeding from his back, in the location where he was flung against the wall by Medupé moments earlier.

"Nothing, man. I can't see anything. Here, lift up your shirt."

Deedat pulled his shirt completely off to reveal his entire upper body. With his hands extended above his head, he slowly turned around in a circle for Ruiz to examine his torso. There was a small red mark on his back from where he'd hit the wall, but he wasn't cut. Nor did he have any cuts anywhere else on his body.

Captain Grey watched the two men with a curiosity that wasn't there a moment ago.

"Let's see your hand again," Ruiz said.

Deedat held out his hand. It was blood for sure. The smear was definite, but it didn't appear to be his blood. It wasn't Ruiz's blood either, nor was it the Captain's or Cody's blood.

"Well, where the hell did it come from then?" Ruiz asked.

Deedat mentally retraced his steps. He explained to Ruiz and the Captain about the events that took place on the main deck, in particular about Percy being hit by the cable, but how he never touched Percy. He was certain of that. It didn't make sense how his hand was bloodied.

Deedat mentioned how Medupé knocked him down on the way to the command center, and that the red mark on his back was courtesy of their unfortunate interaction.

"Officer Medupé?" the Captain asked.

"Yes, sir. I was coming around the corner when I ran into him, and he knocked me pretty good. That's how I hit the wall. He was very sorry though. He gave me a hand up," Deedat said, and then stopped.

"He gave you a hand up?" Ruiz asked.

"Yes, I remember his hand feeling sweaty, but I didn't think anything of it. He looked fine."

"Did he look hurt? Did you see him bleeding?" asked Ruiz, looking puzzled.

"No, he seemed fine, like I said. I didn't notice anything wrong with him," Deedat said.

"Where exactly did you bump into, Mr. Medupé? I want you to take us there right now." Captain Grey ordered, regaining some of his lost composure.

Deedat brought Ruiz, the Captain and Cody to the exact spot where Officer Medupé had knocked him down. With flashlights, the three men scanned up and down the steel exterior of the Reiziger for any signs of blood. Cody sniffed about, not really sure what the men were looking for, but she wanted to help.

They figured the color red would show up quite easily on the white exterior of the ship, but after a long search, the men found nothing.

"Okay, men...here's what I want you to do. Ruiz, head back to the engine room. Purge all the water you can. Leave the pumps running at full speed. Hopefully we can keep flushing the water out as quickly as it's coming in. Close off all remaining bulkheads. If they open up, we won't know...I realize that. But at least if the water is contained, hopefully the negative pressure will make it difficult for any more to force in."

Ruiz gave a salute to the Captain and rushed off.

"Deedat, you head back to the lab. Inform them that I'm on my way. I have to check on a couple of things, and then I'll be right there. Take a look at Medupé. See if he is injured, but don't be obvious about it."

"Yes, sir."

"Right now, I don't want to alarm anyone, so don't mention the breach or the blood. Just wait for me to get there. Is that understood?"

"Yes, sir."

Deedat was about to follow orders and leave the Captain, but instead stopped on the upper catwalk overlooking the main deck.

"What is it, Mr. Deedat? Follow through on your orders."

Deedat turned to the Captain. He was crying again.

"I really tried to save him, you know. I didn't let go. Something was down there. Something was fighting me as I tried to bring him up...something pulled him under."

Captain Grey hadn't forgotten about Blomkamp or Carlito. Quite the opposite - the loss of them, coupled with the loss of Tom and Drew were quickly becoming his worst fears. He should have done something earlier. He should have listened to Dr. Baruti, but he didn't. With the ship taking on water, Medupé injured, Tom and Drew dead, someone destroying the command center, the life rafts gone, and Percy severely wounded, the last thing the Captain wanted to do was focus on the fact that he knew there was likely something in the water. He knew and he didn't warn anyone.

"It wasn't your fault, Deedat. I know that. Now, please, go join the others. I'll be there shortly."

Deedat wiped the tears from his face, saluted the Captain once again, and departed.

27

The night sky was speckled with thousands of shining stars. The moon was nowhere in sight. The air was cool and filled with an unusual sweet smell that mixed with the exhaust of the Reiziger's diesel engines which were still idling. Captain Grey picked up on the scent, but soon disregarded it; he had more concerning things to deal with.

Cody began to bark into the night as she and the Captain crossed over the main deck.

"Shhh. Quiet, girl."

As they reached the MIG IV, Captain Grey checked his surroundings to make sure nobody was watching. For a brief moment, he felt like a fool. Why did he feel he was being watched aboard his own ship? He didn't have an answer to that question, but he trusted his instinct, and carried on with caution.

The Captain put his hand on MIG IV's door latch and opened it. Using his flashlight, he peered inside the vessel to locate the tranquilizer gun. It was gone.

* * *

Stephan gently knocked on Dr. Duiker's cabin door. No answer, so he knocked a second time more forcefully.

A voice came from behind the door, a South African voice. "Who's there?" the voice called.

Amy edged her way closer to the grey steel door and spoke through the hinges, "Joost, it's me! It's Amy and Stephan. Let us in."

Amy and Stephan stood at the door for a few more seconds before they heard the distinct click of the lock, but the door didn't open.

Amy manoeuvred around her brother toward the front of the door, her back toward Stephan. She grabbed the handle and began to open the door. "Stand behind me, just in case," Amy whispered.

Stephan felt awkward about the situation. His baby sister was protecting him. It was strange, but not as strange as her saying, 'just in case'. She had vouched that Joost was a decent guy who'd been given a raw deal. Why would she be scared of him? Stephan almost stopped Amy from opening the door, but couldn't find his voice.

Amy continued to open the door, "Joost?" Amy called as the door opened all the way.

The interior of the cabin was very dark. Amy couldn't make anything out. The only light within the room was very faint at best. The two shadows that projected across the floor of the cabin emanated from Amy and Stephan as deck lights shone from behind them. Amy stepped further into the room, her hand tracing along the wall for guidance. As her eyes focussed in the dim room, she saw the outline of a person, a silhouette barely visible sitting in a chair on the other side of the cabin.

"Come in. Close the door," the silhouette said.

* * *

As Deedat entered the research lab, he saw the five scientists along with Jako and Lefu standing quietly at the back of the room. Everybody stared at the table where Percy lay dead. He was such a big man that his arms hung over the sides of the table. A trail of blood ran all the way from the entrance door to the table. The room looked like a battle zone.

"Gentlemen, I just spoke with the Captain. He said he'd be here shortly," Deedat said, breaking the silence.

"No. I want everyone on board this ship assembled in the mess hall now." Lefu said talking directly to Deedat.

Lefu's eyes glared.

"You tell your Captain to make sure everybody from your passenger manifest is there in ten minutes. I don't want one person unaccounted for."

Dr. Baruti opened his mouth as if he was going to speak, but he didn't. He knew it was impossible to have everybody from the Reiziger present. Tom and Drew Bailey were dead. How would the Captain explain that? At this point, it didn't seem to matter.

Lefu and Jako gave each other a nod as they turned and left the lab. Their sorrow had quickly changed to anger. The scientists all stood paralyzed as the pair left the room.

"What happened out there?" Stuart Radcliff asked to Deedat.

"I don't know. Blomkamp and the captain of the Pemba Koningin went underside to make repairs to the ship. Then something went wrong," Deedat began to tell his story again, as he relived the events in his head.

"I tried to bring them back on deck but something was fighting ROK's tether. I lost them as the cables snapped; one of them kicking back and hitting Percy. There was nothing anyone could do."

"What do you mean something was fighting the tether?" Baruti asked, quite alarmed.

Deedat explained the tug of war that took place between the ROK and the crane, but how he didn't see anything. He said that Mr. Asunda would be the only person who may have seen something, if anything at all.

"I need to talk to Mr. Asunda at once!" Baruti exclaimed.

"Doctor, you heard Mr. Lefu. He wants us to gather in the mess right away," Dr. Conte commented.

"I'll head there shortly. First, I must talk to Mr. Asunda. I must know what he saw. The rest of you...go now!"

* * *

"Can I turn on the lights?" Amy asked as she entered further into the darkness.

"First, close the door behind you," the silhouette replied.

Stephan and Amy made their way inside Dr. Duiker's cabin and closed the door behind.

"Lock it!" the voice said.

Stephan locked the door and stepped around side of Amy so he was positioned next to her instead of behind. He didn't want to feel like a complete weakling behind his kid sister.

Amy fumbled in the darkness to find the light switch beside the door. Fortunately, the layout of Dr. Duiker's room was an exact duplicate of her cabin. Everything was in the exact same location in this room as it was in hers.

Amy flicked the light on. Their eyes quickly adjusted to the brightness. As their vision was restored, they were in complete shock of what they saw. Sitting in the chair across from them, where moments ago they believed was the silhouette and voice of Joost, sat Second Officer Medupé. He sat grinning like a Cheshire cat, and in his left hand, he held a gun – and it was pointed directly at the pair.

Amy defensively raised her hands in front of her face while Stephan summoned his courage and stepped in front of his sister.

"Sit down, both of you! And I won't need to shoot you." Medupé said calmly.

"What are you doing?" Stephan asked.

"Just sit down. I won't ask again."

Stephan and Amy slowly edged across the room toward Dr. Duiker's bed. The bed looked as if it hadn't been slept in since they left Cape Town, a testament to the cleanliness of the old doctor. The pair took a seat on the edge of the bed, Stephan positioning himself to be the closer of the two to Medupé.

Medupé kept the gun in his left hand trained on them. His right arm hung limply at his side and was covered with what appeared to be dried blood.

"I will ask you, and please don't lie..." Medupé began, "Where is the diamond?"

Amy couldn't believe what she was hearing. How the hell did Medupé know about the diamond, she wondered. Dr. Duiker found out because of the thin walls between the cabins. Stephan found out because he met the butt end of Joost's gun, but she couldn't understand how Medupé would have found out any of this.

"How do you know about...?" Amy asked nervously but trailed off her sentence.

Medupé chuckled quietly.

"Oh, my dear, I have known about the diamond for a while, much longer than you. I have been looking for it since we left Cape Town."

Amy and Stephan were confused, but neither spoke. They knew it was best if they kept Medupé talking. At least it would buy them some time until they could figure out what to do.

"You see, my cousin informed me of a diamond that he found a few weeks back. He claimed that this special rough diamond was worth millions. And with a diamond of that value, he knew that others would lay claim to it. He told me how he and his friend had discovered the diamond, and they felt it was right-fully theirs. But if they kept it - which they did - they would be in trouble. I agreed. Why should the rich keep getting richer? Why not let the little man prosper? So the pair asked me to help them escape South Africa without detection. To avoid the hassle of obtaining passports and all the bureaucracy, I suggested that they stowaway aboard the Reiziger. I wasn't sure where our next voyage was going, but they didn't care. They just needed to escape as soon as possible. Besides, I was sure I could convince the Captain to alter his course once we were at sea. Getting them to where they ultimately wanted to go wouldn't be a problem."

"Alter the course of the Reiziger...you? How were you going to do that? And where did they want to go?" Stephan asked.

"It took some planning I'll admit, but in the end everything seemed to come together. It really was quite easy," Medupé waved his gun in the air as he spoke.

"All I had to do was frame the Captain for a crime, create suspicion amongst the passengers and crew, and ultimately a mutiny aboard the ship would take place. The only downside was that I'm not second in command...or at least I wasn't. If I was going to take over from Captain Grey, I had to make sure that the First Officer was also out of the way."

Amy placed her hand over her mouth.

"Oh, please understand, I didn't want to hurt Tom Bailey, and I wasn't sure how I was going to remove him from the picture... but it just happened for me...it was destiny." Medupé laughed and shook his head. "With the two of them out of the picture, the Reiziger would be mine to command as I wished."

"Tom Bailey? You know where he is?" Amy asked.

"Of course. He's in the Captain's quarters," Medupé smiled again. "I found him last night. He was walking the main deck in a daze, hurt and bleeding. I don't know what happened to him, I really don't. I thought perhaps, he'd run into my cousin and his friend and had a tussle, because he kept mentioning an attack. So, I brought him to the Captain's quarters while I thought of what to do next. He kept talking about his brother and some attack, but he was really quite incoherent and badly beaten. Anyway, I took his keys and locked him in the Captain's room. I told him I'd return. And later in the day, I did. But when I came back, what do I find? Wouldn't you believe it? The Captain's personal gun just sitting there - right next to Tom. It really was a stroke of luck. I needed to frame the Captain and I needed Tom out of the way. I had to make an executive decision – so I did. It was much easier than I thought."

"So, you killed Tom with the Captain's gun to make it look like the Captain did it?" Amy said in disbelief.

"Exactly!" Medupé smiled at the pair, hoping they would admire his cunningness.

Stephan and Amy began to squirm in the seats. It was apparent to both of them that Mr. Medupé had lost his mind. Not only was he narrating his monstrous escapades, he seemed to be enjoying it.

"Why is there blood on your arm?" Stephan asked, pointing to Medupé's right arm.

Medupé reacted to Stephan's movement and thrust his gun closer to the pair.

"Whoa! I'm not trying to do anything. I'm just looking at your arm, that's all. You're bleeding."

Medupé brought his arm up to show the pair. It was slit open with a straight gash from inside the wrist to the elbow. The bleeding looked like it had mostly stopped, but the cut was still grotesque. Medupe laughed as he examined his own wound.

"Would you believe it, one of those sons-of-bitches from the rescue ship did this to me! I found him wandering the ship. I asked him what he was doing, and bam! He pulled a blade on me. Can you believe that? These men claim that they are here to help us, and he pulls that kind of shit."

Medupé stopped to consider what he just said. "Help us, yeah right. That's a good one. Turns out – they are bounty hunters, if you can believe that. In fact, our so called rescuers from the Pemba Koningin are men after the very same diamond."

"Are you sure?" Amy asked, trying to keep Medupé talking.

"Oh, I'm sure. I squeezed that piece of information from that dirty bastard before I sent him swimming," Medupé began to chuckle as he recalled tossing Mr. Hogg overboard.

"The most troubling part of that man's story was how they knew the diamond was aboard this ship. I haven't figured that out yet. And I forgot to ask." Medupé paused and his facial expression turned from pleasure to anger.

Nobody spoke.

Medupé stood up and began to rub his pistol against the side of his head. It looked as if he was trying to scratch at an itch inside his head.

Amy and Stephan were at a loss for words, but Amy knew she had to keep Medupé talking.

"Was it you who ruined the communications?" Amy cautiously pried.

Medupé stared at Amy without saying a word. Less than twenty four hours ago, he had seen her hold her own with the Captain. However, Medupé wasn't going to give in to her. He just stared and stared. Finally, Amy broke away from his stare and lowered her eyes to the floor. She didn't want to challenge a man with a gun.

Medupé sneered at Amy as she cowered, "Remember when I escorted you to the command center? Remember when the Captain was called away? Of course you do. And that's because I watched you! I waited and watched the whole time. I watched you leave the command center, and then I went to work. Yes, I did it! I figured the Captain may blame you for the communications being destroyed. You were the last one there. You had a motive. You were angry. Regardless, I couldn't have the Reiziger in contact with anyone. It's hard to make a ship just disappear if you're in radio contact."

"Disappear?" Stephan said.

"Yes, you can't just alter the course of the Reiziger. I was going to take her to Argentina...and then make her disappear."

"Why would you do this Mr. Medupé? You're a respected man aboard this ship. A man of great character," Amy pleaded with the madman, but still avoided eye contact.

"A respected man?" he yelled at Amy. "By who? I don't get the respect of my Captain. I must yield to everyone on this ship. And do you know why? I am the Second Officer, which means I'm only 'third in command'!"

Medupé began to raise his voice louder and wave his gun rapidly.

"For eight years, I've worked on this ship. I make enough money to keep myself in clothes and food...and that's it! I don't get anything else. No opportunity, no life, and no future! When my cousin offered me a chance to make a difference with my life, I figured what have I got to lose? And the answer is... nothing. So I'm going to ask you one last time, and no more bullshit...where is the diamond? Where would I find my cousin and his friend?"

Stephan lightly squeezed Amy's knee, realizing this could be the end for them. Then very softly, he asked, "Mr. Medupé, why do you think we know where the diamond is?"

Stephan's question tipped Medupé over the deep end. Medupé struck Stephan with the butt of his gun, hitting him directly in the same spot where Joost had hit him earlier.

Blood exploded from Stephan's nose as he covered his face and fell to the floor crying in agony.

"I know everything because I followed *her* back this way after I found her creeping around the lifeboat, you idiot. When I saw Dr. Duiker enter your cabin, I slipped into this cabin here."

Medupé pointed his gun at Amy. "I listened to the whole conversation you had with the old doctor. I know that you've been in contact with my cousin's partner, Joost. So, for the last time, where are they hiding?"

Amy began to cry, "I don't know."

Medupé dropped his gun away from Amy and watched her cry. This was the second time he'd seen this woman who came across so powerful, now seem so vulnerable.

Just then, a knock was heard on the cabin next door - Amy's cabin.

Medupé froze. He held his bloody hand up to Amy and Stephan warning them not to say a word.

"Ms. Masterson, Mr. Woodley, if you're in there, the entire compliment of passengers has been asked to the mess hall... again! Come at once." It was the voice of Dr. Conte.

A few other voices could be heard as they passed by the cabins. Amy prayed that Dr. Duiker wouldn't enter his cabin before heading to the mess hall meeting. Fortunately, he didn't. As the trio waited in silence, the sound of footsteps faded into the distance.

Reaching into his breast pocket, Medupé fished out a new handkerchief embroidered with the Reiziger logo. It looked similar to the one he'd offered to Amy yesterday, but this one was different, it was blue instead of white.

"Dry your tears, my dear. We're going for a walk."

Amy took the handkerchief and dabbed her eyes. Sliding from the bed, she put a hand on Stephan's shoulder. "Please, don't hurt us."

"Oh, I won't. Not right away. And as long as you help me find my cousin, Joost and the diamond. But first, we have a meeting at the mess hall. Oh, and don't think that I won't kill you in front of others if I have to. I will. It's in your best interest not to mention anything to anyone. Got it?"

28

Fenyang watched with contempt as scientists and crew began filing into the mess hall. He had just finished cleaning up for the night and wasn't expecting any more work until morning.

"No. You no eat right now. I'm done. You come back tomorrow," he said in his high-pitched voice.

The scientists paid no attention to the small cook as they gathered at the back of the room near the larger round tables.

Stuart Radcliff gave Fenyang a smile and a pat on the shoulder as he walked past. Fenyang flinched at Stuart's touch.

"We're not here to eat. We're here for another fantastic meeting aboard the Reiziger," Stuart said sarcastically. "Stick around Fen - you don't want to miss it."

Fenyang squirmed away from Stuart and shuffled back to the side of the room where he had just finished stacking plates. He cursed under his breath in Chinese, so nobody could understand what he was saying.

"Where the hell are Stephan and Amy? Those two are AWOL again and we're left here to deal with all this bullshit. I'm sick of it." Stuart said grabbing a chair and sitting down like a spoiled child.

"Mr. Radcliff, let's not worry about them. Let's worry about why we're being asked to come here again." Dr. Conte said.

Stuart turned to Dr. Duiker, "I thought you asked them to get supplies for that injured guy in the lab? Didn't you send Amy and Stephan to the First Aid room? Why didn't they come back? Those two are up to something, I'm telling you!"

"Just let it go," Dr. Duiker said.

Stuart looked to the old doctor and realized he wasn't going to get anywhere with any of his colleagues. He figured he'd best keep quiet or he'd hear about religion and life again - something he wasn't interested in hearing any more about. Stuart shut up.

Doctor Duiker shifted his focus from Stuart and leaned over toward his colleague, Doctor Baruti. Quietly he asked the doctor to share with the group why he was so withdrawn over the past twenty-four hours. Baruti thought of lying, but wasn't sure if he could. Captain Grey had asked for his confidence, but Baruti was too worried for his colleagues; he needed to warn them.

Gathering the group close together, Baruti asked that nobody interrupt or make judgement on what he was about to tell them. He warned them that what he was about to tell them would reveal a danger...a danger that they surely wouldn't want to know about, but once he told them, it would be too late.

* * *

Lefu looked over at the Pemba Koningin floating a short distance away. The light from the ship cast a reflection across the water that looked like tinsel hanging from a Christmas tree.

Pulling a cigar from his pocket, Lefu put it in his mouth and began to chomp the end.

"So, what do you want to do boss? Maybe we should just start killing these bastards one by one until somebody talks," Jako suggested.

Lefu smiled and shook his head. As much as he liked that idea, he was afraid to use that tactic because it carried the risk of killing the wrong person, somebody who might actually know where the diamond is.

Jako wouldn't let the idea go. "Boss, Percy is dead. Carlito is dead. This ship is 'slegte geluk!' Let's get what we came here for and get out!"

Lefu chomped the cigar harder. Bad luck? He didn't want to accept the fact that his plan had failed, but it had. The Reiziger was useless to him now. The repairs were not completed. Members of his crew were dead.

Grabbing the side rail with both hands, Lefu leaned his head over the edge of the Reiziger and spat a piece of loose tobacco to the water below. As he did, he caught a sight he couldn't believe...the Zodiac was being untied from the Reiziger with Mr. Asunda the only person on board.

"Asunda!" Lefu yelled over the edge of the ship. "What the hell are you doing?"

Mr. Asunda heard Lefu's voice and began to panic. He grabbed the cord from the outboard engine and frantically began to pull it. Jako responded to Lefu's yell and wasted no time as he quickly climbed over the edge of the Reiziger onto the stair rail. Mr. Asunda noticed Jako coming down the rail toward him just as the Zodiac's engine roared to life. All he had to do was untie the mooring rope.

Jako's stocky body was getting closer by the second. Mr. Asunda's fingers worked feverishly as he unharnessed the small boat. Just as Asunda loosened the final knot, a large splash shot up beside him. Jako had tripped and fell the final eight steps into the water beside the Zodiac.

Unhurt from the fall, Jako managed to quickly get his bearings and began to paddle towards Asunda and the Zodiac.

Mr. Asunda throttled up the motor and pulled the Zodiac away from the Reiziger just before Jako's hand could reach the side.

Mr. Asunda kept the small pontoon style boat at full throttle. The sight of the Pemba Koningin in the distance was his only concern, his only safety.

After what Mr. Asunda recently witnessed with Nelson Blomkamp, he couldn't take anymore. He didn't care about the money. He didn't care about the diamond. He didn't care about the crew he was working with. He only cared about saving himself. Mr. Hogg and Mr. Asunda made prior arrangements while still on board the Pemba Koningin that if anything went wrong while on the Reiziger, they would signal each other that they were going to cut their losses and escape. When Mr. Hogg never returned to the Zodiac, Mr. Asunda knew that he was going to have to make the trip solo.

A shot rang out. Mr. Asunda felt a sharp pain in his neck. Before he could figure out what had happened, he keeled over face first into the side of the Zodiac. He quickly pressed his hand to where the pain radiated, as if by instinct. His neck was warm and wet.

Lefu tucked his gun away, not really caring if anyone saw him shoot at Mr. Asunda. Lefu was sure he'd hit him, as he watched the Zodiac begin to randomly weave through the water.

Jako swam back to the Reiziger and climbed up onto the small mooring platform where the Zodiac was only recently fastened. He was climbing the stair rail, when he heard the gunshot. He stopped and turned to watch the small Zodiac as it labored toward the Pemba Koningin.

Mr. Asunda was in extreme pain. His strength began to drain away and his vision became blurred. He struggled to steer the Zodiac, but kept it at full throttle until he reached the courtesy ladder still hanging precariously from the side of the Pemba Koningin.

As he neared the ladder, Mr. Asunda cut the engine and drifted slowly over the waves until the Zodiac bounced gently against the side of the large ship. Lifting his head off of the side of the Zodiac, he felt secure that he was safe distance from Lefu, and needn't fear another bullet at this distance.

Mr. Asunda clumsily tied the Zodiac to the side of the Pemba Koningin to prevent it from drifting away. His fingers could barely complete the task. He reached his hand to the hanging rope ladder and with all his effort began to climb. One, two, three, four, five - when he reached the fifth rung, his leg slipped through a rung and hooked in behind his knee.

He tried to lift his leg out, but he didn't have the strength to. He tried to talk, but couldn't. His body began to shake. Mr. Asunda dropped his head back as he watched his own blood soaked hands slowly fade to black - while all sound around him muted.

Lefu and Jako watched the Pemba Koningin through the starlit night. They watched as Mr. Asunda managed to reach the mother ship with the Zodiac. They watched as Mr. Asunda began to climb the rope ladder. And they watched his body fall backward toward the ocean only to become entangled in the rope ladder. The body hung motionless. Mr. Asunda was dead. Lefu puffed on his cigar and laughed.

29

Captain Grey pushed open the heavy metal door to the lab. It swung easily and banged into the metal wall directly behind it. The sound rattled through the room like a gunshot.

Captain Grey peered inside while Cody stayed close to her master; her body pressed tight against his leg.

Deedat was sitting on one of the tables in the center of the room. The sound of the door opening startled him and he jumped from the table to the ground. "Holy shit, you scared me, sir."

Captain Grey crossed the threshold of the doorway and cautiously entered. He couldn't believe his eyes. The amount of blood splattered on the floor was immense. He saw that the blood led to the table at the rear of the lab where the body of Percy lay motionless. Cody saw the horror from beyond the threshold of the room and didn't follow Captain Grey inside.

"Where are the others?" Captain Grey asked.

"Lefu requested that we gather in the mess hall. He asked that you bring everybody on board, sir. I was just waiting here to give you that information, and then we'd proceed there together. He's very distraught."

Captain Grey looked to the body of Percy. "That's understandable. What about Medupé? How did his hands look?"

"He wasn't here, sir. I didn't see him."

Captain Grey realized that Medupe had been acting strange. The thought had crossed his mind earlier, but he quickly cast that notion away. Now it was back.

Why did he have any concern over Medupé? The Captain and Medupé had sailed these seas together for over eight years. Medupé was always trustworthy, honest, professional, and diligent. Captain Grey couldn't put his finger on it, but he knew that today in particular, Medupé had been acting out of character. Grey wasn't sure of anything right now, but he wasn't comfortable.

"What about Doctor Baruti?"

"Yes, sir, he was here with the rest of the scientists. Although he looked exceptionally shaken by the loss of Percy compared to the rest. He doesn't look good, sir."

Captain Grey realized that Baruti had seen enough horror for one day.

"My God, what is happening?" the Captain said as he shook his head in disbelief.

"I wish I could tell you, sir."

"Let's head to the mess together Mr. Deedat. First, we'll have to head to the engine room and gather Mr. Ruiz. If we encounter any..." he trailed off.

Captain Grey looked around the lab. The picture on the wall of Albert Einstein caught his attention. It was the picture of Einstein sticking out his tongue for the camera. The Captain just stared at the picture. It felt as though Einstein was mocking him. Captain Grey picked up a beaker and threw it at the picture. Glass shattered across the wall and fell to the floor.

"Why me?" the Captain yelled at that picture.

"Sir?"

Captain Grey had briefly forgotten that Deedat was in the room. He realized he must have looked like a madman, assaulting a photograph.

"I wonder if this is how the previous captain of the Reiziger felt. I don't believe he ever had this much trouble in one day. Yet he ended up losing her. His crew mutinied." the Captain lamented.

"You're not going to lose the Reiziger sir. We'll get her going again. You'll see. Even if there's a breach in the hull, we can shut it out and contain it. We'll get the screws spinning and find our way to the nearest port. Remember, we still have MIG IV. We'll send it down and strictly concentrate on freeing up the screws and get Reiziger moving again," Deedat said with a slightly wavering confidence.

"I wish it were that easy, Deedat."

The Captain walked toward the body of Percy lying on the table. "You said for yourself, something was fighting you below the ship. Well...something is fighting me up here."

Deedat wasn't sure what the Captain meant by the second part of his remark.

"How could I? I knew...I knew and didn't stop the men from going below. I knew and I sent them to their deaths. I knew, but all I cared about was the Reiziger. I was more concerned with not ending up like former Captain Klaustzman. It was my error that led to three people being dead."

Captain Grey looked directly at Deedat. "It wasn't your fault. It wasn't you, Winston. It was me."

"It wasn't you, Captain," Deedat tried to comfort the captain.

"Yes, it was. Dr. Baruti tried to warn me that there was something in the water, but I didn't listen to him. I didn't want to believe it. I thought that if what the doctor was saying was true, perhaps whatever it was, was now dead, and wrapped up in our props. The truth is, something was out there, it is still out there, and for some reason, it's hunting us. I don't know why, but I won't sacrifice another person on board for the sake of the Reiziger."

"Captain, I'll go down in MIG IV. I'll free the screws. Let me try. We have to try something."

Captain Grey shook his head, "No, my friend, that would be a fatal mistake. We have to get off this ship. We must get the crew and passengers to the safety of the Pemba Koningin. It's our only option now. I just pray that the souls of these men will forgive me. And I pray that Lefu and the rest of his team will accommodate us after what has happened."

30

The scientists sat quietly at the rear of the mess hall, looking through the window into the distance. All of them were searching for St. Helena, but it wasn't to be seen.

The early morning sky was beginning to take on a light blue hue as the sun slowly began to rise from the east.

Most passengers suffered through the past twenty-four hours or so with a little less than a couple of hours of sleep, if any at all. The signs of fatigue were obvious throughout the room. Some people were yawning, others were stretching, while a few even fought nodding off to sleep with an embarrassing jerk that left them peeking around the room to see if anyone noticed.

The sleep deprivation psychosis began to taunt everyone's mind, but fortunately it had not yet fully set in. With another day or two of ongoing sleeplessness, complete psychosis would be a reasonable outcome. However, most felt as though it was already upon them.

Captain Grey and Cody entered the mess hall with Winston Deedat and Alan Ruiz in tow. The three men sat at the head table facing the scientists while Cody settled down right next to her master. Captain Grey removed his hat and nodded to the scientists, but he didn't speak.

Fenyang approached the Captain and whispered something in his ear. The Captain shook his head and then waved Fenyang away. Fenyang bowed curtly and was about to leave when the Captain grabbed his hand, pulled him close, and whispered once again. Fenyang bowed to the Captain once again before taking a seat beside his serving station.

Next, Amy and Stephan sheepishly entered the mess hall with Officer Medupé directly behind them. Medupe had a fresh shirt on covering his cut arm, but the arm didn't move very well.

The two scientists were not exactly sure on what they should do. They were surprised to see most of the Reiziger passengers and staff present, and they hesitated on where to sit. Once they caught the inviting faces of their colleagues, the pair quickened their pace to sit with those they felt most comfortable.

"What happened to your face? It looks worse than before!" Dr. Athans asked Stephan.

"If I told you I tripped again, you probably wouldn't believe me, but that's exactly what happened."

"My goodness! Here, let me take a look," Dr. Conte offered, as she rushed to Stephan's side.

"No, please...it's broken, but I'll be fine. I'm just having a bad case of clumsiness lately. I think it's the rocking on the sea that's making me dizzy. And a lack of sleep doesn't help either."

Everybody gave an affirmative grunt to Stephan's comment. Lack of sleep was a bitch.

Medupé remained standing in the front of the room as he continued to watch Amy and Stephan sitting with their friends. He didn't show any concern about them sitting apart from him. He had explicitly warned them: 'If you tell anyone about what I told you, I will kill you both, in front of everyone.'

Ruiz caught Medupé's attention as he pulled a chair out for the Second Officer to join them at the Captain's table. Medupé gave him a respectful nod as he took the chair and lost focus of the scientists. As he sat, he looked to Captain Grey for approval, but the Captain avoided eye contact with Medupé, still upset from earlier.

For the next several minutes, the room began to hum with lighthearted conversation. No one spoke of anything serious. But a few smiles were shared; even a couple of jokes were overheard. The atmosphere seemed to ease everyone's mind.

"Ladies and gentlemen," Captain Grey spoke as he stood up. "May I have your attention please? That would be appreciated. Thank you." The room fell quiet again and all eyes were on the Captain.

His composure was different from the night before. He was standing in the same location as yesterday when he had informed everybody of the missing life rafts. At that time, he was brooding, methodical and somewhat angry. Now, he was passive, slightly humbled, and calm. He spoke softly, "I realize Mr. Lefu has asked us all to meet here, and I'm glad he has, but I don't know when to expect him."

Cody wagged her tail as she stood beside her master.

"But while we wait for him, I regret to inform everyone that the Reiziger is in trouble. Aside from the fact that the life rafts are missing, we are now taking on water, and on top of that, we can't get the screws turning."

"That means the props," Baruti whispered to his colleagues.

"With all that has transpired since we've left Cape Town, I'm advising that we take the necessary precautions and transfer all passengers and crew to the Pemba Koningin. It is for everyone's safety, and therefore, I will ask Mr. Lefu for his assistance with this matter when he arrives. I can only hope that he is willing to help us."

Captain Grey could tell that his passengers and crew agreed with his assessment of the situation, and appreciated a move towards a resolve.

"Don't count on it!" Lefu said as he entered the mess hall from behind the Captain.

The Captain's mood and the developing optimism of the room sunk when Lefu and Jako walked up. They were holding automatic weapons.

"What the hell?" Captain Grey said.

"Okay, now listen," Lefu said. "We're here for one purpose, and it has nothing to do with saving any of you."

Jako fired a single shot into the sky before he entered the mess deck directly behind Lefu. The shot got everyone's attention. Fear spread through the mess hall and no one moved.

Lefu chomped on a nub of a cigar and smiled as Jako waved his gun around, his clothes still soaking wet from his dip in the Atlantic.

Cody was frightened by the sound of the gun. Keeping herself out of view from the men, she slithered under the table over to Captain Grey and nuzzled onto his leg. The Captain slowly sat down and comforted his companion with a firm pat on the head.

"Mr. Lefu?" Captain Grey began to ask.

"Shut up, Captain. Just sit there, and shut up. I don't want to hear from you or anyone else in this room unless I ask you to speak. This ship is under my control. You are of no importance to me Captain, and neither are your crew or passengers." Lefu yelled as he gave Jako a nod.

"You...Get up here," Jako crossed the room with his finger pointed at the group of scientists. He waved it around for a moment before stopping at Dr. Duiker.

"Get your ass up here, now!" he yelled again.

Everybody wanted to prevent the doctor from standing, but they weren't sure how.

Dr. Duiker slowly went to stand and waved his friends down. With his old bones and muscles straining to their limits of exertion, he got up. Once on his feet, he braced himself with his brass cane and stood looking at Jako. "I'm sorry, I'm a bit slower than I used to be," he said.

"What has Dr. Duiker done?" Stuart Radcliff asked somewhat sheepishly.

"What has he done? Nothing, you piece of shit. You want to take his place, pretty boy? Do you? Huh?" Jako said as he pointed his pistol at Stuart.

Stuart backed down and slumped below the table as he shook his head to Jako. Not sure why Jako had singled out the doctor,

Stuart wasn't interested in trading places with him. Instead, he shut up.

"Stand here, old man," Jako demanded as he pointed to the center of the room. Duiker hobbled to the center of the mess deck as ordered.

Jako stood next to Dr. Duiker while Lefu stood on guard by the main entrance to the mess hall. Lefu was holding a submachine gun quite capable of tearing everyone in the room apart with a single spray; Jako was brandishing a pistol.

Captain Grey was looking just beyond Fenyang. Directly behind Fenyang's station was another entrance to the mess hall. To reach the door, you would have to pass through the center of the room. Everyone in the room knew that the exit was there, but it was too far away to safely make a break for.

"What's your name?" Lefu demanded to the old man in the center of the room.

"I'm Doctor Uuka Duiker. I'm an oceanographer."

"A doctor you say? What are you doing aboard this ship?"

Dr. Duiker didn't know where Lefu was heading with his questions, but thought it was best not to be crass to a man holding a gun, so he continued with a civil tone, "I am here to advise our team of when continental plates are shifting, and what type of changes are taking place on a subterranean level. That's my job! I've been doing it for many years. I was asked here by…"

Lefu raised a finger in the air to silence the doctor. Lefu frowned at the doctor and shook his head, slowly rolling his cigar from one side of his mouth to the other. Perhaps Lefu didn't fully understand Dr. Duiker's answers, or perhaps he didn't care. Lowering his finger, Lefu took a deep breath and continued his questioning.

"Doctor, have you seen anybody on board this ship besides the crew or your research team?"

"No, I…um…" Dr. Duiker responded questioningly.

The doctor knew exactly who Lefu and his men were looking for, but also knew that the outcome of giving that information could be devastating for everyone on board. He couldn't reveal his secret. Unfortunately, the doctor wasn't a very good liar, as his hands began to quiver.

Lefu noticed the doctor's body language and smiled.

"Are you sure, Doctor? I think you might be hiding something. Why are you shaking?"

Doctor Duiker didn't speak; he merely shrugged his shoulders and looked to his colleagues for support. Nobody moved.

"I'm only going to ask you one more time, Doctor. Have you seen anyone else on board this ship besides the crew or your team? Anybody at all? In particular, a man named Joost?"

Dr. Duiker shook his head in defiance and gave a little laugh.

"No! I'm sorry. I wish I could help you, but...I don't know what you're talking about."

Lefu again shifted his cigar from one side of his mouth to the other – this time his smile disappeared.

"That's a shame, Doctor. Because I think you're lying. And now, I have no use for you - Jako!"

Lefu snapped his fingers.

Reminiscent of a Saigon street slaughter during the Vietnam War, Jako placed the barrel of his gun to Dr. Duiker's temple and pulled the trigger without hesitation.

The gunshot echoed through the mess hall. The old man's body fell to the ground, his life snuffed out instantly as the blood spurted from the hole in his head. In seconds, the mess deck floor was covered in a sea of red.

Amy screamed, Dr. Conte covered her mouth and cried out hysterically as the rest of the passengers and crew sat speechless, too tensed up from the immediate shock of what they had just witnessed.

"As you can see, Dr. Duiker will not be joining us ever again," Lefu laughed, "So if anyone here has the answer to the question I'm asking, I suggest you share with us now. I plan on going through this process with each and every one of you. Make no mistake – I will find what I'm looking for. Okay Jako, who's next?"

"You, get on your feet!" Jako demanded as he pointed at Stuart Radcliff.

"No, please, no. I don't know anything. I'm just here as a biologist. I haven't seen anything, I haven't heard anything..." then Stuart stopped pleading with the gunman.

Stuart realized that telling them that he knew nothing would get him killed, so he changed his approach. "No wait...actually, I did hear something. I'm not sure what it was, but..."

Stuart was grasping at straws and almost everyone could see it.

Lefu was intrigued. It only took one kill to get the information they desired.

"I overheard *her* talking to a stranger. She must know where he is," Stuart said pointing a finger at Amy.

Amy couldn't believe that Stuart would sell her out like that. He had no evidence. He never saw her talking to anyone, let alone heard anything. Why did he single her out? Was he listening through the walls? Perhaps he did overhear something. His room was one over from Dr. Duiker. If the doctor was correct about sound easily travelling through the walls, then Stuart's account was possible, but was it truthful? Amy couldn't be sure. She realized Stuart was desperate to save himself after seeing what came of Dr. Duiker, but why her? She had never hurt him. Maybe it was because the two of them used to be lovers, but that was over now. Did he carry some sort of resentment towards her? Did he still love her? Was he jealous of her and her research? Whatever the reason, he had just thrown her under the bus and potentially set her up to be killed. Stuart was truly a coward.

"You there, stand up," Lefu ordered from the front of the room as he pointed to Amy.

Amy felt her knees get weak. She had the sudden urge to throw up as she slowly stood up. Stephan reached out to stop her, but she waved him off. There was no point in both of them being killed; these men were ruthless.

She looked down at the lifeless body of Dr. Duiker heaped on the floor. She felt a deep sadness for him. He seemed to know that he wasn't to see the sun again. 'How did he know?' she wondered. She thought of him fondly. He really was a nice man - kind and gentle. What did he say? Everything happens for a reason? This mantra didn't make much sense right now to Amy.

Remembering what was going on, Amy became scared. She didn't want to die.

"Do you know anything of a man named Joost?"

Medupé watched Amy under interrogation wondering if she would reveal information that he too wanted. He didn't stop the proceedings nor did he come to her defence. That much was expected. Amy wasn't sure if Medupé would be happy with her answers, but she had no choice.

"I do. I have met Joost," she said.

The room stared in shock at Amy. She actually did know about Joost. Captain Grey shook his head in dismay, not wanting to believe what he just heard. Stuart Radcliff could hardly believe it himself, as he let out a gasp.

"And what did he tell you," Lefu pressed.

"He told me that he hid a diamond aboard this ship, and that he needed to get to a safe place."

"That's right. But the diamond he has, this very special diamond, belongs to me."

Amy realized that briefly she was somewhat indispensable. Lefu needed her information to find the diamond, so she made sure to choose her words carefully.

"I was told the diamond belonged to two men - Joost and Ramon."

Lefu lifted his submachine gun toward Amy. "You really do know something about my little friend Joost, don't you?" Lefu snarled. "But what did he tell you about Ramon? Has he seen him aboard the ship? Are they still working together? Did Joost give you any of that information?"

"No, he didn't."

"Well, I'll tell you why, little bitch! He hasn't seen or heard from Ramon because I blew his brains into the Atlantic two days ago."

Amy shifted her eyes from Lefu to Medupé. Ramon was dead. The information was irrelevant to everyone else, but to Medupé, it meant that his cousin was dead. Medupé's face turned sombre as he slowly clenched his hands into fists. Under the table, his leg was shaking and he shut his eyes tightly, possibly fighting back tears. Half expecting Medupé to lose his cool, Amy kept watching him. Instead, Medupé looked as if he was taking deep breaths and controlling his anger.

Now would be the perfect opportunity for Amy to reveal Medupé as being Ramon's cousin. Now would be a good time to expose the crimes that Medupé had already committed. But the more she considered, the more she thought better of it. She didn't want the entire room to be caught in crossfire – nobody would win in that situation.

"What is your name?" Lefu asked, still pointing his submachine gun at Amy.

"Amy."

"Amy, where is Joost?"

"I don't know exactly."

"Where did you last see him?"

"I saw him at the bow of the ship, we spoke there in private. He was hiding by the anchor chains when I met him. That was last night. I don't know where he is now."

She was lying. That was where she had her first conversation with Medupé.

As much as Amy really didn't know where Joost was, she didn't want to draw attention to the Savior. What if Joost was only sleeping the last time she went there? No, it was best if she left that detail out. Besides, it may be the only hope for getting off the Reiziger.

Amy worried that Medupé may try to discredit her story, especially after seeing her at the lifeboat, but again, he remained silent. His eyes remained tightly closed.

Captain Grey couldn't contain himself any longer, even knowing that speaking right now could get him killed.

"Lefu, I must speak – it is of grave importance."

Jako looked at the Captain with anger in his eyes. Stepping over the dead body of Dr. Duiker, the stocky henchman walked purposefully toward the Captain. Thankfully, Lefu stopped him.

"No Jako, wait! What is it, Captain?" Lefu said.

"Lefu, I didn't know anything about a diamond aboard my ship. Nor did I know anything about a stowaway. I'm shocked to hear that some of my passengers had information of such, but that's not important to me. I only want to ensure everyone's safety, but that is in your hands now. But, I have to tell you, the

Reiziger is sinking. I just came from the engine room, and we're taking on water fast. I know it may not seem important to you, not as important as the diamond, but if we don't repair this vessel within the next few hours, there will be no ship left. It could take you hours to search this ship, but in that time, this Joost character...the diamond...will all be at the bottom of the Atlantic, gone forever."

As he chomped on his unlit cigar, Lefu considered what the Captain was saying. The diamond would be useless to him if he drowned with the Reiziger.

"What do you suggest, Captain?"

"I am offering a trade. Let my passengers and crew go to your ship, the Pemba Koningin, and I'll stay here and search for Joost with you. I know all the nooks and crannies on board. I could make the search more efficient."

Lefu began to laugh. The Captain thought it was because his offer was unreasonable, since he didn't really offer much in return to Lefu. Then Jako began to laugh too, but he didn't know why. Everyone in the room remained on edge, waiting for Lefu's laughter to explode into anger. But it didn't.

"Amy!" Lefu called to her.

"Yes?"

"How well can you swim?"

31

The morning sun began to rise above the eastern horizon creating a wonderful red-orange fire across the sky. Waves of the Atlantic gently rocked against the Reiziger. The sound of breaking whitecaps could be heard whispering from the sides of the ship.

The entire crowd from the mess deck flowed outside to the main deck. Lefu and Jako held the rear as everyone filed out in an orderly fashion ahead of them. If anyone stepped out of line, they'd be shot. That was the word given to them before they walked out.

Once everybody assembled onto the main deck, not far from the pool of Percy's blood, they were ordered to stop, turn and face the Pemba Koningin, and step up to the guard rail. Some people shuddered thinking that this was going to be an execution. Dr. Conte could barely stand, but Dr. Athans helped her over to the edge of the rail. What an ending - a quick shot in the head, and a dump overboard. But Lefu had other plans for the people of the Reiziger. He surprised everyone as he invited them to see something of interest - something only he and Jako knew of.

Approximately one hundred yards from the Reiziger sat the Pemba Koningin. The ship itself looked exactly as it had when it came to the rescue yesterday afternoon: solid, motionless, and cold.

"Oh my god," Dr. Conte said as she pointed to the side of the ship.

Everyone looked, and saw exactly what Lefu wanted them to see. There, hanging upside down from the courtesy ladder was the body of Mr. Asunda; his arms dangling precariously toward the Zodiac that was secured below him.

"You see, that is what happens if you try to betray me. That is the fate that awaits you if you do not follow my every command. Is that understood?" Lefu barked at the crowd.

Everyone nodded. The sound of some people swallowing could almost be heard above the sound of the waves and the Reiziger's engines purring.

"Now, here's the problem: the Reiziger is sinking, so says Captain Grey. And since my ship is out of reach, I need the Zodiac brought back here while I look for my diamond. So, this young, fit, and beautiful Amy has been chosen by me to retrieve my boat, but she is not going alone. I need two more to go with her. It's a far swim - so three will go, just in case one or two don't make it. I can't see three people drowning. So you, and you, will go as well," Lefu said as he pointed to Alan Ruiz and Stuart Radcliff.

"Why can't we just take the other submersible over there?" Dr. Athans asked meekly.

Lefu shot him an angry look.

"We snapped both cables from the crane, so we can't get the MIG IV harnessed. She's quite useless right now," Deedat responded.

"What about the Savior 5 vessel?" Dr. Baruti begged, hoping to keep the trio from having to enter into the water.

Medupé answered before Lefu had the chance to think of the Savior as an option.

"We can't, I checked her out last night and the throttle mechanisms are cut...somebody sabotaged her."

Amy's eyes grew big. She knew that Medupé didn't want anyone going near the Savior as there was a chance that Joost was in the life boat. On the other hand, if the vessel was in fact ruined, it was entirely Medupé's doing. And if the Savior was ruined, there were now only two ways for Amy and Stephan and everyone to get off the Reiziger - aboard the Pemba Koningin or in a proverbial coffin.

"This is not a debate" Lefu yelled, "I said you and you and you. In the water! Get my boat back here, now!" Lefu fired a burst of his submachine gun into the air.

"And listen - no funny stuff or we start killing your friends, one by one," Jako added.

Lefu didn't expect Jako to speak out of turn, but he liked the idea he presented.

"Please sir, if I may speak?" Dr. Baruti said, "We can't send anybody in the water, there's something down there. Something attacked the ROK submersible last night, something attacked your captain, and I have reason to believe that it attacked a few other people on board this ship before you even arrived. We can't put anybody in the water...it's just plain suicide!"

Lefu stared at the pudgy doctor as he began to move closer to him. As he neared, he pulled out a long knife he kept tucked inside his jacket.

"You mean to tell me that you knew of something in the water...and you sent my man down there anyway? Two of my men are dead because of that withheld piece of information. So yes, to send your people to retrieve my boat may be suicide, but the alternative is murder."

Lefu grabbed Dr. Baruti by the back of the neck and thrust the knife into his abdomen. "You killed my men."

Baruti tried to grab at Lefu as his eyes widened with fear.

"Say hello to Percy for me," Lefu whispered in the doctor's ear as he pulled the knife out.

Doctor Baruti collapsed to the main deck holding his stomach as blood began to spill out. He looked for help from his colleagues, reaching out a hand, but no one moved.

"Nobody touch him. Let the pig die. Anybody moves, and I kill them next," Lefu yelled as he wiped his blade along his pant leg.

Cody began to growl under her breath, steady and unwavering.

Doctor Baruti writhed in pain. He tried to speak, but he couldn't catch his breath long enough to form any words. His teeth were covered with blood and he began to wheeze as his body started to convulse.

Cody raced from Captain Grey to the doctor's side, and rubbed her nose against the dying doctor's face. Baruti cracked a small smile as he continued to gasp for breath. Up until now, Cody had been her usual timid self. She was aware of the cruelty humans were capable of, but had never seen such evil. Not sure if Cody was defending the doctor or if the sight of the knife scared her. She just snapped.

Cody leaped from the doctor's side and jumped on Lefu, chomping down hard onto his arm that held the submachine gun. Lefu screamed in pain as the strong malamute thrashed her head back and forth, her canine teeth tearing into his hand and wrist. Lefu dropped his gun and knife at the same time as he fought with Cody, but she was too strong. He fell onto his back as Cody released his arm and went for the kill lunging at Lefu's throat. Captain Grey watched his companion with pride, and then shock. As Cody reared up and was about to pounce, Jako fired a shot that hit her in the side.

Cody's body flung off Lefu as she let out a whimper that echoed across the main deck. She tumbled twice across the cold steel of the ship, but quickly clambered back to her feet. Jako fired another shot at Cody, but missed, as she ran away limping.

Dr. Athans saw the commotion as an opportunity to help his dying friend.

"Oh, god, please stop this," Dr. Athans cried as he dropped to Dr. Baruti's side and held his head, trying to comfort his dying friend. "I'm here, Bruno. Everything's going to be..."

Dr. Athans words were cut short as he was shot in the back of the head point blank by Jako. The doctor's body instantly collapsed on top of Dr. Baruti.

Lefu picked himself up from the deck and grabbed his submachine gun with his uninjured hand. Jako backed away from Dr. Athans and swung his gun back and forth towards the passengers making sure nobody else made a move.

Lefu's left hand didn't look like it would work again. Blood was dripping from it and the flesh was torn and mangled, yet he managed to feebly pick up his knife with the injured hand. As Lefu struggled to put the knife back into a sheath hidden in his jacket, he turned to the remaining members of the crew. "You sons-of-bitches. You god-damn-sons-of-bitches. I'd kill you all if I didn't need that boat! I said...you, you, and you...in the water. Right now!"

Lefu then yelled at the Captain. "I knew I should have killed that dog the minute I came aboard."

Captain Grey didn't smile or give Lefu any expression to show what he was feeling. Captain Grey wanted to find Cody, to run to her, and comfort her, make sure she was going to be okay, but he couldn't. All he could do right now was take comfort in knowing that in the face of danger, his dog had found her courage.

32

Stephan held Amy's hand tightly as she readied to climb over the side of the Reiziger toward the ladder rail. Tears streamed down his face, as he looked his kid sister in the eyes, probably for the last time.

"I love you Amy," he said.

Amy removed her hooded sweatshirt and handed it to Stephan while she gave him a big hug. She held him close and whispered in his ear, "By the Savior," was all she said as she pressed something into his hand so nobody would notice.

Stephan took the small item, not sure what it was. As he stepped back from Amy, he discretely tucked the item into his pant pocket.

Amy was the first to scale down the ladder to the waiting waters below. Next was Stuart Radcliff, followed by Alan Ruiz.

"Go quickly, be safe...all of you!" Captain Grey yelled to the trio as they climbed down the side of the ship.

"May the grace of God bless you...swim fast, we're counting on you," Dr. Conte added as she held onto Deedat's arm.

The remaining passengers and crew watched as the three unwilling victims entered the cold waters of the Atlantic, and began to swim toward the Pemba Koningin. Tears could be seen on everyone's face – all except Lefu, Jako and Medupé.

Lefu broke the melancholic atmosphere.

"Okay, listen up. We're not going to waste any time. Captain, first off, just so nobody tries any heroics today, I need to know if you have any weapons on this ship. And don't lie to me. I don't take lying to kindly as you're now well aware." Lefu said.

Captain Grey shook his head, "No."

He knew that there <u>was</u> one gun aboard – his gun. But that gun was missing, so there was no point mentioning it. Intentionally, he also didn't mention the missing tranquilizer gun.

Lefu painfully raised his hands into the air as he spoke loudly for everyone to hear. He spoke like a charismatic dictator rallying his troops, and his methods seemed to be working, as everyone clung to his every word.

"I don't want any more bloodshed today. All I want is the diamond, nothing more. All you want is to live, so I'm going to make you a deal. If you find my diamond, I will take you from this ship and deliver you to safety. Make no mistake...I will only save the one person that finds the diamond or delivers me Joost. For those of you that do not want to do my bidding, you may go and hide. But remember, this ship is sinking...and you will die. At least I am giving you a chance. Find my diamond, and you will live."

* * *

Amy struggled in the cold water of the Atlantic. The waves that once seemed so small from the main deck of the Reiziger were actually quite big in the water. The odd wave caught her off guard, filling her open mouth and sending a gag reflex through her system as she choked on the salt water.

Stopping to catch her breath for a moment, she caught the sight of the Reiziger behind her. Eight figures stood along the side of the ship watching while Ruiz, Radcliff and Amy made their way to the Pemba Koningin. Amy knew they had to make it, for if they didn't, six more people would die and one of them was her brother. The Pemba Koningin seemed miles away, but she pressed on.

Ruiz was the best swimmer of the three. He kept his strokes smooth and calculated while breathing in and out with perfect rhythm. It wasn't long before he passed Amy on the way to the other ship.

Stuart was struggling with the task. His strokes were choppy and uncoordinated. Amy was surprised that a young man with such charming features was actually quite clumsy. He seemed to be stopping and starting too much. Amy treaded water as she waited for Stuart to catch up. When he wasn't making forward progress anymore, Amy knew he was in trouble.

"Come on, Stuart!" Amy yelled.

"I can't do this," he cried.

"Yes, you can...you have to."

"I can't, I have to turn back. I can't swim all the way."

"No, Stuart. If you go back, they'll kill you or someone else. You have to keep going. Come on, I'm waiting for you. I'll help you. Just get your ass up here."

"I can't! Amy please, you have to help me!"

Amy grew frustrated. She thought back to the love they once had, a relationship that foiled two years earlier when Amy caught him with another girl from the university. The other girl was a cute blonde in pre-med. At the time, Amy was deeply hurt, but never let Stuart see her cry. Instead, they parted ways but remained friends, at her suggestion. Even though it was hard for Amy to keep things amicable at times, she proved that she was the stronger of the two, and maintained the promise of friendship. She never asked for his love again, and never took him back, even when he begged forgiveness. Repeatedly, she showed that she was stronger than him. And at this moment, she had to prove it once again.

Amy swam close to Stuart. "You have to keep going. If you don't, they will kill somebody."

"Can't I just wait for Ruiz to come back with the boat? I can't swim anymore."

"Fine. Wait here then. Float on your back and save your energy. We'll get you on the way back."

"Amy?"

"What?"

"I didn't mean to set you up like that. I shouldn't have pointed you out to those guys. I just panicked. I didn't want to die like Dr. Duiker. And I didn't want you to get hurt, either. But I didn't know what to do. I still love you, you know? I wish none of this ever happened. I just want to go home."

Amy looked at Stuart floating on his back. Despite the waves of water splashing across him, she could tell he was crying. Briefly she felt sorry for him. She knew he wasn't a bad person, he was just a coward. He was looking to her for strength to get through this. Amy felt anger rising up inside her. She wasn't willing to waste her energy on arguing with Stuart. She had nothing to give him any-more, friendship or otherwise. All she felt for him was regret.

"Listen to me. I'm going to catch up to Ruiz," she said dis-regarding his comments. "Stay here, and whatever you do, DO NOT GO BACK! Do you understand me?"

Stuart shook his head, "Okay. Amy, I love you!"

Amy didn't answer. She swam off and made her way toward the Pemba Koningin.

* * *

Medupé left the main deck heading towards the stern of the ship. Dr. Conte, with Deedat at her side, departed the main deck heading towards the port. Fenyang also exited the main deck, but for once, did not head back to the mess deck. All of them were desperate to find the diamond – desperate to save their lives.

Captain Grey refused to play Lefu's game. He first thought of staying on the main deck, but as he watched Ruiz, Radcliff and Masterson make their way to the other ship; he began to think of Cody. He needed to know if she was alright, or if she was dying. He didn't want to know the latter, but he needed to know. Finally, Captain Grey left the main deck.

Stephan kept his eyes fixed on his sister as she swam out across the Atlantic, her white shirt a barely visible small speck in the vast blue below. He didn't want to leave the main deck. He too refused to do Lefu's bidding. Besides, if his sister wasn't safe, he felt it would be his fault...and he wouldn't want to carry on.

Stephan looked away from Amy to see that all of the other passengers and crew had left the main deck to carry out Lefu's dirty work. Lefu and Jako remained by the guard rail watching the team of swimmers as they made their way across to the Pemba Koningin. Stepping away from the pair, Stephan reached into his pocket and pulled out the item that Amy had given him. In his hand was a tube of lipstick. Stephan grew puzzled. He wasn't sure what it meant, but remembered Amy mentioning something about the Savior. Stephan put the tube of lipstick back into his pocket, blew a kiss out to Amy, and left the main deck.

33

Captain Grey followed the drips of blood across the main deck. Every few steps he could distinctly see a bloody paw print. If not for the blood trail, the Captain may have never found her. The blood ran in a single direction from the main deck towards a small flight of stairs leading to a narrow passageway, the same direction as the Captain's quarters. The Captain quickened his pace as he began to run toward his room. When he finally came around the corner, his door was in sight – but no Cody. He slowed his pace along the hallway, still following the bloody paw prints. The Captain reached his door, but Cody wasn't there. The blood trail carried on past his door.

The Captain knew that the hallway ended twenty feet beyond his doorway. At the end on the hallway there was a vertical ladder on the left that led back to the main deck, and a small storage compartment on the right. The paw prints led to the right.

Captain Grey rushed to the end of the hallway. Kneeling down, he found her. Cody was curled up on a pile of floatation vests.

Cody looked up at the Captain with glassy eyes. Her breathing was shallow and weak. Captain Grey softly put a hand on her head, "It's going to be okay, girl. I'm here. Let me see..."

Cody whimpered as the Captain put his hand on her side. With his other hand, he gingerly dragged the life vest Cody was lying on into the light in the passageway. Her entire backside was blood soaked into a deep, dark red.

It looked as though Cody's right hind leg, around the hip, was the injured area. Captain Grey applied an amount of pressure to stop the bleeding. It didn't look good.

Using the life vest as a stretcher, Captain Grey slid his hands under the vest and lifted Cody up. She was very heavy, but the Captain stayed strong. He nuzzled her close to his chest as he carried her back toward his cabin. Cody yelped a couple of times during the short walk to his cabin, but allowed the Captain to take her.

Once he reached his cabin door, he carefully rested her body against the door as he pulled one of his hands free to retrieve his keys and open the door. He pulled out the key ring and single-handedly fished through the assortment of keys. He couldn't find the key to his cabin...then he remembered. He'd given it to Dr. Baruti and forgotten to get it back. But Baruti was now dead.

* * *

Dr. Conte followed the best she could behind Winston Deedat as he hurried along the port side of the ship. The young deck hand left no rock unturned as he searched for Joost and the diamond. He looked under, over, and inside every available compartment. He meticulously checked behind every wall and along every passageway.

"Mr. Deedat, please. Slow down. I can't keep up with you. We must work together." Dr. Conte pleaded.

Deedat briefly stopped searching and turned back to the doctor.

"We? There is no...we!"

"Deedat, please. You must have some weapons aboard this ship. Can you not defend your passengers?"

"This is a research vessel. It used to belong to the military, but it's not a military ship anymore. Captain Grey abhors violence, so it's really no surprise that we don't have any form of protection on board."

"What are we going to do? Oh, please slow down. Lefu said he would only save the one person who finds the diamond or the man in possession of it. We have to do something. We have to come up with a plan. We must stay together."

Deedat snapped, "I'm trying goddamnit! Can't you see that you're holding me up? Go search for yourself. Like I said...there is no WE! I'm not prepared to die, especially not on account of you and your colleagues. Why don't you go look somewhere else and leave me alone?"

Dr. Conte froze - staring at Deedat as he waved his hands and yelled at her. She didn't want to believe that human nature could deteriorate so quickly. That the preservation of life could tear people apart; strip them to the core of primeval instinct.

Being a woman born before WWII, Doctor Conte had a full understanding of the evils of man. She'd seen it as a young woman, but here and now, in her early sixties, she was witness to it being played out once again. As much as Dr. Conte understood Deedat's motivation - his behavior confirmed that Lefu had suc-ceeded in doing something unthinkable – he had unleashed hell aboard the Reiziger.

Deedat stomped away. He was desperate. Dr. Conte felt alone. Her closest friends and colleagues, Dr. Athans, Dr. Baruti, and Dr. Duiker were dead. Amy Masterson and Stuart Radcliff were on a suicide mission, and Stephan Woodley had to be more con-cerned with his sister's wellbeing than to worry for a suffering middle-aged woman. She shook her head.

With a defeated gait, Dr. Conte shuffled to the port edge of the Reiziger and looked off into the distance. She looked back on her youth. She thought of her family, her friends, her first love, and her children, all things she realized she'd probably never see again. A tear ran down her cheek and dropped over the edge of the ship.

Dr. Conte leaned over to follow the tear down to the water, but instead, she saw something else. She adjusted the glasses on her face. She looked to the sky and then back to the water. Again, there it was. She looked around for Deedat, for anyone. She needed someone to witness this with her, to confirm what she was seeing. She stared closer at the ocean. Dr. Conte saw what appeared to be a massive colony of tiny jellyfish sprouting up near the surface of the water. It was like a rainbow of color radiating just below the side of the ship. There were thousands, maybe hundreds of thousands of tiny jellyfish, bound together so tightly that they seemed to move as one. Red, orange, pink and blue colors mixed, scrambled into a mosaic of protoplasm, each one pressing up against the surface and then falling away for the next to take its place. Dr. Conte couldn't make sense of what she was seeing, but the sight made her smile.

"Oh my, Amy has got to see this..." Dr. Conte said.

"Why don't you show me.," said a voice from behind her.

* * *

Stephan managed to find some of the other passengers as he walked casually toward the Savior. Out of the corner of his eye, he caught Fenyang heading towards the sleeping cabins while Medupé went up onto a catwalk and disappeared toward the bow of the ship. Once everyone was out of sight, Stephan carefully stepped up to the Savior and knocked on its door. As expected, the door didn't open, but this didn't keep Stephan from standing ready in case Joost popped out.

Stephan grabbed the latch on the door and gave it a twist. It was still locked. He then reached into his pocket and pulled out Amy's lipstick. Sliding off the cap he noticed it was a deep red-brown shade; pretty much the only color his sister had ever worn. He closed the lid and put the lipstick away.

What was Amy trying to tell him? What was he supposed to be looking for? Stephan searched high and low around the Savior hoping for a clue when finally a voice stopped him as he was kneeling down just below the Savior.

"Is this where you and your sister found him?"

Stephan turned. It was Medupé.

Stephan carefully rose to his feet.

"Yes, this is where we found him. But I don't know where he is now. The Savior is locked, so if he's in there, we can't get to him."

Medupé smiled at Stephan and waved him out of the way.

"I have a key. Let's take a look."

Medupé put his key into the Savior door and unlocked it. He pulled out his gun and kept it at the ready, just in case Joost was ready for them. But then Medupé stepped back. "You open it," he said to Stephan.

"Why the hell should I open it?"

"My arm is hurt. I can't exactly open the door and protect myself at the same time. Besides, I told you to. Now open it or I'll shoot you."

Stephan ran his hand across his face feeling his nose. He'd already had it broken twice in one day and he didn't feel like breaking it a third time. Keeping his nose protected, Stephan grabbed the latch handle, turned it, and threw open the Savior door.

Medupé stepped around Stephan to the open door, his gun at the ready. He swept his arm around inside the life boat, left and right, up and down. The vessel was empty.

"That son of a..."

Medupé stopped short of a full curse. His mind was racing. Where else could Joost be hiding, he thought. Medupé put his gun back into his jacket and ran off. He didn't even bother to give Stephan a dirty look. Maybe he knew of a better location that Joost might be hiding. Stephan didn't care, he was just glad that he had left.

As Stephan watched Medupé run away, something unusual caught his attention. He noticed a reddish-brown 'X' marked on the side of the support beam for the Savior. Stephan ran to the mark. As he smoothed his fingers across it, the mark smeared. There it was. It was Amy's lipstick.

Frantically, he searched along the support beam front and back. Using his hands, he felt all around it. When his fingers worked toward the base of the steel, he felt an opening. Reaching inside, Stephan pulled out the tranquilizer gun.

34

Ruiz quickly climbed aboard the Zodiac and fell flat onto his back. He remained there for a few minutes while he caught his breath. Looking above, Ruiz met with the dangling body of Mr. Asunda hanging upside down, his face looking right at Ruiz, eyes wide open. Ruiz scrambled to his feet and moved away from the body.

"Help me up," Amy called from the side of the Zodiac, her voice startling Ruiz.

"Oh my God," he yelled out.

Once he realized it was Amy, he quickly pulled her from the water. Amy fell onto her back inside the Zodiac. Her stomach heaved up and down like a newborn taking its first gasps as she caught her breath. There she lay, right below the body of Mr. Asunda. Instead of moving as Ruiz had, she just covered her eyes with her forearm.

"Where is Mr. Radcliff?" Ruiz asked.

"He's staying afloat about fifty yards away. He said he couldn't make it all the way. So I said we'd pick him up on the way back."

"I don't see him."

Amy rolled to her side and poked her head just over the edge of the Zodiac. She searched the ocean from the direction that they'd just come from. She too couldn't see Stuart.

Getting to her knees, she felt a panic setting in. She looked and looked for Stuart floating in the water, but couldn't see him.

"He was just there, not more than five minutes ago. I don't see that he's gone back to the ship...oh god, what if he's drowning. Quick, Mr. Ruiz, start the Zodiac, we've got to save him."

Ruiz shook his head in disbelief, but didn't move.

"He's gone..." he started to say.

"I can see that's he's gone. We have to help him."

"We can't," Ruiz said, "I don't know what it is, but there is something in the water. Something down there took the Pemba Koningin captain and Nelson Blomkamp. I didn't see it, but he did!"

Ruiz pointed at the dead body of Mr. Asunda. "We're all doomed if we don't get away from here. We must leave right now."

Ruiz got up and grabbed the access ladder that entangled Mr. Asunda. Pushing the dead body out of the way, Ruiz began to climb up.

"No, Ruiz. You can't leave them. They'll kill everybody on board the Reiziger!"

Amy popped up and grabbed onto Ruiz's wet pant leg trying desperately to pull him back down. He was too strong and wriggled his leg free. Looking back down at Amy, he kicked to the side of her head. Amy dropped back into the Zodiac.

"You don't get it, do you? They're going to kill us all anyway. Doesn't matter if they get their diamond or not – they'll kill us. The Reiziger is sinking. The breach in the hull is getting bigger and bigger. If we don't get out of here aboard this ship, we'll never get out of here. Now, if you want to come, then climb up." Ruiz yelled down.

A popping sound like firecrackers could be heard in the distance. Lefu and Jako were shooting at them. The whizzing sound of bullets pinged off the steel exterior of the Pemba Koningin. Ruiz frantically scrambled up over the side of the ship.

"They're shooting at us!" Amy screamed. "Ruiz please, what about the Captain? Think about Fenyang and Medupé. You have to help them?"

Afraid of being shot, Ruiz didn't look back, but Amy could hear his voice shouting down from above.

"I'm sorry. Their fate is in God's hands now."

Amy collapsed back into the Zodiac flat on her back; the sound of gunfire still resonating across the water. Amy looked up at the ladder and the body of Mr. Asunda. She realized that Ruiz was right. If she went back to the Reiziger with the Zodiac, she could still be killed. Amy wasn't ready to die, but she also wasn't ready to abandon her brother and friends. Dr. Duiker was right – Amy was strong in her faith, she felt it. Something told her that she had to go back.

Quickly stripping off her wet t-shirt, Amy sprung to her knees and began to wave the shirt like a surrendering flag. Within a couple of seconds, the gunfire ceased.

Amy scurried toward the Zodiac's outboard engine and gave the starter cord a few pulls. After the fifth pull, the engine roared to life. She then untied the rope Mr. Asunda had used to weakly harness the vessel to the Pemba Koningin and drove the Zodiac back toward where she last saw Stuart. When she felt she'd reached the exact area where she last saw Stuart, she slowed the boat to a crawl.

The waves of the Atlantic bounced the tiny boat up and down. The occasional whitecap splashed into the Zodiac's side sending a spray onto Amy.

"Stuart!" Amy called to the open ocean around her.

He was nowhere to be seen.

Her heart felt heavy. Even though Stuart was at times rude, arrogant, and more recently quite cowardly, Amy felt a deep sorrow that her friend was gone. Just then, to her left...about ten yards away, she saw him. He was still floating on his back.

"Stuart!" she screamed, "Hang on, I'm coming!"

Putting the Zodiac into mid-throttle, Amy directed the boat toward him. As she neared, she cut the engine and gently coasted up next to him.

"Grab on," Amy yelled over the side to Stuart.

She let go of the motor and reached over the side toward Stuart. His eyes stared blankly while waves cascaded across his face. As the water covered his eyes, he didn't flinch or blink. Amy frantically examined Stuart's body and saw that one of his arms was gone, ripped off at the elbow. Stuart was dead.

Amy put a hand across her mouth to prevent screaming or being sick. The thought of what Ruiz said crossed her mind, 'There's something in the water'.

Amy looked to the Reiziger now sitting about fifty yards away. She looked to the Pemba Koningin, also sitting about fifty yards away.

"I'm coming, Stephan," she said as she manoeuvred the Zodiac away from Stuart and back toward the Reiziger.

As she sped away from Stuart, she watched his lifeless body floating in the water. She shook her head in sadness and wiped the beginnings of tears from her eyes. When she looked back at Stuart again, his body was gone...and the water where his body once was began to swell. Suddenly, the swell began to move towards Amy. Something under the water was coming right for her. Amy cranked the throttle on the Zodiac wide open. The inflatable leaped across the ocean as its bow barely touched the surface of the water. Looking back, Amy realized the swell had dissipated, but she kept the Zodiac charging toward the Reiziger. Again, she waved her shirt in the air letting Lefu and Jako know she was coming and not to shoot, but it may have been too late... the Zodiac's pontoons were starting to deflate.

When Amy reached the Reiziger, she quickly cut the engines, tied up the Zodiac as best she could to the mooring staff, and began to climb up the ladder rail without looking back. She didn't want to know if there was something behind her.

As she climbed over the side rail onto the main deck, Lefu approached her and offered his uninjured arm to help her get firm footing. Amy didn't accept any help. She firmly planted herself on the deck and backed away from Lefu and Jako. Amy wasn't embarrassed about her body, but she didn't want Lefu and Jako to see her in her bra, so she put her wet shirt back on.

"What happened? Where is the engineer? Why didn't he come back with you?" Lefu demanded.

Amy had to think fast. The gun pointed at her midsection seemed to have that effect.

"He said he wanted to help you," she lied. "He said that without Mr. Asunda or Captain Carlito, you'd need his help. So he was going to get the Pemba Koningin ready to depart, and wait for you. I don't know if it's true, but that's what he said. He said it takes time to get the engines ready."

Lefu paused to consider the explanation Amy just delivered, and it seemed plausible. Jako and Lefu hadn't thought far enough ahead as to how they would move the Pemba Koningin if and when they got back to it. Lefu smiled. If Amy's story was true, it actually benefitted him. And he didn't have to think of it.

"There is one problem though, Lefu," Amy said as she pointed over the side of the Reiziger.

Lefu and Jako looked over the edge toward the Zodiac moored alongside.

"When you were firing your guns at us, you must have hit the Zodiac – it's deflating."

35

Captain Grey, Stephan and Deedat were all returning to the main deck at the same time when they saw Lefu strike Amy with the butt of his submachine gun. She fell to the steel deck like a rag doll being discarded by a spoiled child. Her auburn hair draped across her face as she fought to get herself back up. She braced herself on her elbows, but her exhaustion got the best of her and she collapsed again.

"Stop!" yelled the Captain.

"Amy!" yelled Stephan.

Lefu and Jako took a step back from Amy and gamely reminded everyone why they were in charge; their guns pointed and unwavering at the trio.

Stephan didn't care about the guns as he crouched beside Amy and checked if she was okay.

"He hit me because *he* ruined the Zodiac," Amy whispered. "I'm okay." A large red mark adorned her right temple.

Lefu remained unwavering towards the crowd as Fenyang approached and joined the group from around a corner. He looked defeated and tired. He hadn't found Joost.

"I see none of you were successful in finding my diamond!" Lefu yelled. "You really leave me no choice."

A shot rang out.

Lefu looked to his left and then to his right. Everyone froze. Everybody heard it, but nobody saw it. Lefu looked at Jako just as his partner grabbed his chest and fell to the ground. Immediately, a pool of blood began to form from beneath Jako's stocky frame.

"Put it down, Lefu!" a voice called out.

Fearful that Lefu might turn his gun on them, Stephan sheltered his sister's body with his own. Deedat dropped to his knees and covered his head, while Captain Grey and Fenyang stood bewildered, not exactly sure what to do.

Lefu wildly swung his submachine gun around with his uninjured arm, his eyes searching for the unknown gunman.

The early morning sun from the east blocked his line of sight toward the superstructure that housed the command center. Lefu was certain this was where the shot came from, although he couldn't see what he wanted to shoot at. He began firing randomly toward the upper deck. The sound of bullets ricocheted from the steel body of the Reiziger and pinged in everyone's ears. Lefu managed to empty the entire contents of his magazine before he stopped firing.

Once his gun was empty, Lefu stood quietly. His chest heaved as he panted, his eyes still searched for the unknown assailant. Fenyang lay on the ground dead, caught by a stray bullet courtesy of Lefu.

Another shot rang out towards Lefu and the group...this time, nobody fell.

"Drop it!" the voice said.

"It's my diamond, you bastard," Lefu shouted at his hidden adversary. "I won't leave here without it!"

"Then you will die."

Lefu swallowed hard. He held up his injured arm in front of his eyes frantically trying to catch a glimpse of who was taunting him. The rays of the sun were too blinding. He knew from which general direction he was being watched, but he didn't know exactly.

Lefu slowly crouched down and picked up a new magazine from the backpack still lying on deck.

"I'm giving you to the count of three Lefu, and then you're dead - one, two, three..." the voice called out.

Lefu didn't wait for the count of 'three' or the next shot to happen. He threw down his submachine gun and quickly clambered over the side of the Reiziger's safety rail.

His injured arm prevented him from making a fast escape. With great difficulty, he descended the ladder rail to the awaiting Zodiac. The pain became too excruciating for him as he tried to climb down. Three steps before he reached the bottom, he let go and jumped to the partially deflated boat.

Once inside the Zodiac, he fired up the motor and directed the boat back towards the Pemba Koningin.

Amy, Stephan, Captain Grey, and Deedat all stood by the safety rail and watched as Lefu struggled to manoeuvre the crippled Zodiac across the water. The Zodiac looked like a deflated balloon just barely keeping afloat above water.

Lefu kept the Zodiac at full throttle, but the small boat struggled as the entire outboard engine was getting dragged underwater by its own thrust. The Zodiac had lost too much air from the pontoons to support the engine's weight. The bow of the boat heaved toward the sky while the rear fell below the water line. About thirty-five yards from the Reiziger, the small boat stopped.

Lefu stepped across the mid span of the Zodiac and his feet sank into the thin aluminum plating of the keel like he was walking on soft cheese. Lefu realized he had two options: abandon the boat and swim back to the Reiziger, where the diamond and a gunman are, or swim to the Pemba Koningin – a retreat to safety. In the end...the latter prevailed.

Everyone aboard the Reiziger watched as Lefu dove from the Zodiac and began to swim toward the Pemba Koningin. He seemed to stop every minute to refocus, and continue. His swimming was awkward and choppy. It looked as though he was swimming in a circle. It also seemed like Lefu didn't have the energy or strength to make it all the way to the Pemba Koningin.

"He can only use one arm," Captain Grey said quietly to the others, a subtle smile forming on his lips. "Good job, Cody."

Everyone knew the Captain was right.

After attempting to swim for about five more minutes, Lefu finally disappeared below the surface of the water. Nobody could tell for sure what happened. Maybe something grabbed him, maybe he just drowned. Either way, he was gone for good.

36

Captain Grey knelt down beside Fenyang and checked his pulse. Sadly, the quiet cook was dead.

Deedat mutely walked around the carnage that was sprawled across the main deck. On one side, the bodies of Dr. Athans and Baruti lay one on top of the other. On the other side, was the crumpled body of Fenyang. In the middle lay Jako.

Deedat approached Jako slowly. He knew Jako was dead, but saw that he still held a gun in his hand, and Deedat didn't want to take any chance. As he got close to the body, a shadow passed over the corpse.

"Leave it Deedat," a voice said.

Deedat looked up and there was Medupé. Medupé was with a stranger and was marching this man across the main deck with a pistol to his back. Nobody knew who this man was, nor had they ever seen him before...all but Amy.

"I suppose this is the man Lefu was looking for?" Captain Grey asked.

"It is, Captain. This is the man who has made our entire trip more exciting than it needed to be."

Deedat became enraged. "Look around you, you bastard! All of this happened because of you," he screamed at Joost as he charged at him.

The pair wrestled to the ground while everybody watched. Deedat began punching Joost in the face and head.

"Stop it!" cried Amy, "You're going to kill him!"

Deedat grabbed Joost by the collar and started banging his head against the steel platform of the main deck.

"Stop!" Amy screamed again.

Suddenly, a shot rang out.

Deedat stopped throwing punches and looked back at Medupé. Medupé had fired a warning shot into the air, not at anyone in particular.

'Why would anyone care if I beat this person to death? Death was all around, what was one more?' Deedat thought.

"Get off him!" Medupe ordered.

"What does it matter?" Deedat asked.

"It matters because I need him alive," Medupé said.

Captain Grey hadn't noticed the gun until Medupé fired the warning shot. When he saw it, he made the connection. Medupé was holding the Captain's pistol.

"Where did you get that gun?" the Captain asked, nodding at the pistol.

Medupé glared at the Captain with pure evil in his eyes. The color from his irises had disappeared, swallowed up by the deep black pools of his pupils.

"Where do you think I got it Devon?" Medupé asked, disrespecting the Captain by using his first name. "You should be more careful where you leave your things."

Captain Grey realized what Medupé was saying to him, information that Amy and Stephan already knew. If Medupé was holding the Captain's gun, then naturally he was the one responsible for the death of Tom Bailey.

Captain Grey looked surprised and deeply hurt. His Second Officer had betrayed him, and murdered a fellow seaman. He couldn't comprehend it, but there stood the truth facing him with a 9mm pistol.

"Why?" Captain Grey begged Medupé, searching the face of his long-time friend for an answer that he knew would have no reasonable justification.

"Money and power, my friend – that's why anybody does anything." Medupé smiled. "And this man here, I need him alive, so get off him Deedat. He's going to tell me exactly where the diamond is."

"I'm not telling you a damn thing you bastard," Joost said as he got up from the ground. "We knew we couldn't trust you. Ramon – your own cousin said to be wary of you. Ramon was a good friend of mine, somebody that I trusted with my life. When he warned me about you, I took it to heart. And when he never turned up on the ship, I got scared. That's why I stayed in hiding. I knew I couldn't trust you. You offered us safe passage aboard this ship, but you were prepared to kill us both to get the diamond, weren't you?" Joost asked Medupé.

"I guess you'll never know now because the plan has changed. Now tell me Joost, where is the diamond? Don't make anyone else on board suffer. Tell me or I kill somebody. I saw Lefu use the tactic earlier today...it's really quite effective." Medupé laughed at his comments.

"Holy shit, you're no better than Lefu," Captain Grey exclaimed.

"Captain please, this doesn't concern you anymore." Medupé said.

"I can't believe what I'm hearing. *You* brought this man aboard my ship. You kept him hidden. You knew the whole time. You caused everything to happen," Captain Grey said pointing at Medupé. "You're the reason that everyone is dead...you're the reason why my dog got shot."

It seemed to be the final piece of information that devastated Captain Grey. His posture wilted. He looked at Medupé with sorrow, but in reality, his eyes stared right through him. He was no longer a broken man, he was worse – he was a defeated man. He had been cheated and defeated by a member of his own crew.

He finally realized what former Captain Klaustzman must have felt all those years ago – betrayed by his own crew.

"Why, Medupe...you didn't have to do this." Captain Grey muttered.

"I know, Captain. And you know what? You're right. I didn't have to, but I did. And I'm also going to see it through," Medupé said as he pointed his gun at the Captain and pulled the trigger twice.

Captain Grey fell instantly to the ground.

37

Medupé backed slowly away from the Captain where he lay dead on the ground. Just as he was about to turn around, he collapsed to the ground. His body fell limp like a body without a skeleton. As his face hit the steel deck, the Captain's pistol flew out from his hand. Medupé lay there, his body convulsing.

Deedat and Joost spun around. Amy was on the ground as the events took place. No one saw it happen, but they quickly understood as they saw Stephan, holding a discharged tranquilizer gun.

"Mr. Woodley," cried Deedat. "You've saved us."

"I wasn't sure if it would work, but apparently...it did," Stephan said amazed by his own courage.

"What do we do with him?" asked Joost.

"I don't know. How long does the tranquilizer last?" Stephan asked to Deedat.

"You're the scientist. You would know better than me!"

Amy got to her feet.

"It's most likely a neuromuscular-blocking type of tranquilizer. Probably used on the ship to capture and study threatening animals without doing any permanent damage to them. I've studied a couple different types of these drugs. Their effectiveness can last anywhere from ten minutes to two hours. It's hard to say." Amy said.

"Well, we can't just leave him here. If it wears off quickly. He'll be a problem." Deedat said.

As the group stood debating on what to do with Medupé, something interrupted them. The Reiziger began to lean to the starboard side as well as pull to the stern. Everybody had to establish firm footing as the ship began to rock.

"We're sinking! To hell with this bastard, we must get off this ship now!" Joost said.

"Everyone! To the Savior!" Stephan yelled.

The four worked against the gravity pulling them toward the stern of the Reiziger as they headed toward the Savior. They passed the main cabin bank and across the ship where they found what they were looking for, standing with the door open – was the Savior 5.

Joost and Stephan quickly went to the vessel and proceeded to check her over for seaworthiness. Amy and Deedat followed behind, but as they came around the corner toward the Savior, Amy paused as she noticed the body of Dr. Conte about fifty feet away on the port side. At first Amy thought she was dead, but then the body moved as the ship tilted further backwards.

"Omigod!" Amy exclaimed as she ran to Dr. Conte with Deedat speeding right behind her.

"Dr. Conte!" Amy cried, as she crouched down beside the older woman. Amy gently cradled the doctor's head in her hands. The doctor was bleeding quite profusely from her abdomen.

"Oh, no," Deedat said noticing the wound.

"Amy! I saw it." Dr. Conte exclaimed as she recognized Amy's face.

"What did you see? What happened to you?" Amy tried to calm her friend.

"It was Medupé."

"That bastard!" said Deedat, "Don't worry, Doctor Conte, he's gone now. We've got to get you onto the rescue boat. Hold on to me. Here, Amy, you grab her..."

"No! Listen to me," Dr. Conte raised her voice, stopping the pair in their tracks. "I'm dying. I don't want to die, but our mission was a success."

"I won't let you die. Let us help you get to a safer place." Amy pleaded.

"I saw them, Amy," Dr. Conte said, distracting Amy and changing the subject.

Dr. Conte coughed and a large pool of blood streamed from beneath her body, running down the deck towards the sinking stern. Dr. Conte's eyes fluttered as she spoke again, "They were beautiful, Amy. Simply amazing, and I saw them with my own eyes."

"Doctor, please...what are you talking about? Who did you see?"

"The ferroplasma acidiphilum," Conte wheezed. "They've adapted from what we first thought possible."

"What do you mean you saw them?" Amy stopped and looked at her colleague in shock. "They're microbes, Doctor! Too tiny for anyone to see with the naked eye – you know that."

"I know that, but it doesn't mean that in the extreme environments they wouldn't adapt."

Amy shook her head, "They can't adapt to the point of developing cell walls and becoming something more than a microbe - It would take millions of years of evolution for them to do something even remotely dynamic. Doctor, you're delirious. Please, we have to go. We'll help you. Deedat, are you ready?"

"No!" Dr. Conte yelled at the pair again, and then winced with pain. Blood trickled from the doctor's mouth. The bullet must have pierced a vital organ.

Dr. Conte continued, "I saw them, I know what has happened. They didn't develop themselves. Instead, they developed a symbiotic relationship with another species. No different than an ant and an aphid. But what they've done is much more remarkable – they've bonded *into* the other species. I couldn't believe it myself, but it's true. It's the only explanation."

"What species?" Amy asked.

Dr. Conte smiled, seeing that her colleague was finally starting to believe.

"The jellyfish! At first, I thought they were just jellyfish - Cnidarians. They were all around the ship. But as I watched them rubbing up against the ship I noticed that they were capable of doing something no regular jellyfish could possibly do – they were wearing down the steel that makes up the ships' exterior. They were oxidizing the ship at a phenomenal rate. Within minutes, they managed to pit small holes into the side. A regular jellyfish can't do this...but one bonded with ferroplasma acidiphilum can."

"But what is the benefit to the jellyfish if it is a symbiotic relationship?" Amy asked, still confused by her colleague's information.

"That, my dear, is for you to find out. I have done my part; the rest is up to you."

"Okay, I will. I promise. Now please, come." Amy pleaded.

"No. Don't waste your time on me. You're a scientist for God sake. You know that I'm not going to make it."

Dr. Conte was right and Amy knew it, but she didn't want to accept it.

Deedat reached out and gently touched Dr. Conte's cheek. The doctor looked up at him. Deedat's eyes were filled with tears. "Doctor - I'm sorry. I never should have spoken to you that way. I'm not a horrible person. It was wrong of me to abandon you. I pray that you can forgive me."

Dr. Conte placed her hand over Deedat's hand and gave it a soft squeeze. "Thank you, Winston." she said as she closed her eyes and passed away.

Amy leaned over and kissed the doctor on the forehead. Deedat pulled his hand away from hers, and he too gave the doctor a soft kiss.

Just then, the ship lurched and listed. The bow was lifting up above the water line as the stern of the ship began to sink.

Deedat and Amy didn't know what to do as they watched the body of Dr. Conte slide away from them toward the water. The pair slowly looked at each other and without a word, jumped to their feet and sprinted toward the Savior.

Amy felt like she was running uphill, straining against tired muscles ready to explode. Within minutes, she finally reached the Savior vessel with Deedat close behind.

As the pair neared the Savior, they could tell from the look on Joost and Stephan's faces that something was wrong.

"Medupé *wasn't* lying earlier when he said that the Savior had been disabled. He's destroyed the controls and the batteries. This thing is nothing more than a pod now." Stephan said.

"We've got no choice, we've got to..." Amy began to say before Joost cut her off.

"I'll swim to the other ship," he said.

Everyone looked at Joost like he was crazy.

"No, that's suicide. There's something in the water. You can't go in there." Amy pleaded.

"I have to try. Even if we were to get away on this lifeboat, it's useless. We wouldn't survive very long floating around here. It could be weeks or months before anybody finds us, *if* they find us at all. At least with the other ship, we can travel to safety, or at least radio for help. Their communications should be okay. I'll summon a rescue vessel from her, and come back for you three."

"How do we know you'll come back for us?" Stephan asked.

Joost looked at Amy, gave her a smile, and then looked back at Stephan. Joost's put a hand on Stephan's shoulder and said, "You'll just have to have faith."

Amy rushed to Joost's side, and planted a soft kiss on his cheek. "Please don't go," she whispered in his ear.

Amy wasn't sure why she kissed him. Joost didn't know why she did it either, but he smiled. Without another word, he turned and left the trio standing beside the Savior. They watched as he quickly ran away. Passing the bank of cabins, he disappeared.

38

Stephan, Amy, and Deedat climbed into the Savior lifeboat and closed the door behind them.

The interior of the vessel was sparsely decorated if at all. A blue vinyl bench ran the length of the vessel's right side. On the left at floor level were a row of cabinets. Above them was a small vertical ladder, which led to a control centre at the top of the unit which housed a single white chair.

The main console in front of the chair had a few switches and buttons as well as two control arm joysticks for operation of the propellers. Unfortunately, none of the console was lit up thanks to the batteries not functioning properly.

At the rear of the vessel was a first aid compartment room with a foam mattress bed that was supplied with ample sheets and linens. Storage cupboards adorned the upper rear area above the bed; inside they were filled with provisions and drinking water.

Amy and Stephan took a seat along the bench while Deedat checked that the door was locked. He then hurried up the small ladder, and set to release the vessel. He pulled a lever. Nothing happened. He tried again. Again, nothing happened.

"Son of a bitch! Wouldn't you believe it?" Deedat yelled down to Amy and Stephan.

"Do you need some help?" Stephan asked to Deedat.

"Nothing you can do here. That's the problem with a free fall life boat. You never get the chance to test it before using it."

Amy and Stephan's mouths fell open.

"I don't understand. What's the problem?" Amy asked.

"The mechanism that releases the boat from the ship is not working from in here. It does have a safety release, but it has to be triggered from the outside." Deedat began to explain but then stopped. He didn't speak for a moment. Neither Stephan nor Amy broke the silence. They were scientists, not seamen. They didn't know what to do either.

"We only have one option," Deedat finally said.

Deedat climbed back down from the control area, opened the door to the Savior and stepped back onto the main deck.

"What the hell are you going? Get back in here. The ship is sinking. We've got to go now!" Stephan yelled.

"We can't. The lever is jammed from the inside, but I'm pretty sure I can release her from out here."

"No way. No way. No way." Amy started.

"Listen," Deedat cut her off. "I can release the Savior from out here. You two need to stay inside for safety. Remember, Dr. Conte said that these 'jellyfish' type things were capable of destroying steel. That is why the Reiziger is going down; I understand that now. But *this* vessel is fibreglass – you'll be protected. But only if I release the Savior from the Reiziger; if not, this lifeboat will be pulled down when the ship sinks. It is our only option. Besides, I have something I need to do."

"What do you mean you have something you need to do?" Stephan asked.

Deedat ignored the question.

"Deedat, listen to Amy, you could die if you don't come with us." Stephan pleaded.

"I will swim to the Pemba Koningin after I release you. I will ensure that Joost and Ruiz come back for you."

"But the Pemba Koningin is also made of steel, it could be jeopardized too!" Amy said.

"It looks okay right now. It's our only hope. I have to try. And you two need to get inside of the Savior right now. There's no more time to argue."

Amy couldn't think of anymore reasons to stop Deedat. He'd already made up in his mind what he was going to do, there was no point arguing anymore. Time was not on their side.

Just then, the Reiziger's bow lifted to nearly a thirty-degree angle.

Deedat held on tight to the support frame of the Savior. He was smiling, "I promise, I'll come for you," he said. As he spoke he closed the door to the Savior with Amy and Stephan inside. He reached his right arm to a lever up above the Savior and with his left hand he gave the pair a salute.

Click. He released the vessel.

The Savior dropped very quickly, splashing into the Atlantic and careening underwater like a torpedo being released. The impact was much more severe inside the vessel.

When the Savior resurfaced, it was near the rear of the Reiziger. The Reiziger was sitting partially submerged at the stern.

Amy scrambled to her feet and climbed the small ladder to the control area of the Savior. Looking out the topside windows, she struggled to see if Deedat had safely entered the water on the other side of the ship, but she had no way of telling from her vantage point. Desponded, she climbed back down to check on Stephan. Once again, he was unconscious.

* * *

Deedat braced himself against the deck rail as he walked from where the Savior was stowed. He passed the bank of cabins and entered onto the main deck, witnessing once again the horror of

251

what had happened in the course of the day. Six bodies lay across the deck; five of them were dead, one in a deep sleep.

Winston Deedat thought long and hard about what Medupé had done to the Reiziger, the Captain, Tom Bailey, Dr. Conte and the others, all for greed. This man was the evil of human nature. Deedat's anger began to stir as he stared at the motionless body.

Briefly, he thought of grabbing the Captain or Jako's gun and finishing Medupé. He would put the bastard out of his misery while he slept, but that option seemed too easy. It was too good for a scum of the earth murderer like Medupé. Then Deedat thought of something else. He grabbed Medupé's body, as heavy as it was, picked it up and slung it over his shoulder.

* * *

The Savior bobbed in behind the Reiziger and drifted toward the starboard side. Amy's eyes lit up when she saw through a porthole, a figure swimming from the ship. It was Winston Deedat. He was making his way to the Pemba Koningin.

"There he is!" Amy exclaimed to Stephan, but he didn't respond.

Thanks to Stephan's unfortunate luck, he'd once again been knocked out, and his nose once again broken. When the Savior was released, Stephan had hit his head on the roof of the sealed compartment. Amy had checked him over since, and knew he'd be okay. Yet, after two good bumps to the head and what must have been three broken noses in one day...she felt sorry for him. Best to let him sleep. Hopefully, he'd forget everything that had happened.

Peering back through the porthole window, Amy was fixed on Deedat until she saw that he successfully made it to the Pemba Koningin. She watched as he climbed the side ladder past the body of Mr. Asunda. Once he reached the top, he disappeared from sight. Amy felt an excitement inside her. Now, Amy had no choice but to sit and wait for Joost, Ruiz, and Deedat to come to her and Stephan's rescue.

As time slipped by, she watched both ships drifting further and further away. The doomed Reiziger's bow lifted higher and higher into the air as the rear of the ship was being pulled into the ocean. Air bubbles pressed out from its lower cavities, creating a plume of white on the surface of the torrid waters. The MIG IV submersible tumbled the length of the ship and splashed into the water. It bobbed for a few seconds then it too began to sink. Amy turned away when she saw the bodies on the main deck slide toward the water. She retreated to the bed at the rear of the Savior and lay down.

39

Medupé awoke from his drug-induced slumber with a crash. He wasn't sure what had just happened. His face was numb and his vision grainy. He tried to focus, but an excruciating headache prevented him from doing so. He couldn't feel his legs, his arms or his hips. He tried to fight to stay awake, but he couldn't. His body began to feel like it was tumbling, as if it was floating on a cloud. Finally, he drifted back to sleep.

Moments later, another crash rattled through his ears. This time the sound woke him up completely. Medupé became more alert. He wriggled his fingers and waved his arms the best he could; his elbows were restricted by metal. He blinked his eyes and gently shook his head back and forth. His faculties were coming back, but slowly. He fought desperately to stay awake.

A bright light shone into Medupé's eyes. He reached out to cover his eyes, and felt a large pane of glass directly in front of him. The light seemed to waver and bounce in front of him. He shielded his tired eyes until finally the brightness subsided, giving way to a shade of light blue. The colors felt calming. Medupé relaxed and tried to stand. He couldn't.

His heartbeat began to race, as he looked left and right, up and down, his eyes becoming more alert. He didn't know how he got here, but Medupé quickly realized that he was inside the MIG IV submersible.

The last thing Medupé remembered was standing on the main deck of the Reiziger. He'd just shot the Captain...and now he was alone, inside this tin can.

"You sons of bitches," Medupé cursed to nobody, his numb mouth drooling as he spoke.

He continued to fight off the effects of the tranquilizer as he twisted his body within the tight capsule.

Medupé stopped moving and noticed that the bright light that had shone through the front window of the submersible was beginning to grow dim. It was getting farther away. He was sinking in the submersible; it wasn't tethered to the Reiziger.

Medupé began to panic. He tried to open the door to the MIG IV. The latch turned with ease, but unfortunately, the outside pressure made it impossible to press the door open. He was trapped inside. He raised a feeble leg against the window of the door and began to press with all his might, but the door wouldn't open.

His eyes searched wildly all around him trying to locate a way out, possibly an escape hatch, but he found none. He tried flicking switches and pressing buttons to get the unit to spring to life – nothing happened. Deedat had made certain that the vessel was incapacitated before he put Medupé inside.

Sitting and watching, Medupé observed as the world above him grew darker and darker. He started to scream, but nobody heard him. He thrashed his body about inside the unit, bouncing off the sides of the vessel until he grew tired and sore.

Sweat poured from his brow. The air began to grow thin inside the capsule. The sound of the metal compressing around him began to knock and ping in his ears.

Looking up through the front window, Medupé no longer saw light, dark, or the subtle shades in between. He was in total darkness.

The MIG IV crashed into something, jarring Medupé inside. It crashed again to the other side, knocking him again. His head began to get dizzy. The available oxygen remaining aboard the MIG IV began to dwindle. Medupé's breathing was shallow and rapid.

Not knowing what else to do, Medupé just sat quietly listening. A bang, a crash and a thud echoed in his ears. The sound of the metal being crushed under the pressure of the ocean muffled into the interior of the MIG IV.

Suddenly, a pinhole of water shot at Medupé, followed by another, and then another. The rivet seams of the submersible unit were beginning to give way.

Medupé felt like his head was going to explode. Suddenly, there was a flash of white light before his eyes – Medupe screamed - and then nothing. He was gone.

* * *

Amy woke with Stephan standing over her, lightly shaking her and calling her name.

"Joost, Deedat? Are they here?" she asked slightly daze.

Stephan shook his head 'no'.

Amy got up from the bed and went to the porthole window. She looked out, but didn't see anything. She checked the porthole window on the opposite side of the vessel. Again, she couldn't see anything. No Reiziger, no Pemba Koningin – nothing but water as far as she could see.

"Up top, we can open the top access hatch to look!" Stephan said.

Amy climbed the small ladder to the upper control area of the Savior. On the top portion of the vessel's ceiling was a turn crank type handle clearly labelled, "Emergency Exit", Amy twisted the red painted crank and pushed open the small hatch.

The fresh salty air of the Atlantic rushed past her forcing its way into the Savior. The air outside was considerably more refreshing than the stuffiness inside the life boat. It was invigorating; it felt like new life.

Sunlight beat warm on Amy's face as she squinted across the horizon. The sun was positioned almost directly above her head; it must have been close to noon. Neither Amy nor Stephan knew exactly how long they'd been asleep for, but the ocean felt different to them.

Amy searched in all directions for any sign of the Pemba Koningin or the Reiziger, she couldn't see anything. She desperately looked beyond the swells of the waves for a smaller boat that might be hiding, one that would carry Deedat, Joost, or Ruiz to their rescue. She saw nothing.

"What's happened?" Amy asked.

Stephan stood at the bottom of the ladder leading up to the emergency exit, he was looking out one of the side portholes, "I don't know. Maybe the Pemba Koningin went down. Maybe they didn't get off the ship in time..."

Amy shook her head. She wouldn't accept that as a possibility. "It's possible that we've been asleep for a while. We could have drifted miles from where the Reiziger and Pemba were."

Stephan bit at his lip, "So what do we do now?" he asked.

Amy climbed down the ladder, manoeuvred past Stephan and began to scavenge through the cabinets at the rear of the vessel. While kneeling on the bed for support, she noticed a few blood-stains. Checking her forehead, she determined that they weren't from her. She checked further and found that some of the blankets at the rear of the bed were heavily stained and gathered into a bundle.

Stephan continued to watch the horizon through a porthole for any sign of life. He spotted what appeared to be a bird flying. Then he saw another, and another. He realized he hadn't seen a bird in days.

It was almost ten minutes before Amy returned from the rear of the boat. She was holding a flare gun. Climbing back up to the emergency exit she yelled down to Stephan, "Cover your ears."

The flare whistled loudly as it sailed to the sky, leaving a bent tail of smoke in its wake. Against the clear blue sky, at the extremity of the shot, a blazing red fireball quietly fell back towards the sea, fighting against gravity to stay in the air.

"There are five more flares in the case," Amy said as she descended the ladder. "We'll shoot one up at night and one during the day."

"Then we're only good for three days?" Stephan said.

She looked at her brother with a sadness that he understood.

"If we aren't found in three days, we may never be found. Come here, I need you to see something," Amy said as threw the flare gun onto the blue bench.

Stephan followed Amy as she walked to the rear of the Savior. At the bed, she rolled back the pile of bloodied blankets to expose a gruesome discovery.

The body was hidden amongst the bloodied sheets. She was motionless. Her eyes were closed; the breathing rapid and shallow.

"Is she going to die?"

"I don't know. She's been shot. She's lost a lot of blood. It doesn't look good."

"She didn't deserve this."

"I know, but none of us did."

Cody strained in an effort to open her eyes and raise her head up. She wanted to find the faces to match the voices directly in front of her, but she couldn't find the energy. She was near death. She knew it. She began to whimper as blood continued to trickle from her mouth.

40

Amy and Stephan had been drifting at sea for six days. By the third day, the pair had depleted their supply of flares, their water supply was low, and their spirits were dampened. With no sign of rescue in sight, all they could do was to depend on their faith that someone would find them. Fortunately, someone finally did.

A British Naval helicopter practicing air-sea rescue operations approximately two hundred and fifty miles east of the Falkland Islands found them purely by chance.

Lieutenant Corporal William Walters flew his chopper in the wrong direction, fifteen miles southeast of his waypoint – a simple miscalculation which ultimately led to the discovery of Amy and Stephan.

Ensign Cooper and Corporal Muirhead of the Royal British Navy repelled from the helicopter and found the occupants of the Savior in moderate health. The young lady was suffering only minor bumps and bruises, the young man appeared to have a broken nose, while the dog had sustained a bullet wound.

While in infirmary at Mount Pleasant, the British authorities questioned Stephan and Amy as to how they ended up on board the Savior life boat. Each gave a deposition including an account of what led to the demise of so many. Shortly after, the British Navy deployed a search party to find any trace of the Pemba Koningin or Reiziger – none was ever found.

Amy had no choice but to hand over the 'perfect pink' she had found tucked underneath the wounded dog inside the Savior.

A very brief court case determined that since the reported events had taken place in international waters, the diamond would be returned to Amy's possession if nobody came forward to lay claim. Amy hoped that Joost would appear on her doorstep looking to retrieve the diamond, but he never did.

In the year that followed, Stephan went on to become a physics professor at the University of North Dakota in Grand Forks. He set up a private consulting firm on the side to carry out specialized work in geophysics, in particular, volcanic activity. To this day, he is one of the most sought after experts in this field.

Amy briefly returned to Zeeland, North Dakota – the place where her life began, the place where she grew up, and the place where she planned to die. A year later, she left. She asked Stephan to come with her, but he refused.

41

The Caber research vessel seemed to float across the water, its steel frame unyielding and sturdy against the gigantic waves from the Atlantic.

It was hot and humid. The heat was almost unbearable on this August afternoon, but the passengers and crew didn't seem to notice. As they approached their destination, spirits were high.

"Slow to ten knots, Mr. Deacon." Captain Findlay called.

"Aye, Captain." replied the engineer.

The sound of the engines roared. The ship seemed to apply invisible brakes on the water as the ship began to slow.

Amy watched from the bow of the ship as the crew manoeuvred the mighty vessel toward the berthing dock of the island. As they drew closer, an unexpected feeling came over her. Her lips began to quiver, her legs felt weak, and her eyes started to well up.

"Don't be sad," said Doctor Tanner. "They would be proud of you."

Amy looked at her new colleague and smiled. "Thank you, Doctor. Please don't get me wrong – you've assembled one of the finest teams imaginable. It's just hard to do this without the others. I wish they could have been here, too."

Doctor Tanner placed a hand on Amy's shoulder, "They are always with you. It's up to you to make them proud. Here, please, take this."

The doctor handed Amy a handkerchief.

"Oh, thank you, Doctor. I have one."

Amy reached into her pocket and pulled out a folded blue and white handkerchief. She slowly unfolded it. It was the handkerchief Medupé had given her aboard the Reiziger. Looking down at it for a moment, she began to cry.

"Are you sure you're okay, my dear?" asked Dr. Tanner.

"I'm fine." Amy said as she dabbed the corners of her eyes and tucked the cloth away. "I can do this."

The Caber sounded its horn as it slowed into the berth. The sound of the engines died down as the ship drifted in. Finally, a gentle bump was felt as the ship came to a stop.

Captain Findlay smiled and raised his hands in the air. "Could I have your attention everyone?"

The ten person scientific team and eight member crew all stopped what they were doing to listen to the tall, handsome captain.

"I hope you've enjoyed your voyage...I know it's been a bumpy one, but we're here. I want to officially welcome you to St. Helena!"

Everyone cheered.

Amy rested her hand on the top of the guard rail as she watched her colleagues disembark the ship one by one. Amy was the last to leave the ship for the mainland. At her side was her dog - Cody.

The End.

About the Author

KIRK GRAHAM was born and raised in Vancouver, Canada.

He began writing short stories at the age of nine.

Reiziger is his first full length novel.

In the coming years, Kirk will release his nine truly unique novels, as well as a short story compilation of his most obscure and interesting tales.

Kirk currently resides in the interior of British Columbia, Canada with his wife and four children.

www.kirkgraham.com